Praise for *The Complicities*

"*The Complicities* is a subtle masterpiece. Imagine a voice—lyrical and low, intimate and insistent—whispering in your ear. Half-told truths simmer below the surface, like the uneasy murmuring of a conscience. Mesmerized, you listen. There is menace here in D'Erasmo's disquieted world, and terrible beauty, too. Things are not what they appear to be. We are not who we think we are, either, and yet we are complicit." —Ruth Ozeki, author of
The Book of Form and Emptiness

"A tricky and absorbing tale about crime, punishment, and the lies we tell ourselves."
—*The New York Times Book Review*

"[A] perfect outing . . . With smooth shifts in perspective and understated and precise prose, D'Erasmo demonstrates a mastery of the craft. The result is propulsive and profound."
—*Publishers Weekly* (starred review)

"Urgent and personal, *The Complicities* solidifies D'Erasmo's reputation not just as a skilled shaper of disparate fictional worlds and beings, but as a fierce investigator of how it may feel to live inside them . . . D'Erasmo's writing is tight and flavorful; her thinking sharp; her characters warmly idiosyncratic; her causes timely, complex, and morally freighted."
—*The Washington Post*

"As in all her finely wrought, shrewdly piercing novels, D'Erasmo keeps us recalibrating our perceptions . . . An arresting and intricately spun inquiry into talent, resentment, and risk, love and betrayal, self and community, guilt and retribution." —*Booklist* (starred review)

"A portrait of the art of self-deception." —*Oprah Daily*

"In Stacey D'Erasmo's wonderful new novel, *The Complicities*, the past catches up to the present and overtakes it. All the scattered misdeeds and cut corners and malfeasances come together as crimes, big and small, and the characters either see the criminality or try to ignore it. But this suspenseful novel sees it all, and I found myself enlightened and deeply moved by its compelling story."

—Charles Baxter, author of
The Sun Collective

"A multilayered book about guilt, restitution, redemption, and, mostly, about wounded people."
—*San Francisco Chronicle*

"Slow burning but thoughtful and deftly structured."
—*Kirkus Reviews*

"The prose abounds with lyrical imagery. But its particular strength is its examination of that liminal space between innocence and culpability, leaving readers to judge whether these characters are as innocent as they want to believe."
—*Library Journal*

"What does it mean—in such a corrupted world—to reckon with and atone for our own complicities? Stacey D'Erasmo's latest unspools with the twisty intensity of a psychological thriller and the oceanic depth of a literary tour de force. *The Complicities* is an electrifying novel of powerful moral complexity, from a treasured writer working at the height of her powers."
—Laura van den Berg, author of
I Hold a Wolf by the Ears

"A suspenseful, compelling novel that raises the question: How do we reckon with corruption and our own complicity?"
—*The Millions*

"A thought-provoking examination of the stories people tell themselves and the ways that their actions intertwine, whether deliberately or inadvertently, with the lives of others."
—*Shelf Awareness*

"*The Complicities* had me enthralled. This gripping, human tale of our crimes—financial, environmental, self-delusional—is impossible to put down. D'Erasmo weaves a thriller of a tale, exposing sticky webs of corruption that entangle our lives and fates, even those who fantasize about their innocence, redemption and escape."
—Samantha Hunt, author of
The Unwritten Book: An Investigation

"A superb book club selection . . . Full of small mysteries that deserve lengthy discussions with well-read friends."
—*BookPage* (starred review)

"Possibly D'Erasmo's best novel yet . . . Suspenseful and stunning."   —*Brooklyn Daily Eagle*

"Superb . . . *The Complicities* brings to mind the best of Kazuo Ishiguro's work in how it exploits the distance between the narrator's and the reader's understanding of what's true . . . [A] compulsively readable, complex work of fiction."   —*Identity Theory*

"A powerful interrogation of how individuals justify their actions, an exploration of the ways in which we claim the moral high ground, whether or not we can do so honestly . . . Filled with incisive observations of the human and natural worlds alike, *The Complicities* is a beautifully novelistic exploration of profound ethical questions."

—*Bookreporter*

"A compelling, drawn-from-the-headlines examination of guilt, complicity, and regret."   —*Cape Gazette*

The Complicities

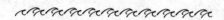

The Complicities

a novel

STACEY D'ERASMO

ALGONQUIN BOOKS
OF CHAPEL HILL 2023

Published by
Algonquin Books of Chapel Hill
Post Office Box 2225
Chapel Hill, North Carolina 27515-2225

an imprint of Workman Publishing Co., Inc.
a subsidiary of Hachette Book Group, Inc.
1290 Avenue of the Americas
New York, New York 10104

Printed in the United States of America.
Design by Steve Godwin.

The publisher is not responsible for websites
(or their content) that are not owned by the publisher.

This is a work of fiction. While, as in all fiction, the literary perceptions and
insights are based on experience, all names, characters, places, and incidents
either are products of the author's imagination or are used fictitiously.

LIBRARY OF CONGRESS CATALOGING-IN-PUBLICATION DATA

Names: D'Erasmo, Stacey, author.
Title: The complicities : a novel / Stacey D'Erasmo.
Description: First Edition. | Chapel Hill, North Carolina : Algonquin Books
of Chapel Hill, 2022. | Summary: "A woman tries to rebuild her life after
her husband's conviction for huge financial fraud"—Provided by publisher.
Identifiers: LCCN 2022014643 | ISBN 9781643751962 (hardcover) |
ISBN 9781643753461 (ebook)
Subjects: LCGFT: Novels.
Classification: LCC PS3554.E666 C66 2022 | DDC 813/.54—dc23
LC record available at https://lccn.loc.gov/2022014643

ISBN 978-1-64375-394-2 (PB)

10 9 8 7 6 5 4 3 2 1
First Paperback Edition

For Daiken, who saw it through

"there where you have landed, stripped as you are."

—from "(Dedications)," by Adrienne Rich

After everything, Lydia framed one of her heart pictures and gave it to me. It's a heart-shape made by a fallen plastic bread bag on the street. You can see the WON along one fold. It looks like it's been run over a few times; the letters are worn. Sylvia gave me the bedspread she had knitted for Alan. The greens in it are subtle and varied, like the greens in a field, and it's soft. Gifts are so complicated, aren't they? Cultures use them as peace offerings, instructions, reproaches, bonds, displays of power. The Roma only give flowers in odd numbers; even-numbered bunches of flowers are for funerals. What's that about? I hung up Lydia's picture. I put Sylvia's bedspread on my bed under the skylight. So I see them every day.

PART ONE

The Whale's Breath

Even now, I walk around with this feeling all the time, I want to say, *You don't know how it was.* I want to lay it all out so the whole shape of it is clear; it's so much bigger and stranger than you'd think. It wasn't what you'd imagine, not for any of us. Not even for him. We were like the blind men and the elephant, so I guess you could say this is me drawing the elephant. Or the whale, as it turned out.

Because—and this is another part of my point, this is what's so frustrating about how stories like ours get told—there was so much that we didn't know because we didn't know one another yet. So much that I didn't know. And the things I knew couldn't help me when there were all these other things that I didn't know were happening. Besides, facts only take you so far. And even facts look different next to other facts.

For example: how big was his crime? Bigger than a breadbox, smaller than Chernobyl. If, let us say, the roof of your local high school gym collapsed during school hours because of shoddy construction, it was that big. So maybe it would be only a day in the national news, unless it was your child who was in gym class when the roof fell in, and then it's the rest of your life, and the lives of everyone you know. It depends on where you're standing.

Of course, I happened to be standing very close, because I was Alan's wife. Noah was just a teenager. In our case, the crime had to do with money—Alan worked in money— but it could have been worse. There are so many ways to go wrong, terrible ways. I'm not saying he didn't commit a crime; he did things with people's money that you aren't really supposed to do, he'd been doing it for a long time, and he got caught. I thought he was clever about curren- cies and exchange rates, but it turned out he'd been doing other things. Anyway, people who were already rich got angry. But the damage, to switch metaphors, is like water damage. It isn't proportional to the crime. It seeps and spreads unpredictably. At first people don't understand why there's a water stain, as it were, on the ceiling, or where the dripping is coming from. And then they do. And then it gets very bad. Life gets impossible, pretty much, and peo- ple have lots of opinions, and they say you destroyed their family's future, but did anyone care about our family and what was happening to us? Why were we suddenly the bad guys?

Although the trial and everything after took a long time, it felt as if in one day my entire life vanished. Alan went to prison. I left him, left what was left of our Boston life, which wasn't much, and came out here, to Chesham, Massachusetts, a lower- to middle-class beach town indistinguishable from the many such beach towns that line the curved upper arm of the Cape. Chesham is on the ocean side, a freckle not far from the Cape's elbow. By then, Noah was in a so-so college in Kansas and refusing to speak to me for leaving his father. My mother had vascular dementia and was living in a nursing home in Vermont. My father was dead. My two older sisters pitied me with all the silent vehemence with which they used to envy me. Our former friends dropped me. I was alone. I had no plan, just an instinct to get out of town for a while until I could figure out what to do next.

I had a little money in my checking account from the divorce, my wits, two suitcases, and a car that I quickly realized would stand out too much in Chesham. I rented a house about a ten-minute walk from the small center of the small town. It was more a shed with electric baseboard heat than a house, a shingled shotgun shack with half-suns made out of painted strips of wood on the front. Darker inside than I would have liked, a low ceiling, a musty scent. A kind of upper half-floor on which the bed—i.e., the futon—could lie, with a plexiglass skylight above the bed. Tacked on at the back of the house/shed/shack, however, was a small addition with a double-paned clerestory window. It was unclear what this room, which opened off of the kitchen, could have been—something to call an extra bedroom for summer rentals? But it was this small, secluded, semi-useless room that contained the house's one beauty that made me rent the place right away. Of all the ugly things I could afford, this one had that long eye set high above, and light slanting down from it.

I sold the expensive car. With some of the money, I bought a little green used Honda that smelled of cigarette smoke inside and had only two working doors, both on the driver's side. The seats were covered in that fake velvety stuff, dull gray-brown, with splotches. The smoke was baked into that fabric, nothing would ever get it out, and anyway, some-how I believed that the smoke was what was holding the car together at all. The hubcaps were rusty, the gas cap was loose, and the windshield wiper in the back window didn't work. The car was cruddy, but it ran, and it provided great cover.

So there I was: alone, forty-nine, still pretty enough: straight blond hair and a straight nose, a slender build. I am physically stronger than I look, even freakishly strong in the arms and hands. My butt is bigger than you might think it would be when you see me from the front. In front, I'm ladyish, but behind I'm a bit of a donkey. In Chesham, I could pass for any number of unremarkable women: soccer mom, boutique owner, high school teacher, whoever. I used my maiden name: Suzanne Flaherty. Around here, that's the kind of name that's so familiar it almost doesn't seem like a

name at all, just a part of the landscape, like a hedge. That
was how I wanted it, because people make a lot of assumptions about someone like me.

I mean, look: sure, you can call me *complicit*, but there's
complicit and complicit, isn't there? It isn't only one thing,
one label that explains everything in every situation. There
isn't complicity but complici*ties*, errors of different sizes,
plus there are other factors, choices that in hindsight maybe
weren't right, but in the moment it seemed different. Other
people have done a lot worse things. Pol Pot. Drug car-
tels. Sex traffickers. And we weren't like those Wall Street
buffoons you've seen, the nouveau riche ones you can see
coming a mile away by the supernatural glow of their teeth
veneers. I graduated summa cum laude from Smith. Alan
was a complicated guy, and he truly was so smart. Incredibly
smart. We sent Noah to Montessori school. We listened to
NPR. Our friends were really interesting people, local artists and a chef and gay guys who went to Burning Man
every summer. We composted before hardly anyone else
was doing it.

No one ever really believes that you didn't know, but
there's knowing and there's knowing. I knew that a good life
cost money, that's what I knew, and I knew how smart Alan
was and how hard he worked. Let's put it that way.

THE UPSHOT WAS that when I got to Chesham, I had no
résumé, even though I've worked hard all my life. My last
job on paper had been as a publicist for a wine distributor,

but that was way back when Alan and I were first going out, and those skills didn't mean much here, anyway. This is a year-round town, not all summer rentals, and it traffics in tangibles: things to eat, wear, use, smoke, or help you stop smoking. A little praying here and there. A rehab center in the next town over. Also, commercial fishermen, Brazilian and Ecuadorian immigrants who staff the kitchens and hotels and the many motels, the Almeida Butcher and a restaurant next door run by the butcher's son, a yoga studio next to a Snip 'n Wave Beauty Parlor, a few CBD emporiums. It was clear that I was going to have to improvise.

I got the idea from that room with the clerestory window. It was so calming in there. It reminded me of a place I used to go to get massages all the time in Back Bay. My favorite masseur was a man named Eagle, who had to be forty-five if he was a day and always smelled of sage. Maybe that's why I rented the house, subliminally. I was standing in that empty room wondering what to do with it, and all at once I remembered the scent of sage. I thought—and I have no idea how this could suddenly happen, but it did, it was a strange time in so many ways—well, maybe I could do that. I could try, couldn't I? What did I have to lose? Who would know if I failed? I found a little online course and it didn't take more than a weekend to do it and then print out a certificate. I framed the certificate and hung it in the otherwise empty clerestory room. Eagle had something like that on the wall in the Back Bay place, hanging under the shelf with all the plants.

I thought of it all as an experiment, something to do in between the life I had left and whatever I was going to do next. Kind of like a hobby. It was easy to set it up. In one weekend I had decorated the room in Early Coven and picked up a space heater and a table that would do. With a twin-size futon on top, and towels and blankets and sheets on top of that, it felt great, just like the real thing. I nailed a face cradle to the table, hammering efficiently. I bought some oils like those Eagle had used and a few CDs of soothing instrumental music. I put up a flyer with those little tear-off tabs on the bulletin board at the small, quaintly shingled library in town. I bought a gauzy, embroidered top made in India and drawstring pants. I pulled my hair back into a simple ponytail.

The first two clients were nothing special, though they seemed satisfied enough when they left. The change happened with the third one. When she came through my front door, my first thought was, Olive Oyl. Everything about her was long and pale: long legs, long arms, long neck, long face, long hands and feet, a long braid of salt-and-pepper hair. Her name was Julie, she said. She was one of two librarians at the small library.

"Suzanne," I said, shaking her long hand. I led her to the clerestory room. "Please undress and lie facedown on the table, under the sheets."

"Oh, cool," said Julie, peeking into the room. By candlelight, the photos of the prairie, the Sphinx, and a beach in Goa looked inviting and expensive and a little blurry in a good way. The space heater hummed cozily.

I closed the door, waited a few minutes, and tapped.

"Come in!" she called out.

I went into the room to find Julie undressed, hair loose, lying on the table under the sheet and blankets, face in the cradle. "Is it warm enough?" I asked.

"Yup." She wiggled her long feet.

"Lavender or plain oil?"

"Oh. Well, plain, I guess."

I turned on the music, oiled up my hands, and put my palms on the base of her long, pale neck. Eagle always started this way with me. My thumbs aligned on Julie's vertebrae. Her body seemed like a slender length of cloth that could twist and slip through a keyhole. She breathed in, breathed out a minty smell. Her back was smooth, white, and narrow, dotted with a few moles here and there. Her shoulder-length hair was ridged from her braid. I pushed down with the heels of my hands. The muscles just beneath the skin were strong, resistant; they felt like pebbles wrapped in leather. I stood on my tiptoes to get a good angle to push down at the place where her neck met her shoulders. Her fingers fluttered under the sheet as I worked. In the flickering candlelight, the sepia grass of the prairie in the picture almost seemed to move in a breeze. The space heater glowed.

"Pressure okay?"

"A little more, if you don't mind, hon," she replied, voice thickened by the face cradle.

I pushed harder, gliding my oiled elbow along the rim of her shoulder blade. Her elbows, eyes up along her body, were rough and red, with deep furrows. The skin above her elbows was rough, too, untended. The muscles in her arms were well developed, but her skin everywhere was the same shade of white, as if she rarely spent much time outside; there was little difference between the color of the skin in the middle of her back and the color of her arms and face.

"Better?"

She nodded.

I re-oiled. Her skin, parched, soaked in the oil. Her right side was tighter than her left side, her right shoulder higher than her left. I figured it must be from right-handedness, but it gave her the appearance of being in a continual state of shrug, even when prone.

"You're new here," she said.

"Uh-huh."

"Where you from?"

"Los Angeles."

"Long way."

"I guess," I said. "Breathe in, please. Hold it. Now breathe out."

I pushed down hard and she sank more deeply into the table. "Ooof," she said. I covered her back and began on her hands and arms. I watched the clock: half an hour head to feet, turn over when you're ready, half an hour feet to head.

Julie's breathing had slowed by the time I was finishing with her left hand and scooting around the foot of the table to begin on her right hand. Her left arm slipped, dangled off the table, so I had to scoot back and gently tuck it against

her side. The gold of her wedding ring gleamed, slick with
oil. A branch rustled against the massage room's clerestory
window. Julie's right hand was rougher than her left. The
nails on both hands were short, unbitten. I interlaced my fingers with hers and moved our joined hands back and forth,
rotated our wrists. Her wristbones were pronounced. All of
her bones were pronounced, long and thin as she was, which
made massaging her feel curiously anatomical, even medi-
cal. The leg-bone connected to the thigh-bone. She was all
perfectly joined structure.

Her feet, however, were a mess. She had large bunions
on both feet, knobs of bone that pulled her feet into watery
diamond shapes and crowded her toes backward onto
one another, like a line of falling dancers. Her heels were
cracked. One ankle looked different than the other, bigger.
Did that mean she had broken it at some point? Or was she
born like that? I coated my hands with oil and rubbed as
hard as I could on her misshapen feet, these stepchildren and
burden-carriers of her body. I didn't know why a librarian
would have such terrible feet, what was in her past or her
genes that did this. I didn't ask. To me they were like duck
feet, some part of her below the waterline, invisible, that did
all the work and took all the weight. I went five minutes over
on her feet.

I covered her feet again with the sheet and blanket. I put
a hand on Julie's shoulder and told her softly that she could
turn over when she was ready. The wind moved over the
prairie in the candlelight. The branch rustled against the

clerestory window. The space heater sighed its hot breath. She woke, snuffled, wiggled down, and turned over. I put the little buckwheat and lavender pillow over her eyes. Her shoulders softened under my hands, nearly leveled. And then it happened.

It's difficult to explain what it felt like. The easiest part to say is that my hands felt hot and alive in a way they never had before. I was doing the things the instructor had showed me how to do in the video, but my hands knew better, they were smarter and more precise than anything my mind could direct. My hands knew, and my arms knew, and my body knew where to stand to get the right degree of leverage and how to push.

"Damn," said Julie. "That's great."

But I already knew that, or I should say, my body knew it. For the first time in my life, I knew exactly what I was doing. I had never felt so competent. I knew right away that I could do this. I could help people this way. It was exhilarating, and it just flowed. I flowed. I knew that I was where I was supposed to be, at last. I rubbed Julie's earlobes and behind her ears, pressed around her hairline. The skin on her temples was so thin that I was almost afraid I would tear it. That was Julie: the battered feet, the elegant height, the fragile skin with the veins beating quietly beneath. I knew what she needed, where to push.

After, I waited for her in the living room with a glass of water. She was so tall when upright, like a walking tree. She looked taller, even, than when she had arrived. She sat down in a chair to put her sensible shoes and thick socks on her hobbled feet, twisted as roots.

"Wow, did I need that," she said. I handed her the glass of water. "My husband just fussed all week. He has multiple sclerosis. Been in a wheelchair for a year now." She drained the glass. "You ever been married?"

"Once. Not anymore."

"You must get a lot of guys in this town picking up on you."

"Not so much."

Holding a hair tie in her teeth, she quickly rebraided her hair, banded it. She was upright, efficient, and slightly reserved. "Well, thank you, Suzanne. This was great. Maybe I'll have another sometime."

"Tell your friends," I said.

"Totally." Julie reached into her bag for her wallet. "Welcome to Chesham."

I nodded and smiled as I put the cash in my pocket. I walked her the very short distance to the door, waved good-bye as she got in her car and drove away, tooting the horn. I went back into the massage room, where the candles were sinking into waxen puddles. The sheets where Julie had lain were faintly marked by the impression of her oiled body, like the shroud of Turin, if Jesus had been really tall. I gathered the sheets and put them in the cotton laundry bag under the massage table, folded the blankets, put the eye pillow away, blew out what remained of the candles, turned off the space heater. I lay down on the massage table for a few minutes, absorbing the ebbing warmth of the room. I got up, left the door open, and sat down in the living room to read a book of poetry by Mary Oliver. The lingering heat and the faint scent of skin and candle smoke wafted toward me. Even as my entire life had crumbled behind me, and my future was uncertain to say the least, I was content. I was entirely content.

The surprising thing was that Julie became a regular client and she did tell her friends. When the first set of tear-off tabs were gone, I put up another flyer with a fresh set. Over the course of about six months, I developed the beginnings of a little practice. It was hardly any money, but I was so excited to have discovered my gift. Finally, I knew why my hands and arms were so freakishly strong, and they got stronger still. With my hands, I cared for the sore and wounded, the flabby and scarred, the small-town real estate agents and retired schoolteachers, who lay on my table. And I realized something, too. Every body—every knot beneath the skin, every scar, every hitch in someone's walk—tells a story, although most of the people who came to see me didn't seem to know the stories that their bodies told. They just wanted, they said, to relax a little. They had stress.

But their bodies were more forthcoming. One lady wore a bathing suit for her session, which amused me until I noticed that the suit had a prosthesis built into it for her missing breast. Her feet were perfect, little toenails like scallop shells. I almost wept. Her muscles were pliant, supple, almost no tension anywhere. She had been through something terrible, clearly, but her body showed no fear, no holding. Bathing suit or no, she was utterly unguarded. A large, dark-skinned man of few words and with a lazy eye lay heavily on the table, his muscles like concrete. It was hard work; I was sweating. He was completely silent. I wondered why he was even there. When I reached the small of his back, though, he began to shake and then to cry. I said, "Hey, hey," sat him up, gave him a tissue. He hung his head, fingers pinched at the bridge of his nose as if he had a nosebleed. "Fuck," he kept saying, curved into himself. "Fuck fuck fuck." He couldn't meet my eye, couldn't finish the massage, and left a massive tip. Another man, who had very abundant body hair, kept trying to guide my hand toward his semi-erect penis as he lay face-up. "Absolutely not," I said, feeling like Little Red Riding Hood admonishing the wolf. "Get up and get out." That happened more than once, to be honest, but I wasn't daunted. A few wolves were nothing compared to all the open souls I was meeting, and helping, on my table. I counted myself lucky to have found my vocation, even at my age, even after all that I had lost.

I needed more money, though, so I got a bartending shift on Tuesday nights at a bar called Waves out on Route 28. I was lucky to get that, too. The usual bartender also worked as a home health aide, and she had just gotten an overnight client on Tuesdays. The married owners, Karen and Jerry, gave me a try-out; I read up in a cocktail book the night before; as it turned out, though, hardly anyone wanted anything much beyond a beer or a tequila shot, served with a smile. I got the shift. At Waves, I served drinks to some of the same people I had seen naked that week on my table, but they hardly ever made the connection. Context makes things visible or invisible. Or maybe they did make the connection, but they didn't want to embarrass themselves, or me. I didn't know, or care. If they were acting like they didn't know me, I acted the same. The customers at Waves told me their stories, too, and all I had to do was lean against the ice machine and nod now and then. I was learning what a powerful thing it is, to be heard. Like my massage clients, the customers at Waves might come in as strangers, but they left as friends.

This was the small time, the narrow time, after the crash, and I have to admit that I sometimes miss it now. In the moment, I was in a ragged sort of shock. I was so lonely. I couldn't believe how fast everything, and everyone, had evaporated; I called Noah every single day, but he never picked up or called me back. The so-so college would only confirm that yes, he was alive, and yes, he was attending classes, but, as they kept saying, he wasn't a minor, and they would certainly let him know that I had reached out with concern. During the small time, it was as if Alan disappeared into a black hole in my consciousness. I couldn't summon him up. There were days when I wasn't sure I could entirely remember his face. Sometimes, my phone rang.

An electronic voice would say choppily, "Will you accept a call from an inmate at Norfolk State Prison?"

"No," I would say, and hang up.

"Will you accept a call from an inmate at Norfolk State Prison?"

"No."

"Will you accept a call from an inmate at Norfolk State Prison?"

"No."

"Will you accept a call from an inmate at Norfolk State Prison?"

"No."

"Will you accept a call from an inmate at Norfolk State Prison?"

"No."

ALAN GOT RELEASED early, but no one told me. The calls stopped coming, but I figured he'd just given up. I was busy surviving. I had a date in my mind for when he'd be released, but I didn't know that that date was already irrelevant. See what I mean about information? Meanwhile, Lydia was falling in love with him. I've tried to imagine what Alan looked like to Lydia, what it all looked like from that angle. When Lydia and I finally met, and later began to talk, it was as if the man she loved both was and wasn't the man I'd loved.

WHAT WAS SYLVIA doing when Alan was released? Ringing up people at the Walmart in Providence, I think. Or was she a greeter? I can't remember, and I don't like thinking of her in that life. Seventy-plus and ringing up plastic crap or handing out the sales flyer at the door—no. No. Say what you want about Sylvia, she's smarter than that. She would have wanted to know that he'd gotten out, because she had kept track of him as much as she could for so many years. Because of the news coverage, she knew when he went in, but no one reported his release. And who else would have told her? I didn't know. Lydia hadn't met him yet, and anyway, she wouldn't have known that Sylvia even existed. I was the one who told Lydia about Sylvia, years later. Alan certainly wasn't going to get in touch with Sylvia; he'd long since written her off. So Sylvia was just standing there at the door of Walmart in Providence, saying "Hi" and "Heya" and "Howdy" and "Welcome." A major part of her story had just begun, but she didn't even know it.

FOR LYDIA, IT began like this:

On her lunch hour, she waited in the line composed mostly of elderly people at the community center in South End. Young, willowy, blond Lydia towered over the rest not only in height but in vibrance. At the front, a handsome older man stood at a metal desk under a banner that read STATE OF MASSACHUSETTS DEBT ADVICE. ASK US WHAT YOU CAN DO NOW! Lydia had her papers in order in a manila envelope. She held on to the envelope with her good hand, the left one. The handsome older man had taken off his suit jacket. Lydia took her hat off, fluffed her hair, bent her head so that her hair fell over her face.

Behind her, a man said, "Free, my ass. What about my time?"

Lydia turned around to smile at him—a gnome, he seemed, with glasses too big for his face, a bit of blue tape at the base of one of the lenses—and he said, "Shit, lady, what happened to you? You look like Phantom of the Opera."

"Fire. Long time ago." Lydia turned back around. *We are only as sick as our secrets*, she reminded herself. She squared her shoulders and shifted the envelope to her right hand, the one with the melted stubs of the first two fingers. Let him look. The line inched forward. An elderly woman in a wool hat with a pom-pom on top was pulling papers out of a brown paper sack. Some of the papers dropped on the floor and the woman bent over awkwardly and slowly to retrieve them. The sight gave Lydia a pang; that could be her one day.

When it was finally her turn, Lydia stepped forward with a smile, extending her left hand. The handsome older man shook it, glancing at her melted fingers, then up at the ruined side of her face, so quickly that it was almost subliminal. He was really something a little different, more off-center, than handsome. Lydia could see that he'd been a cute guy, and now he was an older cute guy, with hair that flopped in his eyes. Lines at his eyes, but a young way of smiling fully. A knapsack rested on the floor next to him; his suit jacket was neatly folded on the chair behind him. In his shirtsleeves and tie, he looked like a candidate come to shake hands and kiss babies. He remained standing, as if he was eager to talk to every person in that ragtag line. The community center around him was grubby and loud, all linoleum and banging doors. How strange that a man like him was here.

"How can I help you?" he said.

Lydia took out the papers, each set paper-clipped and labeled. "I don't have any debt, I hope that's all right. But I want to understand what my company is doing with these stocks in my 401(k) and if I should do something different. Particularly"—she tapped the pile in the middle with a finger on her left hand—"this one. I don't get what this is."

"All right, let's take a look," said the older man. He smiled, revealing an odd brown tooth in front. "I'm Alan."

"Lydia."

With quick fingers, Alan flicked through the papers. After a minute or two, he said, "It's all right. You could have more risk at your age, but that's up to you." He handed her back the stack.

"But what about the weird one?"

"It isn't weird. It's just not doing much. But, you know, you have time. As I said, you could be a little more aggressive, take on a bit more risk." His tone was even and professional, but his eyes roved over her face openly, with a notable intensity. At first she thought he was inspecting the damage, like everyone else, but his expression was more avid than that, as if he wanted to ask her a personal question.

"Should I make them change it?"

"I'd need more information." He wrote his number on a business card. "Here. Call me. We could do this over coffee."

Lydia said, "Mmm."

He held up his palms. "Your choice. I'm just here to help."

Lydia took the card, her papers, and left. She doubted that she would call, but then, thinking of that intense gaze, two days later, she did.

OVER COFFEE, ALAN told her how that pokey stock could be changed and, when Lydia asked, explained that he was doing his community service as a condition of his, well, his *parole*. He said the word as if it had quotation marks around it, looking her very straight in the eye. He was living with his lawyer and his son, who had taken a leave from college to be with him, while he contemplated his next move.

"On parole for what?" asked Lydia, brushing aside the quotation marks.

He didn't flinch. "High-end business practices employed throughout the entire industry. The judge didn't understand the math, basically. Or the law."

"Then how could they put you in prison?"

"Times change. It was like musical chairs, and I was the guy left standing when the music stopped." He laughed ruefully.

"Are you sorry?"

His fine eyes sought hers. "No. Yes. Do you want to have dinner?"

"No," said Lydia. "Yes."

OVER DINNER AT the elegant place with all the waiters— there seemed to be a butter waiter, a bread waiter, a water waiter, among others—he asked her, "So, are you a lawyer?"

"Oh—the firm name. No. I'm a paralegal. And, you know, an artist."

"An artist? Really?"

"Yes." Lydia blushed, but she liked hearing herself say it. She had been trying to do that more. "I make these things with found hearts. Like, something on the sidewalk or maybe in the park that's shaped like a heart—you know, rocks shaped like hearts, or leaves, stuff I see. Sometimes I get them screened onto T-shirts or nightgowns as presents for friends."

"Nightgowns?"

"I like nightgowns," said Lydia, sipping her ice water. The ice-water waiter had brought it, with two slices of lime cleverly criss-crossed, like a lime butterfly poised on the rim of the glass. She paused.

"I'm divorced," said Alan quickly. "In case you were wondering. Just the one son. I was born in Montana." Lydia could almost see it; he moved with the efficiency of a man on horseback who had been on horses all his life. And he was watching her with that same avid look of the other day. What was he seeing? (*Montana?* When she told me this, I said, "Lydia," but she held up a hand. She said, "Let me finish. This is just the beginning.")

"Grew up in Virginia. Single, no children. Ten years sober."

Alan laughed. "And a straight shooter."

"Now I am."

"So, okay, may I ask—"

"Car accident. My fault. No one else was hurt, thank God, but the car was burning when they pulled me out."

"Ten years ago."

"Twelve, actually. I was a slow learner." The butter waiter brought more butter the color of daffodils. Lydia smiled, and Alan smiled. *It's you*, she thought. *Another beauty on parole. Oh, shit.*

"Sounds like you've had it hard."

"People have it harder. I mean, you, too, don't you think? The prison thing, is that why you got divorced?"

Alan looked up toward the ceiling, then down toward his knife. "It was more like . . . my wife, my ex—she wanted the world to be a certain way, and I wanted to make it that way for her. I like to make things happen for people and, frankly, I'm good at it. She was a climber. Very aspirational. But then she deserted me when her dream exploded. She couldn't handle it. Did that ever happen to you?"

"I was the explosion," said Lydia. "I liked it all fast—fast and messy. Most of the time I got dumped when I stopped being the mess for ten seconds. There are people who like the whole broken dolly thing." She buttered a warm, grainy roll with the butter the color of daffodils, wondering what he meant by the way he said "aspirational." Didn't most people want to better themselves? "My mother and my aunt—they raised me—were like professional broken dollies, who were also, you know, Chucky."

"Yeah, I get that," said Alan. "That's tough." He reached across the table and squeezed her right hand. "You had to be smarter."

"I didn't think I was smart. I never thought I'd make it past twenty-one—for a long time I didn't want to—and here I am, an old lady of thirty-five, an upstanding citizen. I'm blessed, really."

"From mess to blessed," said Alan and they both laughed, but all the while he was looking at her from under his lashes.

After dinner, he walked her down the leafy sidewalk to the bus stop, because she said she preferred the bus to a taxi. Just before they reached the bus stop, he paused, turned, touched the side of her face, the bad side, and kissed her. The inner door opened. She said, "Let's give this some time." She wasn't entirely sure why she said that, maybe it was the butter the color of daffodils, this mystery of a man, the wings of lime. She wanted to savor them alone for a while, linger on what seemed so good, but probably—she was no fool—wasn't.

He stepped back, bowed slightly. "As you wish."

The bus arrived, and she got on. He stood on the sidewalk watching as the bus pulled away, his face uplifted in the streetlamp, like a face in a spotlight.

I CAN BELIEVE that Lydia looked like hope to Alan. Lydia is showgirl-tall, and she stands up very straight, because of the rod they put in her back after the accident. The bad side of her face is pretty bad—there are grooves and troughs and a redness that never seems to go away. But the good side of her face is an ingenue's face, with smooth, shiny hair tucked behind one delicate ear. Her gaze is very direct. Her face is her story, right up front and balanced on that very straight spine, and the story is: *I survived myself*. He'd been out maybe a few months at that point, and by all accounts he was less sure of himself. The crash showed. Still Alan, but sagging somewhere behind his eyes. Lydia saw it, that crash somewhere deep within him. I think it moved her. Well, I know it did.

Maybe he fell in love with her because she believed he had a soul and that she could see it, right there, in every room with them. I never thought about his soul, or mine, for that matter; we weren't like that. No one we knew was like that. Souls weren't part of the deal.

ON THEIR SECOND date, they went to the zoo. It was Lydia's idea. She drove her own car there and met Alan at the front entrance. She offered her cheek, the good one, for a kiss, and gave him a quick little hug. She liked the way his shoulders felt under his good coat. He wore no hat, even though the day was cold, just a black wool scarf, knotted at the throat. How old was he? She didn't want to ask, not yet.

"So," he said as they paid and walked in, "the zoo. Can't remember the last time I was here. Maybe when my son was small."

"I like this zoo," said Lydia, although that wasn't the whole story. She didn't want to tell him—she didn't need to tell him—that she intended to get a good look at him in the daylight, in a public place, upright and fully clothed, to be clear, to be safe, to *stay present*, as her sponsor, Naomi, always put it.

"Looks a little run-down," said Alan.

Lydia liked him for that. She slipped an arm through his. "I know. We don't have to stay long." *There*, she said to Naomi in her mind. *I'm present. He sees what I see, here.* "I guess saying that I like it isn't quite right. I'm drawn to it, you know?"

He nodded. "I do. I know what you mean. It's because you're the girl with hell in her eyes." His gaze wandered her face again, and it was as if he was touching it all over. They were nearly the same height, eye to eye, which made his gaze feel that much closer.

Lydia blushed, not from embarrassment, but from the unexpected impact of the arrow hitting home. He already had a name for her, and the name was right. "I guess," she said, looking away.

They wandered the byways of the zoo, but because it was such a cool day, many of the cages were empty. The concrete enclosures were stained, some with browning hay scattered around. It lent the place a deserted air, like a ghost town. It was quiet, hardly any children, just a few adult walkers like them. The faintly rank scent of animals lingered in the air. In one of the cages, a man in a green jumpsuit and big black gloves hosed down the walls, making them shine in the light.

"Looks like the end of the world, doesn't it?" said Alan.

"You say that like you don't mind."

"It's a feeling I've gotten used to," said Alan with a wry smile. Lydia had the feeling that he was older than he looked.

"You have hell in your eyes, too."

He inclined his head. "That I do. That I do."

"Why?"

"I don't know. I think I always have. You?"

Lydia thought. "Yes. As long as I can remember."

He took the hand, the half-melted one in its glove that had been resting on his forearm, and held it as they walked on past the empty cages.

That night, when Lydia said her prayers, she asked God what the hitch was. Murderer? Still married? Multiple personalities? She waited, lying still on the opened fold-out sofa in her studio apartment, but the only image that arrived was of a clearing in a forest. She wasn't sure what to make of that. She got up, blew out the candle, put in her mouthguard (she still ground her teeth at night), and lay awake awhile, but nothing else came. Maybe it meant that she should remain in the clearing and see what arrived.

IN THE WEEKS following, after every time they had sex, Alan would tell her another part of his story. He always came to her little place with the high ceiling, because he said he liked it there, plus his roommates—i.e., his lawyer and his grown son, and here he laughed—well, that would be weird. Night after night, he dropped his knapsack by the front door and came to her.

Sometimes they put the bedding on the floor instead of opening up the sofa. The sheets were bigger that way, and it was like a huge raft floating away from the shipwreck of his old life, and hers. The ceiling seemed even higher. He was lovely naked, a little fleshy as a man his age would be, but he didn't have that strange head-body schism that so many men had, like someone had pasted a stiff-necked head with severely parted hair onto a lumpy collection of parts that didn't particularly like one another. She lay on her side, listening; he lay on his back and told her his life. He said, "I've never told anyone all this before."

His birth mother had been a prostitute and his father was, well, he called himself a businessman, although the businesses seemed to change every few years, and there was always a lot of cash in his father's pockets. He wasn't raised by his mother; he didn't even know who she was until many years later when, as an adult, he had tried to find her. The mother who raised him, his father's second wife, was a cold blonde, slender as a matchstick, who fancied herself a socialite and dressed them both to the nines. He was her prized possession and she never forgave him for seeking out his first mother. It didn't matter. Cancer ate all three of them before he was out of college. His birth mother died two weeks before he found out where she was. She was apparently drinking and drugging right up to the end, forty-eight years old and riddled with despair and disease.

Orphaned three times over when most of his friends were still squabbling with their parents about politics and hair, he figured out early on that he had a gift for finance, which was his blessing and his curse. After he graduated from Tufts, he got into the London School of Economics, but he didn't go because he was already working by then, fifteen-hour days seven days a week. He could have been a big deal on Wall Street, the most important snooty firms used to call him every week offering him higher and higher salaries and begging him to move to New York, but he was a stubborn little bastard, he wanted to work for himself. Which he did. He grinned at his own naivete and ballsiness. Lydia ran her finger along the particular, already so particular, angles of his profile. It moved her that he was trying to impress her with his talk of big deals and big money, like a child.

WHEN I ASKED Lydia if she believed all that, she said, "Well, there were big deals and big money, weren't there?"

"Kind of. But all that other stuff, the London School of Economics, for God's sake . . ."

Lydia shrugged. "I've known people whose lies were a lot worse than that. I've *told* lies a lot worse than that. Listen. I have no explanation for why I didn't kill anyone, including myself, in the wreck that did this to my face. God gave me a chance. Why wouldn't I give that chance to another soul in pain? Do I know more than God about who deserves one? I don't think so."

Sylvia had been a wild child, sure, but she wasn't a prostitute. Alan sometimes exaggerated the good parts of his story, but he also exaggerated the bad parts. It was as if reality colored inside the lines too much for him. And, of course, she wasn't dead. We'll come back to that part.

Later Lydia asked me—texted me, actually, as I was in the line at Whole Foods—"Why did he lie to me and not to you? I don't understand."

"He did lie to me," I said. "Just not about that."

IN THE DARK, Alan told Lydia that he didn't marry well. The day after the wedding, he knew he had married the wrong woman, she was just a version of his stepmother, but she was already pregnant and he was determined to make a go of it. (Thanks for that. And I didn't get pregnant for another year. Lydia could have done the math on that one. But new love puts a thumb on the scale.) Also, everyone in his family was dead by then and who did he have in the world? He desperately wanted a family of his own, a wife, a child, a house, the sooner the better. It was a bad choice, and as the years went by, he consoled himself more and more with drinking and spending and other women and making bigger and bigger promises to more people that they must have known he couldn't keep. That was when he crossed some lines, but, basically, it was all a slow-motion cry for help. He'd had a lot of time in prison to think and read the great philosophers again (again?), and he could see that now. He had always spent so much time taking care of other people, trying to fulfill their outlandish expectations even to the point of going to prison himself for it. His need to please, to be the hero, had cost him everything.

He was very honest about how little he had in the world now. His old house, the big one with all the rooms and pictures and gardeners, was gone. Everything from before was gone, except his son, who was young and loyal and ready to fight the world, and his lawyer, who was helping him get back on his feet. His own business, the one with his name on it, was gone. The old friends—they didn't stay long. Some of them nursed grudges. *I'm fifty*, he said, *and I feel like I'm a hundred and fifty.*

So he was back at the beginning. From prince to pauper. Lydia nodded. She understood that one, being knocked back down to zero and having to start over. That he was at zero: there was no question that that was true.

He was sorry for other people who didn't have his gifts, and yes, he did have a talent, he was born with it, he didn't know where it came from, maybe it was that Higher Power thing she liked so much. Here he kissed her neck. But the thing was that he needed to take care of himself now. He couldn't fulfill people's fantasies of who they could be and what they were owed. No one was owed anything. He told Noah that all the time. He had watched his own father go bust and crawl back to the top a few times, and never once had they missed a meal in his house or dressed in anything other than the finest clothes. That was pride. He knew the first time he saw her that Lydia understood that in her bones. He felt her courage and integrity, her gutsy struggle, and he recognized it immediately. She was his people, he could tell. She reminded him of his grandmother, his father's mother, who left school in the sixth grade to work in a meatpacking plant and was a fighter all her life. (That part did happen.)

Lydia felt that he was her people, too. They were both the people who had lost everything in the fire of their lives, more than one fire, and the fire had scarred them. She was just the one on whom the scars showed.

Lydia felt the loneliness in Alan that shadowed everything he said. As the weeks went by, it seemed to her that an elder lion had entered that clearing in the forest and the lion sat down on the ground beside her and told her his story. He was graceful and powerful and, of course, carnivorous, he had been that in his youth, but she felt no fear of him, because she understood how alone he had always felt in the world, how his loneliness had been his true prison, how desperate he was to get out of that prison. To be fearless like that was her secret gift, it was strength, it was joy. When she was alone with Alan in the dark, talking, the ceiling so far above them as if the apartment doubled in size at night, she knew exactly what to do and say. No one at her paralegal job at Hill, Hill, and Adams, nor her self-starving mother and aunt, nor the people on the street who pitied her for her wounds, knew this about her, about her special power, how expert and exact and brave she was, how she had no fear of the lion. He lay his big, melancholy head in her lap, claiming her, but also in that gesture asking, silently and shyly, Did she claim him? Would she free him from his sadness? She did and she would, stroking his head.

That, then, was the message of the image she had received: to wait in the clearing for this wounded lion. Her wounded lion. Only a woman with hell in her eyes could understand a man like him, who had hell in his eyes, too. She knew he had more stories underneath the stories he told her and she knew they were bad. Many of her stories—most of her stories—were bad, too. And, of course, it was true the other way around as well: only a man with hell in his eyes could understand a woman who had it in her eyes, too. For so long, Lydia could see now, she had been missing a man she had yet to meet, and finally he had arrived.

One morning, she woke up on the raft of sheets to see him leaning, naked, over her small desk, looking at a few of the found heart images she'd printed out recently: the heart found in a toss of tangled string, the heart found in a pile of dog shit, the heart found in a knot in a tree.

"These are great," he said. "May I have one?"

"Have them all," she said. "I have plenty. I see them everywhere."

He put a graceful hand to his eyes, but she could see his tears. She saw him. She knew him. "Jesus," he said, coming back to the raft. "You. You. I want to put a baby in you. Can I do that? Lydia. Please. Can I do that?"

Alan always did love babies.

In the mornings, he put on his suit and tie, picked up his knapsack, and headed out, always before her, to his community service or to meet up with his son and his lawyer. He was an early riser.

On one of these mornings, mostly because the Naomi voice in her head said she should, she googled him. She saw articles about the trial; a professional photo of a younger, thinner Alan clearly pulled from his former firm's website; a mention of him in an editorial about white-collar criminals, the public trust, and too-light prison sentences. A principal of some private school said they might have to close because of the way he'd invested their endowment; what was so terrible about public school? thought Lydia. More compelling was an elderly woman on oxygen, some former soap opera actress, who was afraid of being kicked out of her nursing home because her savings were gone. "I don't know what to do," said the woman. Lydia felt for her, but it was years ago now. Was that woman even still alive? And he'd done his time. Comparisons were made to minor drug offenses and there were statistics about race and class and so on. Lydia noted all this, not rushing through what was there, but none of those articles told her more than she herself knew already about the *why* of Alan. Online, she saw the *what, when, where*, and a bit of the *how*. But it was all about the crime and money and nothing about what had made the man who did those things, nothing asking him why or following up. Why was it news that people wanted lots of money and would do whatever they could get away with to get it? How was that a surprise? He was soul-sick, obviously. Money wasn't the disease and prison wasn't the cure. It was all so typical of the way most people thought about things.

And then it was like once he went to prison he disappeared, he didn't matter to anyone. None of those reporters or judges or anyone else knew the melancholy, thoughtful, life-worn man she knew, talking quietly in the dark in the middle of the night or weeping at her little desk. They were only interested in the old game of cops and robbers. Souls were beyond them. He'd done his time. That was what mattered. She closed the computer, began gathering her things for her own workday. Overall, she was glad she looked, did her due diligence as it were, but now she was free to love the entire man, soul first. She took her umbrella, because the weather said rain.

WHILE LYDIA WAS falling in love with this version of Alan, soulful Alan, I was pounding what pavement there was to pound in Chesham. I had a gift of my own, as I'd discovered, and though I'd gained clients, I still didn't have enough to make rent with money left over. Between the massages and the bartending and what was left from selling the car, I could hold out for a while, but not forever. Traffic to my website with the lotus flowers on water was light. So many people in Chesham were thick, stooped, stiff, crooked. You could see it. But how to connect with them?

I stopped by the library one day to ask Julie. She was reading a book about a caterpillar to a circle of kids for story time. Even cross-legged, she towered over them on the floor. After the caterpillar became a butterfly and the kids scattered, I sat down next to Julie on the carpet and explained my dilemma.

"Maggie and Eddie over at the yoga studio, they don't do a lot of business, either," she said. "More in the summer, sure. I think Maggie's family has money or something. This town." She shrugged.

"But you're a regular and you live in this town."

"Yeah, but I'm from Denver. We have a lot of woo-woo there."

"It isn't really *woo-woo*. It's bodywork."

"That's woo-woo to a lot of people in this town." Julie peered down at me kindly. "You're still new here."

At moments like this I wanted to explain to Julie about how it all really was, but I was never quite sure where to start. I knew how it would sound, and I was afraid her mind would close before I could show her all the layers and complexities.

So I just said, "Yeah."

"And," said Julie, "winter's coming. Business does slow down. Folks pull in. That electric heat in your place." She grimaced. "Annette's going to make you pay for that." Annette was my landlady.

"Right." The caterpillar smiled broadly on the front cover of the kids' book in Julie's hands. On the back cover, a butterfly, also smiling, spread its spotted wings. "Fuck."

"I'll see you Thursday," she said, standing up. "Don't freak out."

I left the library and went back out onto the main street, where the afternoon fall light was burnishing, but the wind had a bite to it. I walked to the end of the street and then slowly made my way back along it, looking carefully at the storefronts I already knew well: beauty parlor, frozen yogurt place, seafood restaurant, CBD shop, women's clothing (coral, aqua, lots of loosely cut shirts in bright patterns), Delilah's the upscale bakery, a strangely vast, old-fashioned five-and-dime that looked like something from a fifties movie set (how were they still in business?), a bookstore with a window full of bestsellers, Almeida the butcher and his son's burger place next door, a thrift store. Functional. Ordinary. Nothing in need of me.

I didn't want to leave Chesham, though. Funny, isn't it? The town wasn't beautiful, or notable for anything. There weren't any spectacular cliffs or extraordinary beaches. No important battles had been fought here. No one famous had been born here. There was one tiny museum of nineteenth-century seafaring stuff—some harpoons, an anchor, a rusty sextant—but it was only open on Tuesdays. Chesham was the kind of town you drove through on your way to somewhere better, maybe stopping to get gas or coffee or find a bathroom. Our old friends would never have come to a nondescript place like this. But I had a grasp on something here, someone to be. I just needed a little more time. A few more clients a week, under the clerestory window. Once people experienced what I had to offer, they'd want to come back. But how was I going to live until then?

I came to the end of the main drag, where the stores petered out and the road wound north to towns with better attractions. I turned back. The next day, I put up even more flyers with more tear-off tabs.

• • •

THERE'S WOO-WOO AND there's woo-woo, right? One night that same fall, Lydia waited for Alan at a lecture. The room was hot with the crowd although the night outside was cool. She had put her bag on the chair next to her, but even so people kept stopping to ask, "Is that one taken?" When she turned to look at them to say it was taken, they tried not to react. She bent her head so that her hair fell over her face. Lydia looked at the door behind her, checked her watch. She was in the middle of the row. He would have to clamber over people after it started if he didn't get there soon. He had said it was a deal he and Noah had to close; he was showing Noah the ropes. The world of deals was intriguing and strange; it seemed not a little dangerous. Well, that was her, wasn't it? She liked that. Her first husband, for instance, the race-car driver (and coke addict), had had a special driving suit with handles on the back so he could be pulled unconscious from the burning car. Except it ended up being her, of course. She was the one who had been pulled unconscious from a burning car and she had been the driver. And she hadn't been in any race except the one she was losing with herself.

Sonny Swan, the lecturer, walked onstage just as Alan darted in. Lydia took her bag off the chair and Alan took his seat, scrolling through his phone and dropping his knapsack to the floor.

"Stop," said Lydia. He put his phone in his pocket, but she could see that it was on vibrate.

Sonny Swan walked onto the stage to some upbeat music. He was a fat, sweaty man, in a bow tie. He always reminded

Lydia of a pill bug. His forehead was shiny and his eyes were small. He wore big, puffy sneakers with orange lights in the heels, like the kind kids wore so their parents didn't lose them in shopping malls. He walked maybe the way an armadillo would walk if it managed to get up on its scaly little hind legs. When he got to the armchair set up for him on the stage, he plopped into it, apparently exhausted from traveling three yards. His feet grazed the floor. He swung them back and forth, blinking orange. Alan looked at Lydia with a quizzical, close to annoyed expression.

"Just wait," mouthed Lydia. She took his phone out of his pocket, turned it all the way off and dropped it in her bag. Alan frowned.

"Love," Sonny said and sighed. "Here's the secret: it doesn't exist. Here's the other secret: it's everywhere. All right? You can all go home now. I don't know what you paid for tickets, but it was too much, whatever it was. No, I know what you all paid for tickets, I know it to the penny, because I love having a big bank account. Overcompensating." He chuckled. "What, you don't know what I mean? You're all creatures of the light out there, you live on breath, you talk to the animals? Bitch, please." Lydia laughed. Alan smiled, a little. "The way these things work is they pay me about eighteen grand and then I get a percentage of the house. My manager gets fifteen percent of all that. So do the math. You don't want to hear that, right? You came here for some wisdom on love and you're hearing about money, my money, to be exact? What the fuck? You could have stayed home and watched me on TEDx for free. You could have gone to the movies, you could be shopping, you could be going out to eat, you could actually be getting a little instead of hearing me talk about it. But you're here. You're still here, because"— and here he bounced to his feet, as if he weighed nothing at all—"because you have this nagging feeling inside, this desire that hasn't quite been satisfied, not ever, not from the best fuck you ever had, not from whatever sucker stood by you for years, not from your god, not from your kids, not from your parents." He paused, scratching his head with the hand that held the microphone, regarding them, as if he was deciding whether to buy the entire lot or just a few of the better pieces. Lydia remembered that gnawing dissatisfaction well. She had felt that for so long, so many years of being lost. Alan was sitting upright now, eyes locked on the stage.

"You're ashamed of it, right? That's why you're here. You're ashamed that none of it was ever quite good enough for you, that you lay in bed at night next to your wife who still had stitches from the episiotomy, or you were watching your kid in the school play lisping his lines in the pilgrim hat, or that person finally said, 'I love you,' and secretly, secretly, you thought, Is that all there is? Remember that song? Some of you are too young. Look it up." He hummed a few bars. "You're not here, none of you, to quote unquote make your relationship work. No one wants a relationship to *work*. You're here so I can tell you what to do about that secret, secret, secret doubt, that, let's be honest, sometimes it makes you kind of angry, that gap. That motherfucking canyon. Maybe it even makes you really angry. And, this is the punch line, you think that me, Sonny Swan, could that even be my real name?, someone who looks like me, a little fat guy with hair in his ears, you think I've got the secret to the jewel of love you could never quite reach with your trembling fingers after you crawled all that way through the cave on your knees? Plus I'm a fag. You know that, right? You did at least google my ass, didn't you? I'm a fag, a screaming queen, I look like this, I grew up in Texas, my father was the goddamn high school football coach, and I'm forty-seven years old which is like being a hundred in my world. I've never even seen my abs. I should probably just kill myself, and, in fact, I tried. A few times. A few times." He walked to the other side of the stage, orange on, orange off, and crouched on his heels in the spotlight. "I don't have the secret formula for love, but I'm a world-class expert on shame, my friends. I know it"—he held up one pudgy hand with hair on the knuckles—"like the back of my hand." He stood up and turned his hand the other way to show his wrist, and anyone could see them in the spotlight, the vertical scars. He kept his wrist there, holding it up, for a long beat.

"Shit," said Alan.

"Once upon a time," Sonny began, "I was a civil engineer. No, really. I was. Pocket protector, wore a tie to work, constipated, the whole deal. Not exactly closeted, I did *say* it, but I didn't have a lot else to say, if you know what I mean. I got sex." He laughed. "I had a brain and a dick and not much in between. I played a lot of Halo at night. But then one night, I hook up with this guy. Young guy, ring in his nose, skinny, called himself Blue." A few people in the audience laughed knowingly. "Right? Maybe you know him. Anyway, we're heading into the, uh, situation and Blue says to me, 'I have to tell you something.' I say, 'What?' Blue says, 'When I come, I'm going to pass out. I have epilepsy, and when I come I lose consciousness. I won't die or anything, I don't want you to freak out, but you should know. Is that cool?' Now, let me tell you, it was *not* cool, I was already freaked out, but I was also hard as a rock, so I say, 'Yeah, sure, should I get a spoon?' And Blue says, 'No, just hold me until I come to.' And then he smiles like an idiot, and I'm thinking this is a big mistake, but whatever. Anyway, sure enough, in a little while the kid starts coming and I'm holding him, he's a tall kid, and I'm, you know, myself, so it's like some fucking ridiculous gay porn *Pietà* but with this Blue maniac and me the furry dwarf and, boom, he drops, right in my arms. Dead weight, and the kid is gone, way, way far away somewhere." Sonny dropped his voice and shook his head, looking up to one side as if he was watching Blue spiral away into the universe, the spotlight falling full on his frightened face. His breath sounded in the microphone. "So far away. I just sit there, his jizz on my hand, thinking, If this kid dies, I'm going to be so fucked. But. A few minutes later, he comes around." Sonny laughed. "He opens his eyes like Goldilocks, says, 'Thanks,' puts his clothes on and leaves.

Never saw him again. Don't get your hopes up. This isn't that kind of love story."

He was back in the chair now, leaning forward. "The next day, I'm back at my desk, pocket protector on, I'm deep in calculations for a certain kind of sonic weapon—oh, did I mention I worked for the Army?—when suddenly, I see it. I see it. Engineering is love. Physics is love. The molecules, the way they move around each other, the way gravity works: it's love. *Money* is love. It's all love."

His voice was soft now. Lydia could feel Alan next to her, tense with attention.

"I start sobbing at my desk, really sobbing, because it was so clear to me, and it was because of that moment, that kid passing out in my arms, putting his fucking life in my hands, the hands of a total stranger, just diving in not knowing if there was any water there or not—the trust of it. It broke me. It broke me right in half. I was shattered, and from that day forward I started telling everyone that engineering is love, physics is love, what's holding up bridges is love, what's fueling the stock market is love, and I've got charts and diagrams to prove it, and Da Vinci sketches, and German equations and I *know* I'm right and so—" He paused, held the pause. "They fire me. Oh, hell yes. Of course they fire me. I had a high-level security clearance, did I mention that? They gave me a cardboard box and half an hour to clear out my desk, and they marched my ass out the door. I was done."

Lydia smiled, her own half-melted right hand in her lap. She had heard this story before, but she never got tired of it. She knew what that was, to be broken in half, to shed a skin and walk flayed in the world. And Alan knew it, too. She knew how smooth Alan looked, but sometimes when she was with him she felt that she was holding not a lion, but a half-feral alley cat, starving and in need of shelter. He needed to hear Danny's lecture as much as she did, and from the expression on his face, it certainly looked like he was listening, hard. It was as if Sonny Swan knew them both, knew their story, and was giving them his blessing at exactly the moment they were ready for it—no, that they *needed* to hear it. The universe was right on time, as always.

"And then," continued Sonny Swan, "my real life began."

Eventually, Sonny Swan did tell them the secret, but it was no surprise and that was part of it, that they'd already had the answer all along. Also, as it turned out, he had a husband, a thirty-two-year-old hedge fund manager named Carlos.

"Ta da," he said at the end, opening his arms, bowing his head nearly to the floor. The man was much more limber than he looked. Applause. Lydia stood up with everyone else, feeling lighter and freer, almost a little giddy. Next to her, Alan was clapping for all he was worth, his damp shirt clinging to his back.

As they filed out with the crowd, Alan was curiously silent and pale. When Lydia handed him his phone, he didn't even turn it on, just slipped it back in his pocket.

"Amazing, right?" Lydia ventured. "He has so much wisdom. And he's so funny."

"Where did you find him?" said Alan.

"The internet. He has a YouTube thing. Are you all right?"

Alan nodded, looking as if he'd just been punched. "That guy," he finally said. "I've felt like that."

"Yeah, me too," said Lydia. "Everyone, I think."

"No, not everyone," said Alan. "I can't believe he said all that."

"He's very open-hearted," said Lydia.

"I guess he's made a lot of money off his act," said Alan.

"No," said Lydia with some firmness, "it's not an act. It's not like that."

Alan put his arm around her and pulled her close. He kissed the top of her head. Neither of them said anything as the crowd, giddily talking and talking of love, dispersed into the night.

YOU CAN, ACTUALLY, find this very same Sonny Swan talk on TEDx. I've watched it. More than once. Why do people pay to go to a talk they can already watch for free? But that's not the point. The point is that I couldn't imagine my Alan being there and having that reaction. I don't mean that Lydia didn't tell me the truth; I think it happened that way. I just didn't know that Alan, knapsack at his feet, clapping and clapping like that for some YouTube guru. It is in gaps like that that he disappears from me, bit by bit, his gaze riveted by something I can't see.

Would Sylvia have understood that Alan? She who must have followed his gaze early on so many times, so closely.

The way you do with your baby. But Sylvia, in Providence, was probably knitting in the evenings after her shift as this was happening. Meanwhile, at the Walmart during the day, she was dropping stitches. She was late coming back from her lunch break. Sometimes she forgot to clock in, or out. There was a sweet, laid-back manager, Babette, who looked the other way.

BACK IN CHESHAM, I felt like nothing was happening, nothing was going anywhere. No one new was calling. My signs with tear-off tabs were tattered or missing. And then one night, I dreamed of turquoise. In the turquoise dream, we were all there. Me, Alan, his lawyer and running buddy Mark, all the others from the glory days. Marietta, who made sculptures out of pipe fittings. Jeremy and Hank. King and Cleo, still together. Noah, too, but Noah at ten, gangly and sweet and endlessly distracted. The restaurant had turquoise walls, inside and out. White tablecloths. A large plate-glass window. The turquoise saturated the walls, but it seemed to saturate the air as well. We were all together, we were leaning toward one another, we were talking—we were more together than we had ever been in real life. Happier. I was as saturated with happiness as the walls were saturated with turquoise.

When I woke up from the turquoise dream, I was full of turquoise. It was an impossible turquoise, denser and brighter than any I've ever seen in life. Awake, though, it made me terribly sad. Above me was a muzzy pair of bird feet, hieroglyphic, on the other side of the skylight. The muzzy bird feet walked this way, then that. I watched them for a while, trying to understand what this peculiar melancholy was, how quickly the turquoise joy had become turquoise sorrow, and what this sense was that something large and fine was out of my reach forever. The turquoise room was within me, but I would never be in the turquoise room again.

The bird flew away, and I got out of bed. That was the day I had promised to go on their motorboat with Jerry and Karen, my bosses at the bar, and their kids. I made a thermos of coffee, bought a bag of premium donuts from Delilah's, and made my way to the dock where Jerry and Karen and their three kids, all in life jackets and sunglasses, were waiting.

"Ahoy! Ahoy!" yelled the kids.

I held up the donut bag.

"Yay!" yelled the kids.

"Now you've done it," said Karen from the bow as I climbed in. "We'll want to drown them in about fifteen minutes." She opened a book called *Life on Mars* and settled in, the day's cold light bright on her face, illuminating her freckles. Out we went, first moseying along the canal, then, as Jerry opened the throttle, faster into open water. Jimmy, the middle boy, stood next to him, eating a massive donut. The littlest girl, Celia, came and snuggled next to me, her face coated in powdered sugar. She put on the hood of her sweatshirt and pulled the strings until her face squished up and only her sugary nose was showing.

The open water wasn't Mars, but it was like another planet. Structures dotted the water—buoys; tall posts topped by the large, untidy nests of waterbirds; a jetty with a large, half-rusted building of some kind at the tip that didn't look as if it could be inhabited by humans; big boats; small boats; a floating plastic bag.

"Daddy!" cried Andrea, the older girl. She stood up. "Get the bag! The dolphins!"

Jerry, behind his sunglasses, said, "Can't, honey. Sit down now."

Andrea, still standing, leaned out over the edge. "It's right there. The dolphins eat them and it's really bad."

"Andrea, sit down," said Karen, from behind her book.

Andrea sat down, crossed her arms over her chest, and shoved her chin down as far as it would go.

"Our little drama queen," said Karen, turning a page.

The boat tilted over the swells, making me a bit queasy. The light wasn't especially warming, and the wind of our motion combined with the wind itself was chilly, but the brightness shifted something in my vision that felt like heat on my eyes, or behind my eyes. The distance was hazy, with shapes that, if I squinted, might be land. Was that Martha's Vineyard and Nantucket? Or was it the Elizabeth Islands, which were owned by the superrich? Whose shores were those near the horizon line? Maybe, if I squinted harder, I could see the bicycles, the little streets and squares, the shingled houses, that loud Nantucket red on pants and scarves and cotton sweaters. Maybe, if I squinted very hard, I could

see my past self, watching Noah play by the water's edge. He
had a bright yellow plastic bucket, and a bright yellow plastic shovel. I would never be there for longer than a weekend
now. Maybe not even that. As I peered into the distance, I
wasn't sure I could see any land at all. I didn't know where
we were, really.

A boat a little bigger than ours, named *Happy Daze*,
passed by. Two women in big red sweaters with red plastic
cups in their hands waved, and the man in the captain's hat
driving the boat honked. We waved and honked back.

WE NEARED THE dock by Captain Pete's, our lunch destina-
tion, where we could tie up the boat.

Andrea said, "What's that?"

"What?" said Karen.

"Down there." Andrea pointed. "All the people. And the
dolphin."

Karen swiveled back around. "Jesus. Honey, that's not a
dolphin. I think that's a whale."

Celia jumped up, pushing her sweatshirt hood off her
face, and clambered over to Andrea. Jimmy abandoned his
post to join his sisters at the side of the boat, and so did I.
Over the heads of the three children, I could see, a ways
down the beach, a gathering of people around a very large,
grayish creature at the shoreline. Although enormous, it
also looked curiously sluglike. Sunlight slicked its surface.
Heading down the beach toward the whale were a Jeep and
two police cars.

Karen was sitting up, her sunglasses on her head. Jerry said, "Oh, man." The boat bumped sideways against the dock. People were standing on the other boats around us. Others were crowded to one side of the deck of Captain Pete's, some holding up their cell phones, trying to get a picture.

"Is it dead?" said Jimmy.

I put my hands on the shoulders of the two little girls, who stood silent. "We can't tell from here," I said.

"Holy shit," said Jerry. "Look at that thing. It's as big as a bus."

"Let's go, let's go!" said the kids, clambering out of the boat and running down the dock to the beach, where they toiled forward against the wind, barefoot, like a children's crusade.

Karen and I followed while Jerry tied up the boat. "That fucking thing better still be alive when we get there," she huffed to me.

As we made our way across the sand, more vehicles arrived and parked around the whale. A person in a uniform, maybe a park ranger, climbed out of a flatbed and hauled a big roll of something down onto the sand. Someone else, woman-shaped, climbed on top of the Jeep, pointing with one hand, holding what had to be a phone to her ear with the other. The scene looked like a military operation. In the ten minutes or so that it took us to near the whale, a truck arrived and people unrolled what turned out to be a snow fence, hammering it in a wide semicircle around the whale. A man in a police uniform unfurled yellow caution tape around the fence. The sound of the hammer blows carried over the beach. Jerry was trotting down the sand toward us at a good clip. I hadn't thought he could run that fast. A crowd had begun to gather; people held up their phones, taking pictures.

We were a few yards away when a great spouting rush, like the eruption of a geyser, sounded. A V-shaped plume of mist shot out of the top of the whale, and then the mist steamed in the cool beach air. The little girls jumped up and down, laugh-screaming. "Mom!" they yelled. "He's smoking!"

"God Almighty," said Karen. The little girls ran to the water's edge and splashed ocean on their faces. Jimmy, hands in his jeans pockets, kept walking slowly toward the animal, surrounded as it now was by the snow fence, the yellow caution tape, trucks, police cars, cops, park rangers, sober-faced people in street clothes taking pictures and writing things down on sheets of paper attached to clipboards, and above it all, the woman on top of the Jeep, who was pointing and shouting. The wind carried her words away.

Like Jimmy, I walked toward the whale, stopping at the yellow tape flapping in the wind. The boy and I were maybe ten yards away from the whale. The whale boomed its geyser sound again, sprayed, misted. The crowd was curiously quiet, holding up their phones, or cameras, or just looking. A little boy said, "How is he going to get back up?" Although it was fall, most people were barefoot. I took off my shoes as well; my feet met the sand, warm with the day's sunlight, cooler just beneath the surface. Two women in sunglasses stood by the tape, one holding a black dog on a leash. The woman on top of the Jeep shouted to one of the men below, who ran to position himself at one edge of the scene with a stopwatch. The little girls stayed where they were at the water's edge, gazing, Karen next to them.

The whale was the largest animal I, and I'm sure they, had ever seen in the flesh not in the confines of a zoo or an aquarium. I wanted to go closer, and not get any closer, at the same time. Its enormous eye, so eerily human but so much bigger, enfolded in flesh, was half-closed. Whales were mammals, I remembered, and that eye was what made it look like a mammal, no matter its smooth mass, its long curve of a tail resting heavy in the sand, bifurcated at the end like a moustache, itself as big as a creature. The eye was set far back along its head and a huge almost-curlicue line seamed its face. The whale rose as high as the Jeep farther up the beach, and its black flippers resting on the sand were as big as surfboards. On its massive head was a whitish growth that looked like a pile of rocks, or maybe lichen, a peculiar too-small crown. Jimmy, close to the snow fence perimeter, craned his neck back, looking.

Jerry reached us, huffing, bending over at the waist. "I think," he said, spitting and drawing breath, "I think it's a fucking right whale."

"What is that?" I asked.

"It's wicked rare. There are hardly any of them left. They live in the waters up around here, and farther north, but you don't see them. I've never seen one." He just stood there. "Unbelievable. Un-fucking-believable."

The whale spouted, loud as thunder directly overhead. "Whoa," said someone behind me in the crowd. The woman on the Jeep shouted and the man with the stopwatch nodded, holding up his hand as if asking the teacher to call on him. On the side of the Jeep it said NORTH ATLANTIC OCEANOGRAPHIC INSTITUTE.

"What happens now?" I asked Jerry. To my surprise, I saw that he was crying.

"Sorry," he said, wiping his eyes. "These big guys—there's like a couple hundred left. On the planet. Now they try to get it back out to sea, but it won't be easy, I can tell you that. You're looking at seventy, eighty tons there."

Had the oddly placed eye closed altogether or was it still slightly open? I couldn't tell. A pelican flew over it, then a few seagulls. A helicopter, like a larger bird, approached and hovered. The whale's tail moved, and I felt it, like a shock, in my breastbone: it was alive. This rare creature, so gargantuan, wanted to live. What were the intervals supposed to be between spoutings? Was it breathing too fast or too slow? I tensed, waiting for it to spout again, counting the seconds. Was that a smear of blood near its mouth? To know that something that big was trying to live—it was nearly unbearable to wait for its next massive breath. I counted, not knowing what number I wanted.

The little girls ran up. "What's it doing?" said Celia.

"Is it going to be okay?" asked Andrea.

"I don't know, honey," said Jerry. "When they beach like this, people have to help them. It might be sick. It might have gotten lost."

"It's breathing, though, right? That's its blowhole, on top?" asked Andrea.

"They have two, actually," said Jerry, surprising me yet again. "Like two noses, but the noses close up when they go underwater." Andrea looked serious, contemplating the two special noses of the whale.

A bulldozer was rolling very slowly down the beach toward the whale, past a few people with fishing rods watching it go by. It was an incongruous sight: the people with their little rods and the clunky mass of machine, like a tank, plodding across the sand. It was as if we had suddenly entered a world where everything was much bigger, no longer in human scale. We were all small and lightweight by comparison.

"You know, girls, those people look awfully busy. Let's go over to the aquarium, see what's going on. I think there are some baby penguins," said Karen as she arrived. "Jimmy!" she called, but he shook his head, waving her away.

"I'll stay," I said. "We'll meet you back at the boat in forty-five."

"Good," said Jerry. "Let's go, girls." He put his hands on their shoulders. The two children and their parents began making their way back down the beach. Andrea looked back a few times.

At the fence, Jimmy and I stood in silence, watching. Others stood nearby, also quiet, standing respectfully at the yellow tape like parishioners at the Communion rail. A young woman in an officey blue dress, but bare feet, set up a camera on a tripod. She wore tags from the local news station around her neck. Every now and then, the whale made its great geyser noise, mist spangled the air, and the man with the stopwatch noted it down. I tried to read his expression, to see if he was worried or reassured, but all I could see on his face was concentration. Jimmy, nearly as tall as me, with his mother's pointy chin, took a picture of the whale, holding his phone sideways.

"Is it going to die?" he asked.

"I hope not, honey," I said.

A cop—a guy of maybe twenty with a blond crewcut—stood at the tape, just watching, like all of us. A middle-aged man and woman spoke German to each other. I went up to the cop and asked, "What happens now?"

"The NAOI folks will try to refloat it. I don't know. It was on a sandbar this morning. They were out on boats all morning, trying to get it out to sea. But now it's come in here." He shook his head. "It's a shame."

One huge flipper rippled, just once. I felt it between my ribs, down my spine. It was trying to live. Like Jerry, I began to cry.

WHEN DO WE know that we love? I hadn't loved Alan the first time I met him. He was our drug dealer at Smith. He turned up on campus from who knows where every few weeks with a briefcase of dope, cocaine, some mushrooms, maybe. He was skinny, had a wide mouth, wore his sunglasses on top of his head and popped his shirt collars. Arresting eyes, I did notice that, and a graceful way of moving. Quick fingers. He was a big one for winking, which I thought was an affectation. He'd slide into one of our dorm rooms, open the briefcase *clickclick*, wink. "Ladies," he'd say, making a sweeping gesture at his wares, an ironic flourish. Sophie was his contact; I always thought they must be sleeping together, or maybe it was just the way she liked to drape an arm over his shoulders while peering into the open briefcase, as if she owned him. Sophie—Sophie's family—owned a lot of things.

I was the girl leaning against the doorway, watching. I bought from Alan a few times just to not seem stupid, but mostly I was doing what I often did then: watching how the rich girls slouched and slumped and draped and glanced and laughed. They seemed to laugh all the time, those girls, like the whole world was just full of jokes. I didn't get the jokes. Some of them were sleeping together, and I didn't get that, either. One of them actually had a little mustache. She was very popular. Another, from Italy, seemed to be some kind of heroin addict. She rarely came out of her room and walked duck-footed, like a dancer. She often roamed the dorm halls in nothing but pink underwear. Being an honor student from Saint Stanislaus Prep in upstate New York hadn't prepared me for much of anything, as it turned out.

When I got to Smith, though, I learned fast. There's well-off and there's well-off. There is a difference between a ranch house and a stone house. There is a difference between Girl

Scout summer camp and a family "camp" that turns out to be a twelve-bedroom mansion on the coast of Maine. There is a difference between poly blend and carefully oversized linen. There is a difference between trying too hard, taking endless SAT practice tests, and seeming not to be trying at all. At college, the rich girls wore thrift-store nightgowns to class, belted, with boots battered from hard use at the stables. In my first semester, I dumped all my close-fitting poly-blend tops and dresses at the Goodwill and headed for the nightgown section. The rich girls all pretended to be Marxists and poets. Even then, I knew that was bullshit, but I didn't say so. I knew better.

So as Alan *clickclick*ed open his briefcase, I was the one leaning against the doorway wearing a man's button-down shirt from Goodwill two sizes too big for me, my hair in a disheveled French braid, pretending that I cared about drugs. I didn't care about drugs, but I didn't care about much of anything else, either. Our teachers at Smith were big on "finding your passion," and they told stories of brave young women who discovered things and created things and saved things; I knew I was supposed to be moved, so I tried to look inspired. It was bad enough that my father was an accountant and my mother was his receptionist. I didn't have to make it worse by having no imagination or ideals. I majored in anthropology and wrote my senior paper on the Roma people and the effect of European bias on their ability to access cooking utensils. I worked hard on my paper, trying to sound outraged about aluminum saucepans.

I ran into Alan a few years after graduation. By then I had that job as a publicist for a Boston wine distributor, making up stories about the ancestry of grapes for managers with bad haircuts. I walked into an expensive bar with a zinc counter near Post Office Square, and there he was, leaning against the gleaming zinc in a suit that was almost too good even for that bar. And who wears a suit to a bar?

"You," he said, pointer finger out. "You are . . ."

"Suzanne," I said. "From Smith."

His gaze on my face was almost too intense. "Yes. Yes. Alan." At his feet was a briefcase, just like before.

"Hello, Alan."

"Drink?" He gestured at the zinc bar using the same ironic flourish with which he had gestured at his wares back in the dorm, but now he wore a shirt with cuffs and his cufflinks shone platinum. When he smiled, I saw that he had a funny brownish tooth right in front, on the lower set of teeth. Why have a suit that good but not fix the tooth? Had he had that tooth before? He had filled out some in the intervening few years, and his face seemed to have broadened. He still kept his hair a bit shaggy, though, brushing the top of his shirt collar. He was handsome, but he was also something else I couldn't quite name. I would say that it was like his suit didn't entirely fit him, but the suit did, actually; it fit him perfectly. It was something else that didn't quite fit. I was interested.

"Sure," I said. I asked for a glass of the rosé that was very fashionable that season. Alan ordered a scotch, keeping that gaze fixed on me, studying me from head to toe. I wasn't sure if I minded or not. He wasn't a winker anymore, though. He seemed to take himself more seriously now.

A bit later, in the taxi, both of us drunk, he put his head in my lap like a child. Also his hand up my skirt. When we got to my apartment, he produced a cut-glass tumbler, engraved with the bar's name, from his suit-jacket pocket. I laughed.

"Now you won't forget me," he said. "Suzanne from Smith." He set the tumbler in the center of my little plywood table from the unpainted furniture store. The tumbler looked so old-fashioned, heavy and grand. A beautiful thing brazenly stolen from another world with the name of its owner written right across it. A ridiculous, obvious theft. Alan tilted his head and smiled at me. I laughed and he laughed, too.

"Did you ever smoke any of those joints you bought from me to impress your friends?"

"They weren't my friends. And no. Were you sleeping with Sophie?"

"She thought so. I mean, yes, a few times, but." He moved closer. "There's sleeping with and sleeping with, you know?" I touched his face. He closed his eyes. I brushed his shaggy hair off his forehead.

"I do know," I said.

He told me things about himself that night, and about what he'd figured out about money, what you could do. He worked for a small brokerage and he'd seen it practically on the first day. It was a thing with currencies and rates of exchange. Lots of people did it. Naked and entwined, we laughed about the world, how easy things could be if you just knew where to look and didn't get distracted by all the pompousness and posturing and jargon and Charvet shirts. The bottom line was what mattered. It was no different than understanding that the rich girls weren't Marxists or poets. None of the emperors had any clothes. "People like us," he said, "just have to be a little smarter. Not a lot, even." His voice was reedy, younger-sounding than his intelligence. He was a clever young man with a striver's expensive suit, a weird tooth, and when had he palmed the tumbler? And why? I confessed that though I knew a lot about wine, I didn't care about wine.

"Who really does?" he said. "Who fucking cares?"

I went farther. Something about that tumbler—it made me want to say things out loud. I told him that I didn't care about the job, and I didn't care about whatever those Smith girls said they cared about so much in the world, plus they were lying, and I didn't have some big passion. I just wanted a really nice life. The rest of it could go screw. Twice.

"Right on, Suzanne from Smith," he said. "You have nothing to lose but your French braid. Do little bluebirds make that thing for you?"

We laughed and laughed, and I knew that he was sad, and I was sad, and there's sleeping with and sleeping with, and being smart and being smarter. We knew which ones we were.

In the morning, I asked him, "So what's in the briefcase?"

Still naked and smeared with me, his shaggy hair even shaggier, he brought the briefcase over to the bed. It was thick black leather with silver clasps that didn't make a sound when he undid them. With that same ironic flourish, he lifted the lid. Inside was the business section of yesterday's *Boston Globe*, a few pens, and a baseball.

"It's my lucky baseball," he said, taking it out and kissing it with a smacking sound.

"Oh, Jesus," I said. "You phony bastard." That was when I fell in love with him, right then. Because that's what the whole business scene was to him: a baseball. He could toss it. For the first time in what seemed like decades, I felt like I was with someone who saw what I saw out there in the world, and could beat them at their own game. I had never understood what the rich girls were laughing about, but Alan and I knew what the joke really was, and that it was on them. This man: I could make a life with him.

We spent the rest of the day in bed; he never really went back to his own place again; we married; he went to work for a bigger firm; we lived well; we had Noah. When Alan cradled Noah as a baby, he seemed to still inside; his innate restlessness slowed, like a top spun down. He looked at Noah with astonishment and almost a sort of skepticism that something so wonderful had happened and was lying in his arms. I thought we might have another child, but I miscarried twice and there was more than enough to do just keeping our little tribe in good form. Noah had reading problems, attention problems; I had to learn about that, and help him after school. Noah hesitated on every threshold, was easily bored, didn't much see the point of printed marks on paper or care how long it took the train that left at eight in Ohio, but five in California, to get to San Francisco going eighty miles an hour, etc. There were private schools to find, tutors to hire, tempting activities, gear for those activities to buy. The three of us took a lot of trips. The dailiness grew around us like vines and all of the vines were expensive—our own vineyard, I guess you could call it. Our own bit of acreage. Other people were way richer than us. Think about all the things they must have done. We were just taking care of our family. We weren't emptying the Federal Reserve or anything, although sometimes I wished we could. Do you know what private school tuition costs these days? Plus the class trips? I sure as hell wasn't going to send my kid to the nuns. And the mortgage, the cars—it adds up so fast. Currencies and rates of exchange are just tiny numbers that change all the time. They hardly even exist, really.

Like every family, we had our challenges. Alan was very patient with Noah, always. He firmly believed that Noah would grow out of his difficulties. I wasn't so sure, watching for any glimmer of Noah's commitment to a task, a book, a team. I was afraid he'd get older and be like me when I was young: sad and indifferent. Unlike me, though, he didn't try to hide it. He dropped things as easily as he left his shoes around the house, apparently confident that someone else would pick them up. I did. I know women complain about things like this, the picking-up after and all that, but I loved the warm, well-lit circle of the three of us. My days were full. It was the good life I had always wanted.

When the crash came, I said, "Jesus, what happened? How could you have made such a big mistake?"

"Suzie," he said. "Come on." His face was mottled. It was more square now, his lips a bit thinner. "Don't play dumb."

"I'm not playing *dumb*. I just don't understand."

He shook his head. "It's these times, it's . . . I thought it would all even out. But it's just, you know, like musical chairs. Sometimes." He paused, looking at the kitchen floor. "The music stopped at the wrong time. Fasten your seat belt. They're going to blame us."

"Us? I did my job. You were supposed to—"

"Supposed to what? Supposed to what, Suzanne?"

I felt very strange. I sat down in the tall chair at the gray-and-blue kitchen island, which still had crumbs scattered on it from our dinner. I gripped the island, so heavy and real, as if its solidity would make what he was saying not true. Through the French doors, the garden was abundant, greens and pinks and yellows. The translucent minimalist bird-feeder seemed to float in all that color, untethered. Alan was still looking at me. "Listen, it's about to get bad," he said. "I have to explain some things. We can fight later."

"We're not like them, though." Had that squirrel been getting in the birdfeeder again?

"Who?"

"Those ones you see on the news, with the briefcases over their faces. That's not us. And I thought . . ."

"What?" He looked at me keenly.

"The currencies and exchange rates, it's just math. How can you be in trouble for math?"

"Suze. Come on. You know better. I mean, even that stuff." He made a seesawing motion with his hand. "But that was years ago, back at Mutual. You know it all went . . . past that."

"No."

"The kerfluffle with the SEC two years ago—you know what they said."

"But they lost. It didn't stick."

Alan sighed. "Mark is coming with some papers tomorrow. He'll explain everything. There will be some things to sign. We have to get on with it."

"Get on with what? I don't understand. I don't understand."

His voice rose. "Suzanne. Stop it with this shit. We don't have a lot of time. There are a few things we can do, things we can move around, but I could be indicted as soon as next week. We have to hustle, like we always have." He reached for my hand. "Plus, obviously, you can't testify against me." He laughed. "Not that you would. I picked the right wingman, for sure."

I pulled my hand away. I felt so peculiar. "I'm not your wingman. I didn't know. If you'd shown me—"

Alan stared at me with an expression that was changing to something an awful lot like hatred mixed with panic. "What? Shown you what? What the hell are you talking about? You see this house. You see how we live, with the trips and the accounts and all the rest of it." He lowered his voice. "You knew I faked those trades. I showed it to you. We *laughed* about it, how you could make it on a computer yourself, how Noah could probably do it."

I went cold. "Well, that was the once. Because of that drop, and the margins, and who she was."

"Where did you think the money came from to put back in her account? She had actually just lost north of two hundred grand."

"How should I know? I don't know anything about money. The numbers, or whatever you were doing—we're not like that. I'm not like that."

Alan swallowed hard. "Suze. You couldn't have believed it was only once. I told you where the money came from, that time. And Mark was over here a million times, you heard what we talked about—"

"No," I said. "No. That's not true." I felt as if I was falling from a very great height, like Wile E. Coyote when he looks down, realizes he's running over a canyon and there's nothing beneath his feet, and plummets. In that moment, I saw very clearly that nothing around me was real, not the birdfeeder, not the house, not the garden, not our lives. It was built on sand. I had thought it was real and solid, but it wasn't. I closed my eyes for a second, trying to take it in. "You're saying I was some sort of accomplice. But that's ridiculous."

"Listen, Suze, *accomplice* is a harsh way of putting it, but you knew enough. I didn't think I had to spell it all out for you every day." He actually looked frightened now, and something like shocked. "We made such a great team." What stories about me had he been telling himself? Suddenly, he seemed a stranger to me, this man to whom I had been married for years, with whom I had a child, shared a life, laughed and cried and puked and came. But this lie he obviously wanted me to agree to—no, I wouldn't do that. I had to draw a line there. "Suzanne?" he said, and he sounded a bit pleading. Was he having mood swings?

My head, and my hands, and my belly, and my skin hurt. I felt like I was dying. I walked out of the kitchen, and once the trial was over, I walked out of that life as well, inexorably, as if pulled on a string, numb but determined. I saw on that day of the crash that, somewhere along the way, Alan had obviously taken a different path, a dark path, and had purposely withheld it from me. This is what I mean about the complicity thing. You have to *know* to be truly complicit, and I didn't. All I knew about was currencies and exchange rates, and I didn't even understand all that much about that. I was busy taking care of our family. I didn't know anything about money. Alan was trying to get me to agree to a lie. Clearly, he had become entranced by ever more fantastical plans and schemes; he wasn't that canny, funny young man with the baseball in his briefcase anymore. I knew on that awful day—and it's peculiar but so important, those moments of clarity in the midst of catastrophe—that what I needed was the real. Only the real, from then on. That was the promise I made myself. I thought: I'll go somewhere small and real where nobody knows me. My old life was built on sand. I'll build a new one.

ALTHOUGH I DIDN'T see it at the time, that string was pulling me to the whale, suffering on the beach. It was a stranger to me in every conceivable aspect. It wasn't even my kind. But the life in it, the huge beating heart somewhere within that vast body: I had to help. I knew what my freakishly strong arms and hands could do now. As I stood barefoot in the sand, counting the seconds between the whale's breaths, I saw that maybe all of our misfortune had happened to bring me there, to meet and help this grand, suffering creature. Maybe there had been a reason for the misery Alan had caused us, a larger purpose. Jerry had said that this whale was terribly rare, one of just a few surviving in the entire world. It was special, hardly ever seen by human beings. It had to be saved. I felt urgent, and unexpectedly comforted, and filled with energy.

As Jimmy and I watched, both of us beginning to shiver in the beach wind, six people in blue vests, boots, and hats came straggling down the sand, and a ranger gestured them into the snow fence to the busy circle where the whale lay. On the backs of their vests it said NAOI VOLUNTEER in big white letters. They clustered around the ranger, listening. The surf lapped at their feet, getting their sneakers wet.

Only six. That was nowhere near enough, anyone could see that. Three of them had to be over sixty, white-haired, bespectacled.

The whale let out a moan and everything inside the circle stopped moving, stopped talking, stopped writing. More than one person in the crowd outside the fence winced. It sounded like the earth itself moaning, like an echo of a sound made thousands of years ago by a glacier scraping over a continent. Jimmy, tight-lipped, looked a little ill. I knew how he felt. I couldn't bear the sound, either. It was a warning, of something from a far bigger place, bigger than all of us.

"Hey!" I yelled to the ranger. "Hey!" I waved my arms around. The ranger, a young woman with a serious/irritated expression, came over to the fence. "I want to help."

"Listen," she said, "this is for trained folks only. You can make a donation right on the NAOI site, we'll let the community know what's going on, but right now—"

"Please," I begged. "Please, please. I'll train. Where do I go?"

The ranger shook her head. "No time for that. We have maybe twenty-four hours to help this guy, you can make a donation—"

"Please," I said, "please. You only have six volunteers—"

She adjusted her hat. "Lady, do you see all these people in here? These are professionals. This is a major stranding. I understand your concern, but the best thing you can do for the animal is let us do our jobs—"

"Please," I said.

The whale spouted.

The ranger paused. It was as if the whale had spoken up on my behalf. "You local? Live here?"

"I was born here. Lived here all my life."

Jimmy side-eyed me.

"Got a car?"

I nodded.

"Got a piece of paper?"

I found the donut receipt and a pen in my bag. "Ready."

"You can call this number, tell them Cindy said to call, you're a local, you want to be a gofer." She gave me a number and walked away.

Another truck pulled up and the NAOI volunteers began unloading big sheets of light-colored cloth. Two by two, they opened the sheets, lofted them and began sidewalking them over the animal as if laying gauze on an enormous burn victim. The woman still on top of the Jeep was yelling something about the blowholes and one of the white-haired volunteers held up a palm to her sidewalking partner. They stood there, the bolt of cloth half unfurled on the sand between them, looking up toward the top of the whale. They needed more help, clearly.

"Smooth," said Jimmy.

"Please don't narc on me."

Jimmy said impassively, "You gotta do what you gotta do."

"We should go," I said, but neither of us moved, watching the volunteers wrestle with the sheets; watching the clusters of people inside the snow fence walk around the whale, writing things down, consulting with one another, talking on their phones. Like the crowd outside the fence, they were taking photos of the whale, too, but methodically, moving up and down the animal's body, stepping over a foot or so, and beginning at the top again. The Jeep inched a little closer to the whale very, very slowly, and the leader-woman got out and climbed on top of the vehicle once more, leaning over the top of the whale. She shook her head, calling out, "We need more cloth."

"I can go," I yelled through cupped hands, and the leader-woman turned her head in my direction, frowning.

"Call that person," said Jimmy.

"Right, right." I dialed, but it went to voicemail. I left a message, trying to sound professional. A professional volunteer.

Jimmy and I watched as the six old volunteeers tried to get the whale covered in the sheets, then I grabbed my shoes and we headed back down the sand toward Captain Pete's. Every few steps, I turned around to look at the great wrapped figure, stranded on the edge of land and sea, surrounded by the Lilliputian figures of people and cars and trucks.

When we docked that afternoon, I got into my car and drove down Route 28, filled with the presence of the whale, the almost frightening, wondrous power of its misting breath. I pulled into a Home Goods parking lot, went inside the cavernous store, and bought as many towels as I could carry. A teenaged Home Goods salesman helped me lug them all out to the Honda. "You having a lot of guests for the weekend?" he asked. I got back to the site and, towels piled up to my chin, made my way over the sand to the inner circle of whale people. It was getting dusky, colder, and the wind scraped at my face.

I arrived at the snow fence, quite close to where the leader-woman was talking on the phone. She was apple-bodied, fortyish, with a broad, open face and brown hair in a tight bun at the base of her neck. She looked like a Quaker minister, or what I imagined a Quaker minister to look like: sober, capable, unadorned. She was listening to whoever was on the other end of the line, shaking her head.

With relief, I dropped the towels at her feet. My hands hurt, my fingers hurt, and my face was starting to hurt. I needed a jacket.

She glanced at the pile of towels with an expression like, *Who the hell are you?*

"It's a donation," I said. "You need it, right? Cindy said I could be a gofer. I'm local."

"Thanks," she said. She pointed at one of the volunteers, and he jogged over, stepped over the fence, hefted all the towels inside the whale circle, and stepped back inside.

"What else can I do?" I said, but she was already walking away, leaving hiking boot impressions in the sand.

● ● ●

WHEN I GOT back home, I clicked around online. I saw photos of scores of small whales beaching and dying on the coast of Chile; a whale stuck going the wrong way up an inlet in England; a whale in a pool of blood on the sand; five people waist-deep in the sea, pushing a whale the size of a sailboat. This was happening in so many places, this kind of thing, and to other marine mammals, too—dolphins and porpoises and seals who weren't swimming right. As oceans all over the world got warmer, it was happening much more often. I teared up, glad that no one could see me here in my drafty shed with my two suitcases, my cheap furniture, my bunged-up hands and my divorce, getting weepy over the environment. I know the word *anthropomorphism*. None of that stopped the tears from flowing over my face, scraped from this long day's sand and wind. I was so late, and the feverish oceans were so vast. What had I been doing all this time? What did it matter about schools and gear and window treatments and exchange rates when this was all going on? How could I have been so blind to what was really happening in the world? Our concerns were nothing, compared to all this. The ocean was alive, it was an entire world unto itself, and it was grievously endangered. This was what mattered. This special, special being had landed on our shore, like a king, in pain and in exile, trying to alert us to the enemies attacking his country: us.

My phone rang. It was a man from the NAOI, brusque-voiced, lots of background noise, telling me to be at the site at six thirty the next morning if I still wanted to help. I stopped crying, turned off the computer, and made dinner. Then I climbed up my loft ladder and went to bed. I set the alarm for six.

BY THE TIME I got to the whale at six thirty, scarfing down coffee and a leftover Delilah's donut in my shambling, smoke-reeking car, the scene was already bustling again. The whale lay in its wet sheets, which glowed pinky-orange in the dawning day, and a mismatched patchwork of wet towels. The leviathan looked like another sun, fallen to earth on the broad, flat beach. Surf swirled around it. Around the whale were the cops, the rangers, the blue-vested volunteers, and now people in jackets that said NAOI on the back, along with a slender Asian woman with a nose ring deep in conversation with the Quaker-faced woman who was in charge. Outside the snow fence, a tall, sunburned man with a shaved head and a massive backpack crouched in the sand peering into a camera with a telephoto lens. Julie was there, blue-vested and in a wool cap inside the snow fence. She called out, "Hey!" I spotted a young African American man with a clipboard and ran around the edge of the snow fence to where he stood.

"I'm here," I said. "Suzanne Flaherty. I'm a gofer."

He checked his list. "Okay, can you go get us some things? We need them ASAP. And don't forget receipts."

"Yes, yes. Tell me."

"Ten five-gallon buckets, a hundred feet of sisal rope, two of those, twenty pairs of utility gloves, twenty shovels, fifteen portable lanterns we can set up on the beach tonight, and food. Whatever food. Lots of it. Might have to do a few food runs. Give me your phone." He called his phone with mine, and handed mine back to me. "Text me when you're back. I'm Tyler."

"Got it," I said as I scribbled down the complicated list. "What's the plan?"

"High tide is four thirty a.m. tomorrow, and we're lucky, it's a full moon, so it will be even higher. If this guy can just stay with us that long, Annie—the boss over there—has a way she thinks we can refloat him. Maybe." Tyler crossed his fingers.

"Who's that person with the nose ring?"

"That's Dr. Chang. Big-deal marine-mammal vet, she flew in from Oregon. She's the shit."

"Poor thing," I said, looking at the whale. "He must be so confused."

"Go," said Tyler.

I WENT TO the Home Depot, moving up and down the aisles with a cart the size of a small car, loading in gear. Charging my purchases, I felt incredibly necessary. I smiled at the cashier, who didn't smile back. Once I had crammed it all into the Honda, I went to the deli in the strip mall and bought as much food as I thought I could fit in the car. There was barely room for me in the driver's seat and I couldn't see anything in my rearview mirror but bags and boxes and shovel handles. I drove back toward the site with my hazards on, my palms sweating with excitement.

I pulled onto the side of the road near the site, texted Tyler, and began unloading everything onto the sand and scrub. Two volunteers in blue vests came slip-sliding down the low, grassy dune, pulling a large wagon with fat wheels and slats on the sides. One of them was Julie. "Where's your vest?" she said, then, to the white-haired man with her, "Roger, let's do the equipment first, then the food." She and Roger began stacking things in, fitting them quickly and precisely. "This is not a drill, right?"

"How's he doing?" I asked.

"Pretty good. His respiration is close to normal, which is amazing, and that vet said she thinks he's young. She can't see any major injuries, but that doesn't mean much. Could be internal."

Roger, surveying the cartload, said, "I think we can get one of the pumps on this round."

"Yup," said Julie, popping one into a space I hadn't seen. "His callosities are great. Like a pile of frosting."

"His what?" I didn't have time to remember that I should be pretending that I knew what I was doing.

"That thing on his head." Julie twirled her fingers over her head. "Callosities. The sea lice make them."

I made a face. "I haven't been around a live-whale stranding before," I confessed.

"Well, me neither," said Julie. "Not like this. This is a once-in-a-lifetime kind of thing."

"It is," said Roger, picking up the wagon handle.

This is what it must have been like, I thought, when

Chesham was a seafaring town, a whaling town like so many around here, and the doings of the sea mattered to everyone, young or old, rich or poor, all races. They had that mysterious vast force at their doorsteps, beneficent and cruel, in common. This town, and all the towns now strung out behind the strip of massive stores, once looked toward the sea and its horizon. They were connected to the earth, and to everything that lived on it. Standing by the side of the two-lane highway with deli bags and Home Depot bags and boxes piled nearby, I smelled the salt in the air with a new keenness.

It took four wagonloads to get everything down to the site, plus me carrying in my arms as much as I could, trudging over the dune and down the sand. Julie and Roger laid things outside the snow fence and up the beach like nurses arranging equipment for a surgeon, the gear divided into piles by category: shovels, pumps, ropes, lanterns, gloves. They put all the food into the wagon, digging a hole in the sand for the handle, then covering it with sand and a pile of tarps. I arranged the food as they had the equipment, putting the chips in a heap, grouping the sodas together, stacking loaves of bread in their plastic bags. The wind sang in my ears. When we were done, the three of us stood near our makeshift staging area, watching the scene. With all of the people, the equipment, and the vehicles surrounding the gigantic, shrouded figure, it looked as if they might be building a whale rather than rescuing one. Dr. Chang, masked and gloved, lifted a flap of flowered towel and gently palpated the animal's side, but no one else touched it at all. What was it like to touch the whale? I desperately wanted to be where she was, to be close to the enormous sides, the enormous breath, but at the same time felt that it would be almost wrong to touch it, like profaning something sacred. It was a strange miracle that it was here, like those statues of the Virgin Mary that weep blood. Who would dare to get close to a miracle?

The bulldozer, its huge shovel up, was parked farther away from the site than any of the other vehicles. A man climbed out and went over to Annie, nodding as she spoke. The whale spouted, and Julie and Roger high-fived each other. "He's hanging in," said Julie. "That's our guy."

Roger squinted. "Yeah, he's doing all right. He's doing all right."

"Now what?" I asked.

"I'm not sure," said Julie. "Annie said they'd be monitoring all day and they're going to have to do something more to keep it wet, but it's kind of a waiting game."

Dr. Chang reemerged near the whale's tail, speaking into a phone that she held flat on her palm.

"Tyler told me they're going to get the fire hoses to mist it," said Roger. "I want to see that."

"Will they take all those sheets and towels off?" I said.

Julie shook her head. "You can't. The sun, the wind, birds—they'd all get at it. It has to be protected."

"That's so strange, isn't it? Something that big, being so fragile?" I said.

"It's only fragile on land," said Julie. "In the water, it's different. Did you know they can hear through their teeth?"

"Wow," I said. I wondered what its teeth were hearing now, and what it thought those sounds were. Did it understand that we funny little forked creatures were trying to help it? Did he feel alone?

Roger squinted. "That thing rolls on you, you're dead," he said. "That flipper could knock you clear to Tuesday."

"How long do they live?" I asked.

"Sixty, seventy years," said Julie. "Like a person." Out here, beneath sky and beach, she didn't seem as tall as she did on the massage table. She sighed. "I'm going to need to go back to town, come back this afternoon. Dan has a doctor's appointment." But she didn't move.

The activity inside the snow fence had slowed; the sun had risen higher; the sheets were no longer orange, but beige-ish. Folks were beginning to gather again outside the snow fence, holding up their phones to take pictures. Out at sea, a large boat that said CAPE TOURS idled, with little figures of people crowded on the side facing the whale. A few people from the whale-rescue operation came over to the wagon and began eating chips, bagels, popping open soda cans. No one talked much. We all watched the whale. It spouted. Everyone smiled. We kept watching.

What I remember now, what I'll remember all my life, is the quiet. The scientists talked to one another and wrote things down, but except for the random shout of a child farther down the beach or a few bars of some pop song from a radio caught by the wind, we, inside and outside the snow fence, were quiet. We all stayed standing. We just stood there, looking. We knew we were in the presence of a rare, mighty being unlike any we had seen before. The dogs on leashes, standing by their people, lay down in the sand. The caution tape flapped. The surf crashed and hissed. Every now and then, a foghorn sounded. The whale spouted. At least once, its tail moved, and I felt it everywhere, electric, almost painfully resonant. Time, measured by the spouting breaths of the whale, slowed.

I HAD A client at noon, so I went back to town, like Julie. As we left the site, I offered to drive us both back later that afternoon, and she said yes. She'd be ready at four. So now I had a sure way back into the rescue operation. In town, a table was set up outside Delilah's with blown-up photos of the whale and posterboards with Sharpie drawings of fish with crosses for eyes and glitter letters reading SAVE THE OCEAN! MARINE MAMMALS ROCK! EMERGENCY BAKE SALE TODAY! SUPPORT THE NORTH ATLANTIC OCEANOGRAPHIC INSTITUTE! The table was filled with cupcakes, cookies, and donuts; a big glass jar sat at one end, already half full of money. Two of the teenage girls I'd seen working at Delilah's stood behind the table, one with a dolphin painted on her forehead, the other with a whale, spouting exuberantly, painted on her forearm.

"Hey!" called out the dolphin one to me. "Want to help save ocean life today?"

"I'm already helping," I said, feeling buoyant. "I'm on the volunteer team."

"Right on," said the whale one, holding up peace fingers. "We support you. Free coffee all day for volunteers."

"Thanks," I said. "Keep up the good work."

A local news truck was parked a few doors down from Delilah's, the back open, a man with coiffed hair sitting on the bumper, looking glum.

"How's it going?" I said to him.

When he lifted his face, I could see the makeup not quite reaching to his collar. "Ah," he said. "Not good. They've cut off access to the beach around that big guppy out there. We're trying to get a helicopter. Got one?"

"Mine is in the shop," I said. "Sorry. Have you been to the bake sale?"

"Twice. The tall one is my daughter."

"Good luck," I said.

I got home with just enough time to set up the room, turn on the space heater, and change into my massage clothes. My client was Ted, a young man who was a developer. Ted and his company were much hated around town, sadly, for good reason. His company was bad, and Ted, as far as I could tell, was bad, too, in the way of people who see the entire world through its financial topography. I had been to a lot of dinners in my former life with guys like Ted. I had thrown excellent dinner parties for tables full of guys like Ted. They spent their lives staring at ticker tapes, their very heartbeats speeding up or slowing down depending on what they saw there. Prisoners of numbers on screens. Ted's body was compact, muscled, and smooth.

From the face cradle, Ted said, "Did you hear about the whale? Jesus Christ! A freakin' whale! My kids are going nuts."

"Lavender or plain?"

"Plain. Not too much."

I didn't particularly like Ted, but I liked to touch him, because he was so springy. His body was like a young dog, always ready to jump up and catch the ball. Naked on my table, he was just a regular guy, average in every way. When he put his clothes on, he put on his ruthlessness, too.

"I've been out there helping all day," I said.

"Good for you," said Ted. I could tell he was starting to get drowsy. He usually fell asleep before I had even reached his calves.

"They can hear through their teeth."

"What?"

"Yeah, it's amazing. Their teeth pick up sound waves."

He sighed. "Weird." A minute later, "I lifeguarded a bunch of summers, back in high school."

"Uh-huh." I carefully folded the sheet over his midsection. Bare, the power of his legs was innocent, all capacity without motive.

"Can you do shiatsu?" he asked.

"I haven't been trained in that," I said.

"Guy I work with loves it."

"Mmmm," I said. "Breathe in." I pressed hard on his springy, furry shoulders. "Breathe out."

Conk. Out like a light. His body yielded fairly easily, although it didn't retain the suppleness very long. Whenever I went back to a section, it had bounced back to its former state, already having forgotten me.

Ted tipped very well, I have to say. But as he drove away, I thought that it couldn't be right, that guys like Ted raked in cash while the NAOI held bake sales to raise money. How many cupcakes could they possibly sell to rescue the ocean?

After Ted left with renewed energy for destroying what little remained of Chesham's charm, I called Noah, who, of course, didn't pick up. "Honey," I said into his voicemail, "it's the most incredible thing, there's this huge rare whale that's beached out here, and I'm helping out. I wish you were here. Remember the Monterey Aquarium, those stingrays? And you went as a stingray for Halloween? I made your costume? You'd love this—I've never seen anything like it. Please call me." I hung up. Later, I could send him a picture. If he could just see how big it was, how much bigger it all was than us. If he could just see that, he'd be able to let go of some of his displaced anger at me. Humanity itself came from the ocean. All life, in fact. We could stand together at its edge, the way Jimmy and I had. We could help, before it was too late.

Julie and I were both excited as I drove us down the strip toward the whale. We had both brought sweaters and scarves and winter coats for the long night ahead. Tyler texted "bring more food" so we stopped at the strip-mall grocery store and loaded up. We filled the back seat of the car with grocery bags. How long, I wondered, could a whale go without eating? I had also brought all my towels—I only had four—and a roll of paper towels, I wasn't quite sure for what. Julie told me she had promised to take lots of pictures for her husband on her phone.

"How long have you lived here?" I asked her.

"This is Dan's hometown. We were living in Denver early on, but we moved back here when he got sick so we could be close to family. It's been a big help. What brought you to our little town?"

"I needed a fresh start and I like the beach."

"Huh," said Julie, looking out the window. "I'd go straight back to Denver. I'm a mountain girl."

There was clearly an unspoken *if* in that sentence. I wondered if the mountains explained her feet, or if she had done other work before becoming a librarian. "How did you get involved with the Oceanographic Institute?"

"Dan's folks are into it. You met his dad this morning—Roger. That lady with the white hair, that's Dan's mom, Shelly. Roger, his grandfather—all fishermen. Going way back. Before Dan got sick, he was big into sailing. Had his own twenty-two-foot O'Day. I mean, we still have it, but he can't go out alone anymore."

"Right," I said. I wasn't sure what an O'Day was, but it sounded like a boat.

Roger met us by the side of the road with the wagon and we filled it with grocery bags. I took the handle this time. It took a hard pull to get it going, and keep it going, over the sand. Julie and Roger pushed as I pulled the handle, both hands on it behind my back, leaning forward to trudge.

"How is he?" asked Julie.

"Well. His breathing is slowing down some. They've been misting him all day, and we're lucky that it isn't hot. Ten hours to go-time. Hard to say."

Down on the beach, in addition to all the people, the bulldozer, the police cars, the NAOI Jeep, and a van that said NOAA on the side, there were also two firetrucks, an ambulance, and a white tent about the size of my old dining room, which is to say: big. Flowers were piled against the outside of the snow fence; the crowd was now watched over by a ranger in a ranger hat. The whale in its dampened sheets and towels lay at the water's edge, vast and silent.

Just beyond the ambulance was a big pile of what I almost thought at first was a herd of little whales or dolphins, also stranded, but I realized that they were long, inflated plastic tubes, each one about six feet wide. "What are those?" I asked Roger, dropping the wagon handle and rubbing my already sore hands. The woman who I now knew was Shelly was making her way over to us along with a few other volunteers in blue vests.

"Pontoons. That's how we're going to do it. Even so." He shook his head. "I don't know. But Annie and Dr. Chang think there's a chance it could work. People have done it in New Zealand."

"What are we going to do with them?"

"That's how we're going to push the whale."

"We can't just push on it all together? Isn't the bulldozer there to push it?"

"That's not what the bulldozer is there for," said Roger.

"You can't ever, ever touch it," said Julie. "Didn't they tell you that? Not with bare hands. Their skin is super-sensitive."

Roger said, "At high tide, we're going to push on the pontoons set all around the whale and refloat it. See that guy?" He pointed to a man in a green jacket. "He's Army Corps of Engineers. This is major."

A figure on top of one of the firetrucks aimed a hose up and at an angle high above the whale; a plume of mist settled on the whale's back and, as the figure moved the hose, along the animal's sides and down toward the great tail. Then back again.

"Plus," said Julie, "it could be carrying something—a disease. We don't know what's wrong with it, you know?"

I hadn't been thinking that anything could be internally wrong with the whale, our right whale. I had thought of it as a visitor from another realm, a creature from a vaster order of being who had strayed into our smaller, earthbound terrain. Something very special, like the Northern Lights. A miracle. It had maybe taken a wrong turn because the ocean was too hot or too cold or too stormy. But of course it could be that it was sick, even very sick. And contagious. Still, wouldn't that make it even more urgent that we get it back to its world? What enormous clock was ticking within the enormous body, covered by that fragile skin, like the *Hindenburg*?

The whale spouted; how long had it been since its last breath? I felt terribly impatient, and a little angry that we still had so many hours to go before four thirty in the morning. It needed to go home. It wanted to go home. This was a slow-motion emergency. The enormous creature was suffering and we were giving it firetruck-mist and walkie-talkies and rubber tubes, and if we failed, a bulldozer was going to push it somewhere like trash. It made me feel sick and angry to think of it.

Julie put her hand on my arm. "Suze, let's go on into the tent. It's getting cold out here."

It was crowded inside the tent, but it felt quieter because the beach wind didn't blow there, and the collective body heat warmed the space. Tyler, looking older than he had this morning, was moving through the crowd with Annie, both of them pausing every few steps to talk to one or another person in a NOAA jacket or a ranger uniform or a blue vest. The atmosphere was purposeful and tense. All the food we had brought was laid out on a folding table to one side and I was pleased to see how much of it was already gone, empty bags and wrappers scattered around. If nothing else, I could help feed the team, although I felt desperate to do more. In one corner of the tent, the man in the green jacket from the Army Corps of Engineers was deep in conversation with Dr. Chang. Neither of them looked happy. Outside the tent, the wind was picking up.

As the night came on, Annie and Tyler divided us into squads. First out of the tent were the official people in uniforms who were going to set up the site for the big push: digging a huge trench, positioning the pontoons, calculating weights and masses and points of leverage. Next out of the tent were five other marine-mammal vets who had come with Dr. Chang, all in waders, knit hats, tight black gloves, and masks. Next out were paramedics and ambulance drivers, who were going to wait in their ambulances for any of us who might slip or drown or be knocked to Tuesday by seventy tons of disoriented, homesick whale. The bulldozer driver leaned against the food table in his shirtsleeves, eating a brownie. He looked familiar to me; he was a regular at Waves, I realized. Always ordered a double bourbon, sat by himself. I stood with the other volunteers, waiting for instructions, drinking coffee out of a paper cup, although I hardly needed it. Energy coursed through every part of me.

There were eight of us volunteers left in the tent—Roger, Shelly, me, Julie, a young man and woman who also looked familiar although I couldn't place them, and two beefy guys with beards. Men out here tended toward the thick; tonight, that was useful. Tyler handed out white waders with built-in boots, one huge flat size, along with hats and gloves for anyone who didn't have them, and masks. I took off my shoes and stepped into my waders awkwardly, fumbling with the suspenders. The waders smelled of rubber. Annie told us what we were going to do. She, too, was covered head to toe; there were circles under her eyes. Her voice was light in timbre, but firm in tone. She spoke deliberately and slowly, as if we were a class taking notes. She kept repeating the phrase "our window," as if there were a window on the vast, dark, windy beach outside, a temporary window large enough for a whale to pass through it. Annie made it clear that we only had that one window, one window in time, and most likely if that window closed and we failed, there wouldn't be another one. Not for this whale, and not for us. The chances of seeing a right whale again here, alive or dead, were minuscule.

Annie would tell us what to do when through a bullhorn. We would set up the portable lanterns, maybe help deepen the trench, and when the time came, when instructed and only when instructed, we would push on the pontoons. We were not ever to touch the whale directly under any circumstances, for any reason. We were to keep our masks on at all times. We were a team, and we had to keep track of one another. Once it started, Annie said, she wouldn't be able to watch us. We had to do that. You count your own heads, said Annie. Tyler handed out whistles. If anyone was in trouble, we were to blow the whistle as hard as we could. I put my whistle around my neck. Then Annie made a curiously small, subtle gesture with her hands, sweeping us all out into the night. Our empty shoes littered the tent floor behind us.

Just outside the tent, as my team trooped toward the site, I called Noah one more time. "It's happening. We're going out now. You can't imagine what this is like, it's so big and incredible. I love you." Then I ran, the rubber waders squeaking, to catch up to the others.

Our first job was to set up the portable lanterns. Tyler showed us how. He began setting little flags at intervals where the lanterns should go. We fanned out in the growing darkness. I put the light in the sand and bent over awkwardly to hold the lantern steady with my foot while twisting it with both my hands. Sandily, it gave, lit. The light was surprisingly strong: an industrial light that hurt my eyes. I put my gloves back on and anchored the lantern as firmly as I could, scrabbling at the wet sand farther down. I went back for another light, went to the next little flag, took my gloves off, stepped, pushed, and got the next lantern open. Light. Still, I wasn't winning the race against the dark; I was barely lighting a few square yards. By light four, I was sweating into my bra. The wind began to feel welcome on my face and hands even as harsh as it was. As I placed the lights, I kept looking up at the whale; the trench next to it was deepening fast, the ungainly, strangely similar shapes of the diggers sinking below the earth. I could see that if the animal rolled onto them, they would be gone, like miners in a mine collapse.

For the first time since all of this had started, I was afraid. I was afraid of the whale, I was afraid for the whale, and I was afraid, too, of something else, of the immense forces all around us that we didn't understand. We were in the middle of something that was already rolling over us, taking us under. The sound of the ocean was loud. Who would be able to hear a whistle blow over that? Who would care? I twisted the lantern in my hands even harder. I made myself look at Julie, at Roger, at Shelly, each bending to their task. One light. Another light. Another light. A small glow spread slowly, illuminating this open-air hospital with just one massive, silent patient from another atmosphere, wrapped in sheets. The diggers tossed up shovelfuls of sand. The pontoons were gathered around the whale, looking as if they, too, were waiting for instructions, but from the animal.

Once the lanterns were set, Tyler gestured us volunteers back into the tent. Everyone else remained outside with their shovels and computers and trucks and gear, their knowledge. Tyler said, "Get yourselves something to eat. Chill out. It's a few hours yet."

Although I wanted to stay near the whale, it was a relief to be out of the wind and the cold. I took off my hat, my coat, and my gloves and sat down in a folding chair. Shelly, sitting next to me, took my hands in hers without a word and began warming them. Hers were veined, age-spotted, and bony. The blood coming into my cold fingers was almost painful. Around us, the tent was a mess of backpacks, notebooks, computers, shoes, an open first aid kit, half-eaten sandwiches, half-empty cups, headsets, and some machine that beeped. One of the beefy guys stretched out on the floor, eyes closed. I flexed my hands.

"Thank you," I said to Shelly.

"You're new here," she said.

"Yeah," I said.

The tent had the atmosphere of a waiting room, and it was a waiting room, of a kind. A few people played around with their phones. Roger read a newspaper. Had he brought it with him? The young man and woman shared a set of headphones, listening to something on a phone.

The hours passed.

Finally, Tyler returned, saying, "Okay, suit up." We gathered ourselves into our hats and gloves and determination, and we filed out of the tent after him. At the site, the tide was now nearly to the whale, and the trench had a broad canal leading to the water. The canal and the trench were both full of seawater, the trench beginning to overflow. The whale was no longer covered in fabric, and I thought I saw it rock, very gently, in its shallow bed of rising sea. It spouted, and we volunteers cheered.

The site was full of people, as before, but now they were occupying specific positions, like players on some sort of sports team or maybe actors waiting for a curtain to go up. The pontoons were perhaps three feet away from the whale, set in a semicircle. Tyler arranged us along the pontoons, interspersed with the official folks, all of us in our waders, our gloves, our masks, and our serious faces, trying to blink away the sand that was blowing in our eyes. The tide was coming in faster and harder, grabbing at our ankles. The whale rose above us, and it was definitely rocking now, as if impatient to be off. I was terrified and exhilarated. I put my hands on the pontoon.

Rising water splashed on my chest, splashed icily on my face; my lungs filled with the smell of salt. My feet had chilled; my calves were growing cold as well. Shelly's face nearby was pinched and white. She appeared to be taking deep breaths, hanging on to the inflated curve of the pontoon. Her lips were moving. Was she praying?

I could see the whale's great eye up close. It was closed, but I could see the profound grooves around it, the curve of the mouth below. I couldn't even bear to imagine what it would be like if that great eye opened and saw me, saw us at this moment; I longed for it and dreaded it at the same time. A lightning strike of fear torched my nerves. All at once I wanted to run, to get away as fast as possible from the vastness and tremendous force of the creature, but instead I kept my gloved hands on the pontoon, and then I swear the whale breathed through my arm. The whale's breath went through me. Oh, God! I felt the animal breathe. I willed it to live. I willed it to live. I willed it to live. The terror turned to energy. I sent all the energy I had down my arms and through my hands toward the gargantuan body of the animal. I knew I was in the right place, at the right time, doing the right thing. It was as if I had been deaf all my life and was suddenly able to hear music.

I don't remember hearing Annie on the bullhorn telling us all to push, I only remember leaning forward with everyone else, pushing with all my strength into the pontoon and then the sensation of the beginning of the floating, the massive turning, the surprisingly quick feeling almost of chasing after it, chasing after a moving mountain, chasing after an ocean liner, the pushing into the water, into the deeper water, deeper still, salt water rushing cold around my midsection, the big white moon above, yelling everywhere, a nearly overwhelming desire to go with it, grabbing for purchase on the slippery rubbery sides, unable to hold them, and then it left us for its own world.

WHEN I WOKE up the next day on my futon under the sky-light, every part of me hurt. Every muscle, every tendon, every joint. My palms were blistered. There was sand in my hair, sand in the sheets. My face stung from what felt like sunburn—moonburn—but must have been the effect of the wind blowing the sand on me for all those hours. Back in Boston, I could have paid a lot of money to have my face resurfaced this way. It was noon. I opened and closed my hands under the covers, lifted my arms, bent my knees. I held the tops of my pained feet in my sore, blistered hands. I was wearing long johns; my hair was thick with sand and salt. The tip of my nose hurt. I touched it and found scratches there. I had been crying hard when the whale slid away into the dark ocean, everyone yelling and cheering; I must have wiped my nose with a sandy glove, maybe more than once. I wasn't hungry. I felt profoundly satisfied and complete. A helicopter beat its wings somewhere. Closer by, the sound of hammering, faint music from a radio.

I crawled slowly out of the loft and, clinging to the ladder, got downstairs. I made coffee, took two Advil, and ran a bath as hot as I could bear, adding Epsom salts. I took the coffee in the largest mug I owned into the bathroom with me, shut the door to keep the steam in, and setting the mug on the floor beside the tub, lowered myself into the hot, salty water. It hurt. The salty steam on my face hurt. Everything hurt. But I was so very happy. I sent the whale a silent benediction for its journey, the king returning to his own country.

I had clients scheduled that day. What was I going to do about my hands? The water in the tub swaddled me, brined me. I ran more hot water. Was this what the whale felt like? Had the cold seawater felt as salvific to the whale as the hot, salty water felt to me? Even reaching my arm out of the water to get my cup of coffee was unpleasant. I held the mug in both hands, elbows and forearms submerged. Suddenly I was starving. The keen edge of that hunger made me giddy, strangely delighted. It was wonderful to be so hungry. I would make myself the midday breakfast of a lumberjack.

Finally, reluctantly, I emerged from the tub with an amphibian slither—although much less gracefully than your average amphibian—dressed, bandaged my hands, made the eggs and bacon and toast. I wanted the taste of the salt, the fat, the meat, the bread. I was going to have to cancel my clients, even though I needed the money. The thought of my bare hands meeting bare flesh, even my own, was painful. I felt so proud of what we had all done, but also, I had to admit, forlorn. I missed the whale, I missed the warm and drafty tent, I missed the rough beach at night and that tremendous, rare, silent creature in our midst.

I ate my breakfast slowly. I thought that maybe I should get a dog, or maybe two dogs, rescued greyhounds, and train them to go into hospitals or something. Maybe I should plant seeds outside, make a garden, or keep bees. The old turquoise room might be gone, but this rough new life had given me a sense of purpose. The crash, awful as it was, had led me here and I was grateful.

When I had finished my breakfast, I stretched, pulling my arms and legs this way and that, swaying and bending. I opened and closed my bandaged hands. I considered going back to bed. I called Noah to tell him all about it, knowing that he wouldn't answer. No matter. I would keep calling until he picked up. His birthday was in two days; surely he'd pick up then.

I collected the slender *Chesham News*, which came out twice a week, off my doorstep. There on the front page of the newspaper was the whale, wrapped in its sheets, flanked by trucks and ambulances, surrounded by laboring volunteers. I could see myself, there by tall Julie, bundled up and smiling. The headline said WHALE RESCUE ON LOCAL BEACH. The whale, said the article, was a right whale, a male. Right whales were very endangered; there were about four hundred left in the world. A whale is also called a cetacean—which sounded to me like *martian*. Anne Morris, incident commander at the North Atlantic Oceanographic Institute, could say with reasonable confidence that it had made its way here from much farther north, that it had gotten separated from its pod somehow, and that a massive rescue effort among NAOI, NOAA, the Army Corps of Engineers, Chesham's first responders, and a team of local volunteers had moved it out to sea at high tide in the wee hours of the morning. Renowned marine-mammal veterinarian Dr. Iris Chang explained that cetacean strandings were becoming more common in our area; in fact, they were becoming more common worldwide. She invited the public to a talk she was giving at the North Atlantic Oceanographic Institute next week titled "Our Oceans in Peril." Donations were welcome. Potential NAOI volunteers for future strandings were directed to a special website.

I folded the paper on the table next to my dirty dishes. And me, I thought proudly. I had been among them. I had proof.

As I was gingerly washing up the breakfast dishes with my bandaged hands, a knock came at the door, first lightly and then harder, more urgent. I opened the front door to find Julie on my doorstep, crying. I squinted in the brightness of the morning.

"Julie? Is it Dan? Did something happen?"

She shook her head, weeping into her hands. I brought her inside, sat her down on the couch.

"Honey, what is going on?" She didn't take off her coat, but sat hunched up in coat and hat and gloves, like a tree bending in a thunderstorm.

"It came back in, and it's dead."

"What?"

She lifted her face, eyes red, crying. "It didn't make it. The tide brought it back. Or they think it might have actually swum back, that it was trying to beach to die. They do that. But it doesn't matter what happened, because it's dead."

"No, no. It was breathing. It was moving. It was trying to live, not die."

She shook her head. "It's true. Dan has a police scanner. It's all this big mess now. It's way down toward the power plant somewhere."

"Oh, Jesus. What do we do now?"

She shook her head again. I took her hand and we just sat like that for a while, me in my long johns, she in her coat, neither of us saying anything, the branch rustling on the clerestory window in my massage room. The door to that room was open and this house, this shed, was, after all, not very big. I could see the prairie from where we sat. I could see the Sphinx. In the morning light, you could tell that they were pictures from magazines, in drugstore frames.

Julie held out her phone to me. "Look, here."

On her phone was an email from the NAOI explaining that the whale had died and where, along with a list of what was needed for the next morning:

Education/Outreach volunteers
Knife sharpeners
Sample packagers
Experienced cutters
Caterers
Safety Officer
Photographer
Recorder
Miscellaneous helpers

"What is all this?" I asked.

"It's for the necropsy. They have to find out what happened, why the whale stranded and died, what its story was. It's pretty brutal—you don't want to see all that."

My heart was the wheeze of an accordion closing. My bandaged hands were cold and the bandages were wet from washing dishes. A darkness, like cold rushing seawater, rose inside me.

PART TWO

Whalefall

The next day, although I didn't know it then, Noah spent his twentieth birthday with Lydia, Alan, and Mark. That was the first time Lydia met Noah. She knew the occasion was both a welcoming and a test, so she framed one of her best heart photos, a heart made of light cast on the side of a wall. The wall was actually the side of a McDonald's and the light came from the way a ray of sun had refracted off a discarded plastic bottle in the parking lot, but the color of the brick close up was a weathered red-pink, illuminated by the light, which rendered it seraphic. It looked like something spotted in Venice or at the Taj Mahal. She made the whole thing, with the frame, big enough to be respectful, but not so big that it would seem like she was trying to dominate any rooms. If Noah wanted to put it in a drawer or hang it generically in a bathroom, he could, no harm, no foul. Lydia wrapped the present and tied a green bow around it. She arrived at Mark's apartment at a graceful five minutes after the appointed time, in a good skirt and blouse and heels, hair swept up. Standing at the door, she reminded herself to stay present, to breathe, and not to be attached to whatever happened next.

When Alan opened the door, his face lit up. "You look wonderful," he said softly. He put his arm around her. "Come meet my gang." They went down the hallway, joined like that, arrived in the living room that way, too. Standing in the living room to greet her were a young man who looked quite a bit like a younger, thicker version of Alan, and an older, paunchy man with a lined face and a keen gaze. Alan must have warned them about her face, because neither appeared to notice it, or her damaged hand. Noah looked like he'd just been woken up from a nap by a loud sound. His hair was messy, his jeans low, the way the kids did, but he was also wearing a preppy button-down shirt with a tie, clipped on slightly askew. He shifted from foot to foot in place. He hovered in the room, looking as if he was waiting for someone to give him permission to sit down.

"Welcome, Lydia," said the older man. "I'm Mark. What can I get you?" He gestured to a bar cart nearby.

"Just some sparkling water, if you have it." Lydia set the present down on the coffee table. "You must be Noah."

Noah said, "Yeah." He kept an eye on his father. "I'm glad to meet you." He stuck out his hand, which turned out to be damp. Although he was taller than Alan, and beefier, his handshake was tentative, as was his gaze.

"I hear we have a deal to celebrate tonight, too," said Lydia.

"Our first one," said Noah. "We're a team now."

Alan put an arm around Noah and Noah beamed. "My kid," said Alan. They all sat down, glasses in hand, on the black-leather and chrome furniture. Lydia smoothed her skirt over her knees. She felt a bit like Snow White visiting the Seven Dwarfs, except there were only three and they were full-sized. But they were all looking at her as if she were going to organize them or make them all dinner or burst into song. "Congratulations," said Lydia.

But then Noah leaned back with his drink. "Dad says I don't have to go back to school. That's my present."

"I said you don't have to go back this year," corrected Alan, glancing at Lydia. "He's going to help us out, learn a few things about business."

Mark swirled ice in his glass. "As you know, there's been a lot to . . . rebuild. Finding new opportunities—"

"Those bastards took everything," said Noah, leaning forward again, focused. "Fucking vultures. They took the *silverware*." He slammed his hand on the glass and chrome coffee table.

"Noah—" said Alan.

"I hear you," said Lydia. "It must have been awful."

"It was extreme," said Noah. "What they did. They banged on the door at six in the morning. Tell me why that was necessary."

"It's a goddamn puritanical country," said Mark. "No one wants to know how the sausage gets made."

"Right," said Lydia.

"These two have been in the trenches with me the whole time," Alan said. "Taking bullets, both of them." He raised his glass.

"And the deal was—" began Lydia.

"Our first one," said Mark. "You know what the crime is? The *crime* is Alan being barred from what he's better at than most people alive. Thank God we've got this one here." He nodded toward Noah. "We're going to teach him everything."

"We're a team now," repeated Noah. His tie, Lydia noticed, had a pattern of little Yodas on it. Was that ironic? Noah didn't look like an ironic type. He continued: "But why can't Dad teach economics somewhere? Be a professor in a business school? Or, like, advise people? Help raise money for cancer kids or whatever." He looked at Lydia as if she might actually have the answer. His expression was so open that it was funny, in a way. It touched her, Noah's and Mark's faith in Alan and their loyalty. They were all trying so hard. The man, her man, had done his time. This was the camp of the comeback kids. She was so happy to be there with them, to be, maybe, part of the team, too, dodging bullets in the trenches.

Lydia took Alan's hand and he squeezed hers tightly. "I know how special this guy is. I know how lucky I am." They all smiled at one another and she knew she had passed. For the rest of the evening, they talked about ordinary things, relaxed and laughing. When Noah opened his present from her, he immediately posted a picture of it online with a caption that read, "From my dad's bad-ass lady, yo." He showed it to her on his phone. It couldn't possibly be cool to post a picture of a shadow-heart taken by your father's "bad-ass lady." Lydia gave Noah a big hug, which he returned with awkward claps on her back.

THE LYDIA ALAN met, and then Noah and Mark, was so earnest that no one would believe she was once the kind of person you wouldn't leave alone in your house. She wore her ten-year sobriety chip on a chain around her neck, tucked inside her modestly buttoned-up shirt when she went to the office. Her work was interesting enough, like untying and retying little knots, and the pay was more than she had ever thought she could earn with just a GED. A GED at twenty-seven, no less. She could pay her rent. She had bought her own fold-out sofa. As a senior paralegal, she got her own cubicle, which she kept very neat. She liked the pens, index cards, paper clips, and the little sticky flags that showed people where to sign documents.

She assumed that the lawyers and her other coworkers at Hill, Hill, and Adams wondered what had happened to her face and her hand, but she didn't tell them, and they had never asked. It was both a long story and a very short one and, in any case, it wasn't their business. She also had a superstition that if she started telling the story anywhere outside of meetings, she'd get sent back to Virginia to her mother and her aunt and their cult of competitive fragility. Vampires, they fed on misery, proudly displaying their own, faking it if necessary, and creating it in others as much as possible. They'd break their own legs and beat you with the cracked bones just for the spiteful pleasure of it. That fetishy long hair surrounding those ravaged faces, like weird little Victorian girls who had been dead for a hundred years but didn't know it. Lydia still had nightmares about them. It had taken her a long time to stop delivering the brokenness to them that they craved. Somehow, she was afraid, irrationally she knew, that if she told the story to civilians, her mother and her aunt would hear and, like ticks, fatten up on the blood. They were addicts, too: misery addicts. Even her nearly burning to death wasn't enough for them, they wanted more, but Lydia was done being a supplier. If she ever forgot her promise to herself, all she had to do was look in the mirror.

After the accident, she had resigned herself to being single. But over the years since her near-death and rebirth, she had discovered how many people were actually into a slender, young blonde with a half-melted hand and a fucked-up face. There was no question: it turned them on. More misery junkies. She knew that something about it drew Alan, too, and she had had a thread of suspicion about that, but on the Sonny Swan night he had passed a test that she hadn't even quite understood she was administering. They had passed each others' tests now.

So, on a Tuesday about a week after Noah's birthday dinner, she carefully inserted the small photo she had taken of
pebbles forming a heart-shape into the plastic disc, snapped
the disc shut, and fed it onto a key ring, which held a set of
keys to her apartment. She put the key ring in a box and
wrapped the box in dark-blue wrapping paper. Around the
box she put a gold cloth ribbon, which she tied in a luxuri-
ous bow. No one bothered her or asked what she was doing,
because she was, after all, a senior paralegal. If she wanted
to spend some of her time at work wrapping presents, she
had earned the right. She pulled the bow tight, fluffed up the
gold loops.

DESPITE JULIE'S WARNING, I went to the necropsy early the
next morning after the whale had beached again. I felt that
we had failed the whale; in fact, that all of humanity, our
kind, had failed all of the whales. Like sitting shiva, going
to see the body was the honorable thing to do. I drove down
to where the whale was, a deserted, thin strip of beach past
Miller's Point. I walked up the pathway to the beach. A cop,
an older white guy, stopped me. "Ma'am, I'm going to have
to ask you to stay back. Professionals only." As with the rescue scene, here was a small white canvas pavilion. Flowing
in and out of the pavilion were maybe twenty-five people,
one with a camera, several of them volunteers in their NAOI
blue vests, others carrying buckets, backpacks, talking on
phones. I didn't see Julie or Shelly, but I did spot Roger's
gray head. There were no onlookers on this clear, early

morning. The bulldozer sat near the pavilion. A strip of yellow police caution tape cordoned off a very broad swath of beach, and two other cops leaned against police SUVs, watching. Everyone was masked. The whale lay about halfway up the beach, still intact. The bulldozer man must have had his moment. The animal's face was all the way down in the sand, heavy and motionless. You could hardly see the lines of its eyes. I knew that it was dead, but when I saw its face like that, I fully believed it. Everything inside me sank, feeling heavy as the whale itself.

I spotted a lifeguard stand past the pavilion, outside the cordon. I pointed. "Can I go sit over there?"

The cop glanced, sighed. "All right. But do not, I repeat, do not come any closer. When they open up that guy, the air inside can be toxic. Do you have a mask?"

I shook my head.

The cop muttered into his walkie-talkie. One of the other cops reached inside the SUV and then trotted over with a mask. "Here you go. You can walk over that way. Get over there now, before they start cutting."

As I made my way along the edge of the dune to the lifeguard stand, I understood the other reason why everyone was masked. On the second day after the whale's death, it was a gargantuan, stinking corpse. By *stinking*, I mean a smell so overwhelmingly putrid, so extensive, and so dense that it was as if a spaceship of the newly dead had crash-landed on Earth, spilling rotting bodies for miles. Even on the low dune a hundred yards away from it, I vomited. When

I was done vomiting, I put on my mask. It cut the smell by
quite a bit, but not entirely. I scrambled up into the lifeguard
stand.

A few minutes later, the NAOI Jeep pulled up and Annie
got out along with an older man with black hair, masked, in a
puffy green jacket carrying a drum. All of the activity inside
the pavilion stopped. The man with the drum sang and beat
a rhythm as he walked around the whale, pausing at intervals to bow; he seemed to be taking things out of his pockets
and burying them in the sand near the whale. Sometimes, he
lifted up his arms, singing to the sky. Meanwhile, Annie was
suiting up in waders, gloves, boots, goggles, arm shields, a
face shield over her mask, and a big apron. She held a long
knife crosswise at her hips, clearly waiting respectfully for
the man with the drum to finish. Tyler, carrying another
long knife, emerged from the pavilion, along with a short,
redheaded woman holding a camera. Roger, also carrying
a long knife, emerged as well, standing next to Tyler and
Annie. The three with the long knives were covered head to
toe, like astronauts.

The man with the drum walked away from the whale,
nodded to the onlookers, then got back into the NAOI Jeep,
shut the door, and rolled up the window.

Annie, Roger, and Tyler went over to the whale. A volunteer in a NAOI vest followed with a wheelbarrow full of
small plastic containers and a few buckets and carrying a
clipboard with sheets on it. Annie stood on a bucket and
then cut a rectangle the size of my clerestory window in the

side of the whale. The blood gushed out, reddening the sand, reddening Annie's knee-length apron. She lifted the flesh away and, stepping down from the bucket, quickly lopped off pieces of the slippery mass and put each piece into a container, closing the lid with bloody gloved fingers. More blood; so much blood. When she reached her arm into the window she had cut, I had to look away, trying not to vomit again. When I looked back, Tyler and Roger were busying themselves at other parts of the whale, cutting, and calling things out to the volunteer with the clipboard, who appeared to be checking off a list. The redheaded photographer took photos of every cut, efficiently dashing from spot to spot. The other volunteers in their blue vests stood in the pavilion, watching. A little folding table had some coffee urns and a few trays of food on it, but no one went there to get anything. How could they?

I kept looking, looking away, looking back, in quick glances. I felt as if I was being turned inside out; I felt that it was my duty to witness this, but it was very, very hard.

Within an hour, the trio had finished their work. The whale—and I can hardly bear to say this—became a thing, skinned and riddled with gaping holes, chunks of it sealed into plastic containers, the containers undoubtedly labeled and dated. The volunteer with the clipboard drank a cup of coffee. Annie, Roger, and Tyler walked into the ocean in their bloody waders and aprons. The surf turned pink. Then they came back up the beach, took off the waders and aprons, and Annie spoke to the assembled group in the pavilion, probably thanking them. The volunteers began packing up the untouched food, striking the pavilion, gathering anything that had been left on the sand. One of the white-haired ones, a woman, folded up the waders and aprons and put them into a duffel bag. All the while, the whale lay in its own blood, which spread around it on the sand like yards and yards of red robes.

I watched until they all drove away in their cars and Jeeps. No one seemed to remember that I was there. The cops left up the yellow caution tape, and they drove away, too. I just kept looking at the leviathan, slashed all over. Its pink tongue was as big as a mattress. Julie said it had probably come to die, but that breath: it had been so strong, and the sound of it, like a didgeridoo, an aquatic trumpet. That was the sound of life, wasn't it? Maybe it had just been disoriented. We would never know for sure if this rare creature, this special emissary from another world, had come to us to live or to die.

When everyone was gone, I lifted up my mask, just for a second. The stink nearly knocked me over. I put the mask back on quickly, but I was glad to have that last breath of the whale in my nose and in my lungs. I didn't believe it would kill me or hurt me, and it didn't. Instead, it lingered within me for weeks.

I THOUGHT WE'D all light candles for a while near the corpse, something like that, but by the third day after the whale's death, a legal fight had begun. As I soon learned, when a whale died, people wanted to get rid of the whale's body, fast. But when whales died on the beach the way ours did, and they weighed seventy tons—or more, some weighed even more than that—they became unmovable dead weight. Trying to push it back into the sea would be like trying to push a building into the sea. People around the world had tried all kinds of things when a stranded whale died— blowing it up, putting it on a truck and carting it away—but none of it worked that well. The county wanted to cut it up with chainsaws immediately and get rid of it—either haul the pieces off to a landfill or dig a really big hole to bury it where it had beached. Seventy tons of dead, rotting, putrid whale wouldn't make people want to visit Chesham. But Julie told me that even if a sufficiently big hole in the sand could be dug, when they dug those holes, the whales some- times resurfaced.

Meanwhile, Annie and Dr. Chang desperately wanted the intact skeleton. A massive, full right-whale skeleton such as this one would be a coup for the North Atlantic Oceanographic Institute and besides, they argued, wouldn't that be a tourist attraction, too? A special team needed to be brought in to filet the whale, essentially, and then another specialist had to take all those bones, lay them out in a field, thoroughly clean them, and reassemble the whale skeleton so it could be exhibited at the Oceanographic Institute. The basement could be fully renovated and renamed Cetacean Hall. The county disagreed: who was going to pay for all these special dead-whale people, plus the renovation? There were other places on the Cape that had whale skeletons; the area didn't need another.

The Oceanographic Institute was drastically under-funded. They'd never be able to sell enough cupcakes to pro-cess the whale skeleton and create Cetacean Hall. Because our whale had washed up dead on a mostly uninhabited area, Dr. Chang suggested a third option: letting the whale rot where it lay. When enough of the flesh had fallen from the bones, or the money had been raised for the special team, the skeleton could be extracted, cleaned, and preserved intact. The county balked at that idea and revved the chain-saws. The Oceanographic Institute filed suit. The battle was on.

In town, people pulled sad faces over the untimely death of the whale and the general state of the global climate, but before too long general opinion swung around to the firm sense that beach season was crucial for the local economy and that the NAOI, in league with the outsider Dr. Chang, was putting its luxury environmental concerns ahead of the public interest. The pro-developers and the anti-developers finally agreed on something. Some racist opinions were heard. People recited the weight of the whale with a kind of pride—seventy-three tons!—as if it were a fish they'd caught. Petitions were drawn up and sent to the Oceanographic Institute, but Annie and her team dug in. They had sup-porters as well, fewer but very earnest. The court delib-erated. I signed all the pro–Cetacean Hall petitions. I did my jobs. The callouses on my hands seemed as if they had always been there. When Karen and Jerry and the people on the barstools at Waves called Dr. Chang names and talked about values and outside influences, I dried glasses, wiped down the bar.

I was more on the side of Annie and Dr. Chang, of course, but I felt that everyone was more or less missing the point. Something extraordinary had been among us. Something almost never seen on land. Something miraculous that went far beyond all these fights that basically just came down to money. I kept finding myself heading toward Miller's Point, going to see the whale. I had to go alone. Even if I had had close friends in Chesham, which I didn't, I still would have gone alone. The wreck of it was awful, but it also drew me; it had an attraction that was magnetic.

To be honest, I'd always been squeamish. When I had to take Noah to get stitches that time in Greece, I nearly fainted myself. I don't like those movies where crazed killers go after people with chainsaws. But the whale was a magnitude of being I'd never seen before, that no one in Chesham had ever seen or was likely to see again. This weird, gargantuan king, this miracle, lay out there on cruddy Miller's Point, where discarded beer cans and cigarette butts littered the dune. I had to keep looking, even though I often had to look away. The creature was as rare and powerful in death as he had been in life. I did wear my mask, but the stink of the whale stayed in my nostrils, accompanying me everywhere. It was a horrible smell, and I treasured it. It was the smell of a grandeur beyond our puny human concerns.

I knew the whale's best option was to become an educational exhibit and be useful, but really, I just wanted nature to take its course. I googled those possibilities. It would take about five years for a whale to decompose fully on land. On the bottom of the ocean, it would take thirty. On the bottom of the ocean, the body of the decomposing whale would become an underwater farm as other animals ate it and bacteria made the bones into home for strange worms with no eyes. They called this process *whale fall*. On land, the whale would simply rot in the air piece by piece. Eventually, the rancid smell would evaporate and the flesh would disappear, leaving only the creature's architecture: the undulating spine at the top, the grand curve of the ribs, the empty hall of the interior. It would become a cathedral and an open-air ossuary, both. We would be able to walk around inside it. But neither of those futures would ever happen now.

AND THEN, ON one of the first really warm days: "Suze, I'm on my way to the Cape, I'm going to stop by. I'll be in the center of that town in about an hour." It was Mark. In forty minutes, he called again. "I'm at a café here. It's called Delia's, Della's, something like that. Polka-dot awning. I'll wait until two."

I put on my sneakers and walked into town, reminding myself to breathe with every step. I had the terrifying thought that he could be here to tell me something about Noah, but a call like that would come first from the so-so college. Or the police. I dragged my feet like a sullen child. I passed the small Victorian house with the sky-blue porch ceiling; the flat-roofed, one-story house surrounded by the chain-link fence; the big house with the American flag hung from its screened front porch. The sidewalk was cracked, rucked up in places by tree roots underneath. This was my town, not Mark's. Neither he nor Alan knew anything about this place or the whale or my new life here.

When I opened the jingling door at Delilah's, Mark stood up. He was like the coarser version of Alan: a heavier jawline; no irony in his smile; ugly, expensive loafers; and, today, a Red Sox cap on his balding head.

"Suze," he said. "You've dyed your hair."

"Actually, I stopped dyeing it. No one out here knows how to do that kind of blond." I shrugged.

"Oh, okay. Shall we sit down?" he said, as if we were in his office and not the café in my town. But I sat down.

He overflowed the white wrought-iron chair where he sat. It wasn't that he was so large. It was his constant movement, the jiggling leg, the peering around, that made him seem too big for the chair, for the room, for his cup of orange-mint tea when it arrived. At the same time, he made Delilah's look cheap, saccharine, and insistent. There were polka-dot bows on the curtains. The cake slices were too big. Mark's open-neck shirt was white with a few pale-blue threads care-fully placed at irregular intervals. His face was seared with lines. It was clear that he came from the world where clocks ticked, important money was made and lost, and only chil-dren had time for big pieces of cake.

"How are you?" he said.

"I'm all right." I looked him straight in the eye. "I'm good here."

"Yeah." He flicked the little tea tag with its instructions for finding happiness within and smiled. "It's a hike, getting out here to your, mmm, retreat."

"You?"

He winced. "There's been a lot to do."

"I'll bet." I folded my hands, waiting for him to play the first card.

"Why wouldn't you take his calls?"

"What was he calling about?" I continued to look him straight in the eye.

He dropped his gaze. "Something has come up."

I didn't say anything. I reminded myself that Mark didn't have my current address. He had no idea how close we were to my house. He didn't know the name of the girl behind the counter—Gigi, who was watching our conversation with unabashed interest, like we were characters in a television show. She had a polka-dot bow in her hair that matched the curtains.

Mark steepled his forefingers at his mouth, then pointed them at me. He scratched his head. He sighed. He shifted on the chair. "Have you spoken to Noah at all?"

"Jesus—"

He held up a hand. "He's fine. I mean, about what's been going on."

"Noah won't talk to me. I call all the time."

"Hmm." Mark carefully put the teabag onto his spoon, set the spoon next to his teacup. "So you don't know that they released Alan early."

"No." Inside my heart rabbited. Gigi was frankly staring. This was going to be all over town by sundown, my connection to some sort of ex-con, or maybe I was an ex-con myself.

"Good behavior," said Mark. He sipped his tea. "You're not hungry? Thirsty?"

"Why are you here?" I called his hand, sat up straight, my stomach fluttering. Gigi, behind Mark's back, was making indecipherable hand and face signals that I think meant, *Are you all right?* I tried to frown her away. She held up her phone, pointed to it. I shook my head as imperceptibly as I could.

"I'm here," said Mark quietly, "about the money you took."

"That account was in my name."

Mark looked me in the eye. "On paper."

"Those were some crazy days at the end. I signed everything you guys asked me to."

"Where is it?"

I didn't reply.

Mark leaned forward. "Listen to me. This is important. It's the restitution."

"The government, the creditors, whoever, got that. The house, everything—they got that."

Mark shook his head, the edge of his Red Sox cap nearly at my nose. I could smell the orange-mint on his breath. I could see the fatigue on his face. "They did. But that was for the criminal case. Some fuck filed a civil suit. A couple fucks. We tried to get rid of it, I'm still trying, but the judge—we're screwed. There's going to be more restitution, almost certainly. We need that money. If he can't pay it, he's screwed forever."

I shrugged again.

"Suze. Let's talk straight. You left, right? You walked away. You didn't pay. He paid."

"Well, he was the one who did it. I didn't know that was what he was up to. I thought it was currencies and exchange rates."

"Bullshit. He says he told you."

"No, there was this one thing one time, but . . ." I leaned forward and practically whispered so Gigi couldn't hear me. "I didn't know he was just taking people's money and giving it out to other people as profit when they asked for dividends. How would I know that? It's too complicated for me."

"It wasn't complicated at all."

"I didn't know." I folded my arms, to guard my breath, which had become scant. "No one can prove that I knew all that."

"You're splitting hairs, and it's time for you to do the right thing here. Not to mention—all we have to do is drop a word to the Feds about the account. In your name."

"You can't do that," I said, but I knew that they certainly could, and would. Mark had me cornered. How naïve I still was, to think they hadn't noticed. Of course they had; they were biding their time, just like me, until they could dig up the account themselves. And continue with their schemes. And right then, at that exact moment, the stink of the whale blew inside me full force. I choked back a gag, but that decayed breath: it was telling me what to do, the right thing to do, and filling me with the power to do it. "Anyway, it's gone."

"You're lying."

"Nope." I was done with all that, done with being dragged into their crimes. I knew what really mattered. "I gave it to the ACLU."

Mark's hands shook as he set down his cup of orange-mint tea. "You gave $850,000 to *lawyers*? Is that a joke?"

"No," I said. "They fight for our freedoms."

"What about Noah? Did you think of him before you threw money that wasn't even yours away? Where is your fucking honor, Suzanne? You've fucked us all."

"Please keep your voice down. What does he owe?"

Mark leaned even closer. "It's looking like one point two, give or take. And what's with the 'he'? It's 'we,' don't you think? Jesus, Suzanne, what's wrong with you?" His gaze was shiny-sharp, but I didn't care. I felt, briefly, invincible.

"You know what? I didn't know what he was doing. I didn't know about this whatever do-over with the restitution. So now the money's gone where it can actually do some good. I can't get it back. And Noah doesn't need to drink from that toxic well."

"Alan was trying to call you."

"Well, maybe he should have sent a letter. Written it on a postcard."

"Suzanne," said Mark, "you had no right."

I didn't say anything.

"What about all the so-called 'victims'? Do you know how many they've got on the civil suit? Three hundred fifty-two. They're claiming millions. Millions, Suzanne. Houses, cars, businesses, pffft." Mark waved a hand, looking disgusted and skeptical, but also defeated. "Everyone's got a sob story. Very sad stuff in the depos. Very sad. I could send them over if you want to read them."

"Like you give a fuck about them. Like that's what you thought you were going to do with the money. He did it. He can figure it out."

Mark buried his face in his hands. His tea with its merry tag about open-heartedness had gone cold on the white wrought-iron table. He lifted his head and looked me in the eye with what I can only describe as contempt. I looked right back.

"I'm done," I said. "It's all done now." Leaning over, I took off his cap, kissed him on the forehead, then tossed his cap and a few dollars down on the table.

I left Delilah's and walked home feeling victorious. It wasn't dark out yet and the night was warm with the approach of summer. I took off my sneakers. Warm, rough road; cooler, smoother sidewalk; soft grass; dirt.

When I got back to my little house, I opened my computer right away and skipped through the world, went around the curves, dodged behind the waterfalls, went into the cave, opened the boxes within boxes, and checked on the money. It made me laugh, sort of, to think that Mark had believed me. The ACLU? What connection did I have to the ACLU? Of course, the money was there. If you pay attention, a lot of things aren't that hard, as Alan had explained to me that very first night that we were together.

Sometimes, bravery comes to you when you least expect it. Maybe I was a Smith girl, after all. There's bravery and there's bravery, right? The breath of the whale had shown me the way. Hiding the money had been a little complicated, but it was incredibly easy to make a whopping donation anonymously to a marine-mammal organization—more cupcakes than could be sold in all the bake sales in the world. A right-whale-sized donation. Take that, Ted and all his kind. It took less time than it had taken to try to save the whale. In less than thirty-six hours, with one last keystroke, I was free. Without a net, but free. I made sure to give them every last cent, to wash that money clean and send it into the future, to fully commit to my new life. I might not have been able to save our whale, but I could help others like him, and their world.

WHAT IS RESTITUTION? Legally, it means that the people who won their case have to be paid back. Of course, they can't be paid back, not in full. The government makes a calculation, its own ratio. When the government first informed us of that calculation after the first trial, a line appeared on Alan's forehead, as if his skull was buckling under the pressure. When I left Alan with his newly indented skull, Noah called me a traitor. With all the righteous certainty of a twenty-year-old with a backward baseball cap, middling grades, and dubious personal grooming habits, he told me that he wouldn't speak to me until I apologized to his father for leaving. From Noah's point of view, that was pretty much the only restitution that counted. Restitution, like all money, accrues interest, even though it's money owed, not money saved. The debt grows like something organic. And the government never, ever forgets about you, even when everyone else may have.

What is restitution? Ethically, it means to repair, to restore, to mend what has been broken.

What is restitution? A numerical impossibility. An ideal. A failure already, legally.

What is real restitution? I don't know. And, anyway, it wasn't my fault. Hadn't I already paid with everything I thought was my life?

What is restitution? Don't we all, all of humanity, owe the earth something? Isn't there a larger picture here? I kept going out to Miller's Point to where the whale lay in state. Every time I went back to the whale, I remembered my values, and what it means to live accordingly. I yet smelled the stink. It was bracing, and it reminded me of what was what, what mattered, and what was real.

• • •

I DON'T KNOW what Mark said to Alan about our conversation. I do know that Alan moved in with Lydia. He brought his books, his phone, a few good suits, and toiletries. He didn't need even half the space that Lydia cleared for him in her closet and dresser. It was marvelous to her that a man whose life had been so big and complex was now as neat as a soldier, all his possessions barely enough to fill a footlocker. He said that since prison, he'd gotten used to traveling light. He said he'd come to prefer it.

Lydia liked his, their, lack of stuff. It made her feel that the two of them could pick up and leave anytime they wanted, turn the key and go anywhere. She realized that she had been missing that feeling. For so long, she had been dutifully doing her job and paying her bills on time, going to meetings, seeing a movie now and then with her friend Caprice, sleeping with the one they called the Bald Dude when she felt the impulse. The Bald Dude was drama-free, good in bed, and never fussed about wearing condoms. When she had sex with the Bald Dude, no one banged on the door to ask if everything was all right or what that smell was. And then, like Blue, she put on her clothes and left.

It was a little strange to have Alan there when she said her prayers at night. Before, when he was over, she would just have a quiet moment in the nude with God once Alan fell asleep, and a longer session once he was gone the next day. She hadn't lived with anyone since before the accident, before this channel in her had opened. But now, on their first night of living together, there was Alan, barefoot, yawning, his knapsack tucked under the little drop-leaf table. She was going to have to tell him.

Lydia said, "So there's a thing I do—I hope it doesn't weird you out."

"Do you need time in the bathroom?"

"No, no, it's not that kind of thing. It's a, you know, God thing." She felt so awkward; how funny, that it was easier to have sex with him than to talk about this part of her life. She pointed up. "Prayers."

"Oh. Okay. Do you want me to leave you alone?" He looked around. "I could go in the bathroom. Should I close my eyes?"

"No," said Lydia. "I mean, you could—do you want to join me?"

"Join you?" Alan looked as if she had suggested that he insert a tampon for her. "No, I'll just sit over here." He picked up his phone. "Take your time. I can put earphones on."

"It's not a talking thing," said Lydia. "But I am going to kneel."

"Sure, sure," said Alan, scrolling through his phone. "Do your thing."

Lydia knelt, closed her eyes, and did her best to let the world recede so that that space opened. She tried to forget that Alan was right there, on his phone, breathing, waiting for her so they could go to bed. She tried not to clench her shut eyes. It was a little weird, like the feeling of someone reading over your shoulder, but she pretty much got there. She reminded herself that Alan was preoccupied with text messages or news bulletins or whatever. When she opened her eyes again, though, Alan wasn't on his phone. He was staring at her with a mix of curiosity and a certain amount of admiration, as if she had suddenly broken into Swahili or Cantonese.

"Hi," she said.

"Can I ask—which God are you talking to?"

"Which God?"

"Right, like—Christian, Jewish, whatever. Which one?"

Lydia sat back on her heels. "I don't really think about it that way. It's just, you know, the divine. It's kind of like what Sonny Swan was saying about love? I mean, he said it in a funny way. But it's just everywhere." She got her mouth-guard out of the side table drawer. "Should we go to bed?—What?" He was still looking at her quizzically.

"Have you always been like that? Is it a family thing?"

"The only things my family believed in were cigarettes and spite. Maybe it was always there, but I also think that God threw me out of that burning car to crack me open, you know?"

Alan, barefoot, tilted his head. "Huh. Do you go to church?"

"Different ones, sometimes. Temples, whatever. I kind of do my own thing. I don't think the various doorways matter all that much. They all go to the same place."

"You seem so sure."

His tone was sad, and Lydia didn't know how to reply. "It's not really like that."

"What is it like?"

Lydia reached out her hand. "Honey, come sit here."

But he shook his head, looking away.

NOAH LIKED LYDIA. He told me later it was a little weird for him at Mark's, but it was better than being at school. Those kids in college with their juvie problems and complaints had no idea what it was like to stand in the smoking remains of your family home, knowing that the war was far from over—in fact, that it had just begun. At that shit college in Kansas, he had felt so much older than the rest of them. He was never going back, except maybe to give a speech and get an honorary degree.

He saw the calls from me, but . . . the look down and away. The blink. You know. His father needed him. They were moving on. Noah was always exceptionally gentlemanly toward Lydia, pulling out her chair at the table and asking about her day, even though half her face was so jacked up. He got used to it after a while, although he did try to sit on her good side, generally. She was sweet, like a babysitter. She was a very organized kind of person, too; she made lists. Noah liked the lists and he wanted his dad to be happy and they all had a lot of work to do. Here a sidelong glance at me, as if what I'd been doing during this time wasn't real work. Real work was what he did with his father, for his father.

• • •

ALAN SURPRISED LYDIA as much as she surprised him. He could, on the one hand, read the stock market like a psychic. He made predictions and his predictions were nearly always right. He would say, "See, I told you we could have made a killing, look at that," or, "Don't buy that, it's going straight down," and two days later, down it went. As if she had any extra money to just play around in the stock market on her own. But he also seemed to get a lot of pleasure out of doing the little things of daily life with a kind of precision and flourish. For instance, he seemed to consider it his job to bring in the mail every day from the mailboxes downstairs. He was always very interested in the mail. When she got home from work, she would find it carefully fanned out on the table. "The mailman didn't come until four," Alan might say disapprovingly, as if receiving catalogues and credit card offers were matters of great urgency. About money, all he said was, "Don't worry about it," and paid half the bills, or more. He said it was better if the accounts just stayed in her name; it was her house, after all, he said respectfully. Lydia was good with that. She put the money he gave her in a savings account. He curled around her at night after she said her prayers and put in her mouthguard, his nose in her neck. Every morning while she was showering for work, he folded up the sofabed, put away the bedding, and had coffee waiting for her in the kitchen area. Then he put on his suit and tie and left.

The way Alan was wise and vulnerable, old and new at the same time, moved Lydia. Sometimes he seemed to drift away somewhere, he looked troubled, and she knew just what that felt like, not to know yourself or the world in the way you once did, or thought you did. She knew that strafed feeling, that sensation of nearly being skinned alive, like a shaved cat. Only half-recognizable to yourself. Anyone who saw them from behind as they walked down the street would think it was a certain kind of story, the elegant older man and the tall, younger blonde. But if that same person overtook them and saw them from the front, it would be clear that this wasn't the old story at all. It was a different story. The story was theirs, and theirs alone.

Maybe so.

NEARLY EVERY DAY that summer in Chesham, as the battle over the whale remains raged in town, I got into my smoke-stinking car, drove past where we had all been, our team, all the teams, and kept going another forty minutes to the rocky bit of land with not much beach. I pulled off onto the side of the road in a clump of trees, and climbed into the lifeguard stand. No lifeguard would be here this summer. In a wide perimeter around the whale, the yellow police caution tape flapped unconvincingly. From that place, I had a good view. I could see the whale whole. The stench of the rotting whale was still so overpowering that my eyes watered. I sat in the lifeguard stand covered in sunscreen, wearing a mask, a long-sleeved shirt, and a wide-brimmed straw hat I got at the hospital thrift store. I took off my shoes. About another half mile down was a big plant of some kind, lots of no-color towers and a concrete rectangle of a building. It always looked as if it was covered in mist, but I think that was the distortion of the distance.

Day by day, I got more used to looking. The birds came first. Many seagulls, but also some other smaller birds, black and gray, whose names I didn't know. They nearly covered the whale some days, feasting on its guts. The whale lay on its side on the sand, mostly skinned, squares and rectangles and incisions cut into it all over, its great tail half-twisted. It looked like it had been murdered somewhere else and then thrown onto the beach by giants who were aiming for the ocean and missed. Even half-covered by the crowd of hungry birds, what spilled out of the whale—lots of red and purple, squiggly, a mass of guts seeping over the sand—was hard to look at. The skin of the whale sank here and there in random declivities. Were those places where organs had been? The great eye was closed forever, become just a curve. The ridges on the whale's underside seemed more prominent, almost like bones themselves.

The seawater came in, covered the lower edge of the entrails, then uncovered them again. Seagulls flew away with strands of the entrails dangling like red seaweed. When the wind blew my way, I smelled the awful, awful smell. When the wind blew the other way, I could imagine that the sea was slowly cleaning the great corpse, that the salt would purify it, although sometimes the good salt scent mingled with the sour chemical scent of the power plant in the near distance.

It was very quiet, except for the wind. No volunteer tent, no trucks, no unwieldy lanterns, no buckets or boots or shovels or flares, no people, no one with a drum, no pizza or donuts, no one guarding it. The flutter of bird wings; their calls. No sheets. The whale was limp, twisted, bare to the sky, and compared to the sky it was small, like the shadow of a small cloud. The sea was darker near the shore, then lighter farther out, then darker again. Along the shoreline, the shells of horseshoe crabs. The sound of a plane now and then. My own breath rising and falling.

I looked at the whale, looked at the entrails. Nearly every day, I made sure to look. The whale looked like it was deflating, becoming heavier and heavier and heavier on the sand, incapable of flotation. I wanted to weep, and sometimes did. Who had done this thing, how had it happened? Had Annie found out? If I were a detective on a television show and this were a person, I could investigate, but there was nothing to investigate. There was no question. There was just the fact of the extraordinary creature, rotting.

By Labor Day, the birds and the water had carried quite a bit of the mass of entrails away. Now the bugs came, so many of them that the mass sometimes looked like it was moving. The carcass seemed to be sinking, to be sagging and tumbling in unevenly, like a house rotting. Watching the whale rot seemed to be my duty. I had to go, and I always went alone: a divorced lady with limited options, in a thrift-store hat, who sat in an old lifeguard stand with a plain steel thermos of coffee nearly every day, watching a very big, very rare, dead animal fall apart. What a pair we were, the whale and I.

One day, I helped Jerry and Karen take the kids to the aquarium. It was hot outside on the boardwalk, cooler and shadowy inside. A small beluga whale, not much bigger than a dolphin, swam up to the glass, looked at all of us with its wide-set dark eyes, then swam away.

I taped up a line-drawing of a whale in my massage room so I could see it as I worked. It inspired me. I pushed on the muscles of my neighbors; I held their feet in my hands; their faces in repose were like the faces of children. I knew I was doing them real good. If I got ten clients a week, that would be four hundred dollars, plus another hundred and twenty at Waves (I had picked up another shift), more or less. It was all cash, so that was over two grand a month. My rent had been $900 in the low season, but now in the high season, it was $1500. My landlady, Annette, seventy years old with a smoker's cough, never failed to let me know that she was doing me a favor, that she could get twice that much, but single ladies needed to stick together. Cough. She, too, preferred to be paid in cash, in person. Cough. Thank you, honey, see you next month.

But I rarely got ten clients a week. The remains of the divorce money got me across the gap, just, but by the time the whale was gone, that would be gone, too. This time, gone meant gone, full stop. When I didn't have enough clients, I also had too much time to see how low the popcorn ceiling was in my drafty rental. I had too much time to notice, again, the scratched linoleum that covered the entire floor and that I could never scrub to anything better than dull. There was one corner of linoleum just by the little stove that curled up inexorably, revealing dirty plywood underneath. That corner filled me with dread. I tried never to look at it. If I went out and walked around to get some air and perspective, when I got back that curling corner was always there waiting for me, smiling its creepy smile. When I didn't have enough clients, I was all too aware of the ticking of the clock on the stove, and on my life. I could do the math on the money in my sleep. I made more flyers, with pictures of lotus flowers in water, and put them up around town. The season began to turn.

ON AN OCTOBER day when it looked as if the town was going to get a decision in its favor, I drove out to the whale to say goodbye, heart sinking. So far, it had been an eight-client week. Instead of climbing into the lifeguard stand as usual, I stayed near the dune, a hand to my eyes. What was left of the whale's insides was black, nearly flat, covered in bugs. A scrap of sea-foam clung to the blunt end of what had been the nose. The smell remained, somewhat lighter now, or maybe I had become more accustomed to it. The skin lay unevenly on the carcass, like a blanket being pulled off, or put on. A few feet of the long curve of tailbone were bare, sculptural, final—a curve that wouldn't be changing again. I pulled a sheaf of dune grass and a yellow flower from the dune and lay the bouquet in the bend of the tailbone.

I stayed there a bit longer and then left, but by the time I got back to town, the case had already been done and undone. Julie texted me. Someone had filed something somewhere, somehow. The NAOI and Dr. Chang were still holding their own. A new client called for an appointment. The light scent of whale stink filled my nostrils as if to say: still here. That night, the lights were on in the library and people were heading up the steps. I walked past, smiling, on the other side of the street. I could do another day.

EVEN NOW, EVEN after everything, I imagine peaceful evenings during this time for Alan and Lydia. Maybe Lydia worked on her heart pictures on her computer, adjusting the colors, cropping and re-cropping, naming the files: Knot-heart 1, Knot-heart 2, Dead Pigeon Foot-heart, Necklace-heart, Spilled Paint-heart, and so on. Alan, across the small room in glasses, read the *Wall Street Journal*, a print copy, from beginning to end. He often texted Noah as he read, since Noah was the one who could do transactions and other kinds of business for them both now. Mark had figured out how to make Noah an Inc, which Noah thought was hilarious and he also loved it.

One night, Lydia asked, "Do you mind? About what happened."

Alan looked up from the paper, tilting his head. "Mind? Yeah, of course. It's not like it's *fair*. But the kid and I are doing great." He smiled. "Those idiots won't have the last word, don't worry."

Another night, Lydia asked, "What was it like, you know—in Norfolk?"

Alan didn't even look up. "Something no one tells you about prison: it's boring as shit. Getting raped would at least break up the afternoon. I just talked to my lawyers a lot." He turned a page. "I graduated early."

Lydia didn't think that was the whole story, but, like the rape joke, she decided to let it go. He would tell her more when he was ready.

Another night, Lydia asked, "Was it really a lot of money? Like: ridiculous?"

Alan said, "Do you want some mint tea?" Lydia nodded. When it was ready, he brought it out and said, "Yes, what I earned and then had to pay was a ridiculous amount of money. It was all ridiculous. It was a ridiculous era. I can tell you about it sometime. But that's all over now. I paid my debt to society, and then some."

Lydia reached for his hand; it was warm from the mug of tea. "You did. But this isn't boring for you? I mean, this apartment is small, and . . ."

"I'm not bored," said Alan. "I love this place." He kissed her palm. "I've never been as happy as I am with you."

Lydia wasn't entirely sure she believed that, either, but the funny thing was that he really did seem content with their basic life. They had breakfast together in the mornings, she went off to Hill, Hill and Adams, and he worked on business things with Noah during the day or went to do his community service in the community center where they had

first met. If he missed his old, big, dramatic life, it was probably like the way she missed speedballs, like the way retired
astronauts miss outer space: the air up there was just too
thin, and the probability of burning up in the atmosphere
when coming down too great. They were now grounded,
sober people, people who understood what it was to nearly
die of wanting to stay so far above the earth for so long.

ON A DAY that felt like a return to summer even though it
was deep fall, on a scanty six-client week, I could see from
my stand that there was far more tailbone of the whale visible
now. The skin had fallen in between a few of the ribs, exposing the upright curves. The animal was still mostly a messy
heap of skin, flesh, and various stages of rot. The clean, dry
ampitheater of the skeleton was still entangled in the meat of
the creature, like a crowd surrounding royalty. I called Noah,
but of course he didn't answer. How much longer would he
blame me? I put my head in my hands and cried.

Suzanne, get the fuck up. Where had that come from?
It sounded like my mother, my mother when she was stolid
and perpetually aggravated and telling me and my sisters to
stop whining. The keeper of accounts. I kicked at the side
of the lifeguard stand, tears in my ears. Get the fuck up and
do what? I was trying, wasn't I? What was I supposed to do,
knock over a bank? Here I was, transformed and transfor-
mative, but no one could tell.

But I got the fuck up, the same way I had always done
what my mother said, however resentfully. Or maybe it was

the whale telling me to get the fuck up, to remember what I had to give the world, one body at a time. I trudged back across the sand and drove back home to the shed, which was not only colder during the day but slightly dank, as if the cold was bringing out the damp. I made more flyers with tear-off tabs, but I improved the flyer. I made a bigger type-face with a new pitch:

CHANGE YOUR BODY, CHANGE YOUR LIFE
BODYWORK WITH EXPERIENCED PRACTITIONER

As usual, my mother was right. The phone finally rang.

THAT WINTER, THE clients came, steady as a tide coming in, sometimes twelve or thirteen a week. I got better at my work; the better I got, the more confident and relaxed I got. I raised my price to fifty dollars an hour, and still they came: Otavio, the owner of the burger place, whose arms were scarred by kitchen accidents; Otavio's husband, Sterling, who was slight and funny; James, the pediatrician, who limped and rarely smiled; Julie, of course, who often stayed to chat after; her father-in-law, Roger, who sometimes farted on the table and held my hand a little too long when saying goodbye; Sharon, who worked at the stable out of town, giving lessons, and always smelled faintly, pleasantly, of horses; her twin sister, Susan, who worked there, too. They had had the same knee surgery, on the same knee. They had the same complaints about what the stable was feeding the horses and the incompetence of the lazy vet who charged too much. They both had calves so locked that I could barely push into them.

Everyone paid in cash, which I kept in a strongbox in one of the kitchen cabinets. If I shook the box, the bills inside made a light shushing sound, like the rustle of leaves, interspersed with the clinking of coins for which some people had dug in their pockets. Annette always took the bills from me without counting them, saying, "I trust you, honey," which she almost certainly didn't. She meant: "Don't screw me around, ever." I always made sure to pay her right on the first of the month. Clients became regulars. The shed stayed warm all winter.

On a particularly cold night, the man I came to think of as the twisty little man arrived for an appointment. It was four o'clock in the afternoon, but it was dark already, with a cold, wet wind. I opened the front door to him—his name was actually Dean—standing on the step bundled up in an ankle-length down coat, a large fur hat, thick gloves, and a long, green scarf wrapped several times around his neck. He was very short, perhaps five feet, just. When he came in and took off his hat, his scarf, his coat, and his gloves, tossing them with a strange familiarity over a chair, I could see that his face was oddly shaped, as if someone or something had lightly compressed it in a rickety vise.

"Suzanne," he said, nodding once. "Dean." He held out his hand, which I shook. His grip was firm. "Shall we?" he said. "I'm on a tight schedule."

"Of course. The room is right through here. Do you have any particular areas you'd like me to work on?"

"Ankles."

"Ankles?"

"Yes. I was a ranked figure skater in my youth, and it left me with fragile ankles. Overworked." With that, he walked away into the room with the clerestory window and closed the door behind him. I tried to remember the part of the online course that had to do with ankles. Extension, flexion, rotation: I could do that. His clothes on my chair were sumptuous. The long, green scarf was a thick cashmere. The down coat was so dense and well-made, with grommets and pockets and zippers, it could have kept a horse, or at least a pony, warm.

I tapped on the door.

"You can come in," he said.

Inside the room, he lay facedown with the sheets already folded to his hips. The candles glowed in the early dark; the cold, wet wind whispered outside the window. I turned up the space heater, since he was already half-naked.

"Lavender or plain oil?"

"Plain. Not too much."

"Right." I oiled up my hands and put one on the nape of his neck, the other on the small of his exposed back, which was curved with scoliosis. He was warm, with a thrumming energy. When I moved my hands down his back, I felt the strength of it, each muscle crisply defined. Maybe he really had been an athlete, although the scoliosis—I doubted it. I rocked him a bit, my hands spanning his ribs, then tapped around on his back with light thumps. He was like a drum— not, as they say, tight as a drum. That's not what I mean. I mean that he was firm and resounding; his skin had surface tension. He obviously worked out, but I had the sense that he also worked in, that he drove energy inside himself, concentrating it. I wanted to get to that energy. A few dark hairs lay like threads on his tailbone. When I eased the sheets down, I saw that his legs had the fuller half-moons of hamstrings and quads that skaters do, indeed, have. I worked down his legs, his knees, his feet.

I encircled the ankle bones of his left foot with my thumbs and forefingers. His fingers, palms up along his sides, curled. His breathing slowed. I put a hand on the sole of his left foot, cupping and then rubbing along the length of it. I bent his knee. His body warmed, softened, and the air between us grew warmer as well. He was breathing slowly, but I knew he was awake because of a slight tension in his neck. I lowered his left foot. He lifted his right leg and foot, anticipating me, his right foot grazing my hip, as if accidentally. A current passed between us. I thought of the wolf man, but this was no wolf—or was he?—and I wanted him to stay. I worked on his right foot, then held both his feet in my hands, ever so gently shaking his legs. I took longer than I should have. His hamstrings rose. I felt myself drawn forward. One of the candles guttered, then went out. The room grew darker.

I could have leaned farther toward him, but I held myself at an angle, the weight of his lower half in my hands, pulling at the muscles of my arms. It was an awkward suspension, but also, as my muscles tensed to hold myself there, an exciting one. I could go forward or back, but I wouldn't be able to maintain that angle long. He sighed. I put his legs back down and walked to the top of the table. I stood there, looking at his dim shape in the candlelight. The current continued to pass between us. I didn't want him to turn over, because I didn't want to know whether or not he was hard. Either way, it would have been a problem.

What I mean is: joy. I felt joy with the twisty little man. Joy in the dead of winter. Joy in the moment of not knowing whether or not he was hard. After all my struggles: joy came to me with this stranger. I welcomed it. At the very end, the part where I stand behind the person and rest my hands on their forehead, he opened his eyes and looked straight at me. Neither of us said anything, or moved, but inside I thought, *Please, please come back.*

He never did.

I WAS BEGINNING to feel part of the community, a healer. Once, Annie even came. Her coworkers had given her a holiday gift certificate—I made them myself on translucent rice paper—and she arrived on January 2, which seemed like a great omen for the year to come. She pulled up outside my place in the NAOI Jeep. I was opening my door before she could knock.

"Hi!" I said.

"Annie," she said, holding out her hand for me to shake.

"I helped out with the whale," I said, shaking her hand. "I'm Suzanne."

"Oh. Okay." She looked around, then down at her boots. "Well, thank you. We do rely on our volunteers." She reached in her coat pocket and handed me the gift certificate. "So—"

"Right, right. You can leave your coat and boots here, and then the room is just through there. I'll knock to make sure you're ready."

"Got it."

A few minutes later, I entered the warm, candlelit massage room. Annie was facedown, sheets tucked in close to her body, her arms outside. The ice on the clerestory window made the room strange, a bubble that could be floating through the air or on the sea or in outer space. I turned on the music and gently moved Annie's arms—first her right, then her left—inside the sheets. I put my hands on the nape of her neck and pressed. I was so happy to be helping her in this way, to give back.

"What are you doing?" she said.

"It's just—it's how I start. It's a centering thing."

"All right. Go ahead."

"Anything especially tense or painful?"

"Nope. My staff gave me this." She sneezed.

"Tissue?"

She pulled out an arm and took the tissue, wiped her nose, then held her arm out to the side uncertainly, holding the tissue.

"It's okay, I'll take it." I tossed the tissue in the little trash basket and retucked her arm under the sheets. I began working on her back, kneading and smoothing, digging with my thumbs. Between her shoulder blades was a tattoo of a smiling octopus, tentacles reaching and swirling in all directions. Why an octopus? Why smiling? I wanted to ask her, but refrained. There were so many things I wanted to ask her.

"Actually," she said, half-muffled by the face cradle, "now that you mention it, my brachioradialis could use some attention. It's been complaining."

"Of course," I said. What the hell was that? It sounded like something that lived at the bottom of the sea, a species of coral or anemone. "What kind of movements make it complain?"

"Just everyday stuff. I mean, you've seen what I do."

"Uh-huh." Directing ambulances? Hiking over sand? Cutting open the whale? I started to sweat. I redoubled my energy, pressing forcefully everywhere I went on the theory that someplace had to be the brachioradialis.

"Ouch," said Annie.

"Sorry."

After a few more minutes, I just couldn't help myself. "What's happening with the court case?"

"Ah, those fuckers. We'll lose."

"What? No, no. You and Dr. Chang—"

"Listen, I'd love to win. I would. But we're making it uncomfortable for them. People like them." She shook her head a little in the face cradle. "They don't want to know anything about anything."

"Yeah." I ran my elbow along the inside of her forearm.

"Oh, thank you," she said. "All those buckets." That must be it, then, I thought, feeling victorious. She continued, "Whales make people really sentimental. I don't know why. Everyone's all boo-hoo about the whales until it might affect their money and then, boom, they're done. I've seen it a million times. Hypocrites."

Not me, I thought, warmed by the knowledge that I'd put all that money where my mouth was. I longed to tell Annie that as well, but it would prompt too many questions. "Right," I said.

She relaxed under my hands. "I see why people like this," she said.

"Good," I said. "Breathe in. Now breathe out."

At the end, as she was putting on her socks and boots, her face flushed and the marks of the cradle on her forehead, I said, "I go out and visit the whale a lot."

She nodded, then squinted. "What for?"

"To, well, to see it. To see what's happening."

"Decomp," she said. "You aren't touching anything, are you?"

"No, no." A silence fell.

Lacing up a boot, she said, "Thanks for the spa day. Please don't touch the whale." She tipped me a few dollars, nodded once more, and left.

• • •

LATER, MUCH LATER, Noah showed me the photo on his phone: Noah, in a suit and a proud smile; Mark wearing a boutonniere; and Lydia's friend Caprice, tattooed from wrist to shoulder on both arms, standing in front of city hall. The night before the wedding, Lydia sent the Bald Dude a considerate goodbye text, and deleted his number from her phone. The wedding was on New Year's Day. Lydia wore lace gloves and a hat with a veil, which Alan lifted to kiss her at the end. Caprice and Noah clapped, and Mark took them out for a fancy lunch. They ate lobsters and toasted, Lydia's glass filled with sparkling water. Noah even wore a real tie, tied by his father that morning.

I DIDN'T KNOW about any of this at the time. I was working on the butcher, the baker, and the candlestick maker of Chesham. If I had been walking by city hall that day and seen them coming down the steps, happy, on their way to lunch, I wouldn't even have waved. Maybe I would have called out to Noah. But I wasn't there. And he wouldn't have left his father's side, anyway. Maybe I would have thought, Alan, do you think you're starting over? Really? Maybe I would have thought, Young(ish) lady, do you know who you're marrying? Maybe I would have been generous enough to silently wish them luck and mean it. But I doubt it. Healing takes a long time.

ONE NIGHT A few weeks after they were married, Alan turned to Lydia in the fold-out sofabed and said, "Let's go to Paris."

She looked at him in surprise. "Paris?"

"Have you ever been?"

"No," said Lydia. "I don't even have a passport."

He waved a hand. "That's easy. And everyone should have a passport."

"Well. I do have a lot of vacation days saved up. But the tickets—"

"I've got that." Alan smiled the new, broad smile that showed his brown tooth. Lydia always thought of it as the tooth he got from his first mother, the dead, addicted prostitute—a woman she easily could have become herself—and kept in memory of her, or maybe as a warning. He didn't say that, but Lydia thought it was so.

"Don't you have to get permission from your parole officer?"

"Easily done. I'm no sort of risk. I want a honeymoon with you. A conjugal vacation."

"You're not in prison anymore, honey," said Lydia.

"Yeah," said Alan uncertainly. Then, "What do you say?"

"I say . . . well, all right."

"All right, then," said Alan, and it was done. They would go to Paris.

THE PAPERWORK TOOK longer than they had expected, but, finally, they arrived, just in time for the beginning of spring. The white buildings all looked regal; the street signs were uniform and inscrutable; they took a boat ride on the Seine and a guide with a thick accent told stories of the French

Revolution. Alan, her husband, bought Lydia a long, dark dress in a boutique with flowers in the window. The woman who ran the boutique put up Lydia's hair in a silver clip; Alan bought the clip, too. They walked hand in hand down a cobblestoned street to dinner that night, and Lydia twirled in the dress in front of him. At dinner they ate a cold pea soup that tasted the way a hill in early springtime looks.

Lydia had three guidebooks with her, all of them bristling with the little translucent flags that showed people where to sign documents. Every morning, she put on her glasses and consulted the books, serious as a rabbi consulting the Talmud.

"Chocolate, taxidermy, or a medieval church, husband?" she might say, putting rhubarb jam on her croissant.

"Taxidermy, wife."

And off they would go in search of the taxidermist, getting lost two or three times before eventually peering at the carefully arranged window display, a strange and subtly perverse zoological diorama, and deciding not to go in. Even the taxidermist looked rich, the name of the shop in gold cursive on the window. "It's been here since 1835," Lydia said. "Same family." Alan wondered aloud how much taxidermy you could sell, to have a shop like that for all those generations. What else did they sell, under the table?

"No, no," said Lydia. "They're the real thing. Chocolate. It's on the next street."

But it wasn't on the next street, they got lost again, and stopped to order crepes at a window where you could watch the man make the crepes, smoothing the circle of batter on the griddle with a little wooden paddle. Lydia closed her eyes and inhaled the floury, buttery scent of the crepe, trying to hold it in. Remember this, she thought. Remember this. Or was that me who thought that, when Alan and I went to Paris for the first time? First time for both of us.

"We should live here," said Alan, as they continued on their way, warm, paper-wrapped crepes in hand.

"We can't live here," said Lydia. "I have to work. And I don't think they'd let you move out of the country, anyway. Not yet."

Alan fell silent. His face seemed to change shape. She kissed him on the cheek. "It will be all right. You're a smart, smart man. There's a place for you."

"If you say it, I believe it. Maybe I could learn taxidermy." He lay his head along her neck like a child, and they walked like that, awkwardly, laughing, taking messy bites of each other's crepes.

LYDIA HAD ONE of her war dreams on their next-to-last night in Paris. In the dream, she was crouched in a bombed-out building, dead bodies everywhere, gunfire, soldiers were coming, but she wasn't sure if they were on her side or the other side. In fact, she didn't know what war this was or what country, if she should run or stay where she was, and maybe she had a gun or maybe she didn't, it kept changing. All the terrors were indistinguishable from one another. Her limbs, in the dream, didn't work very well. She could hear a child crying for help. She began making her way toward the child, as she always did at this point in the dream, but there were flashes and tumbling mortar and the soldiers, friends or foes, were getting closer. Maybe her leg had been blown off, she didn't know and she couldn't bear to look.

She woke, breathing hard. She took out her mouthguard. "Alan," she said. "Alan." But he wasn't there. Lydia turned on the light. The hotel room gazed blandly at her. His phone was on the little table next to the petite striped sofa. She got up and looked in the bathroom, but she knew he wouldn't be there, and he wasn't. She pulled the balloon shower curtains back, feeling foolish. Lydia lay back down in bed, unsure what to do. It was three thirty in the morning. She got back up and opened the curtains, peering up and down the charming, empty street with its white buildings and its balconies. Already, the night outside the windows was threadbare. She left the curtain open, as if Alan might fly in the window, like Peter Pan. She lay back down in bed, pulling the covers over her feet. She stared out the window at the indigo sky. Her last thought before she fell asleep again was that if he had gone off somewhere into oblivion, she could still make it back home, she still had a job, after all. She still had a place to live. The shame would come, of course, but Caprice would help her. Naomi would understand, although Lydia dreaded seeing that understanding look on Naomi's face. Naomi would only understand the bad part of the whole thing.

But when she woke up some hours later, Alan was asleep beside her, in running shorts and athletic socks, bare-chested, smelling of sweat. A pair of sneakers, still laced, lay akimbo on the carpet. She didn't know he'd brought them. Or had he bought them somewhere here? The room was hot with sun. Sunlight illuminated everything, and it lit him up, too, every hair and fold and mole. She could see every inch of him as if magnified, but she had no idea who this was, this midnight runner. Had he even really been running? She wasn't sure what she wanted the answer to be. She didn't know if she should let this one go. She hadn't put her mouthguard back in and her jaw was sore; she must have been grinding her teeth in her sleep, waiting.

Over room-service breakfast, Lydia gathered herself and said, "So, last night . . ."

"It's a thing I've started to do sometimes. I don't know. I like it." He looked at her almost with embarrassment, as if he'd been caught doing something silly, juvenile. "I'm sorry. I guess I should have left a note."

"Where did you go?" she asked as if curious, as if she wasn't, just a little, testing him.

"Along the river. I figured that way I wouldn't get lost. I actually ran around the Eiffel Tower. Twice." His face was open, bright.

Lydia decided to believe him. She got the guidebook with its fluttering translucent flags off the table. "Last day, husband," she said. "Candles, pastry, or parrots?"

ON THAT DAY, it could have been that day, I walked right up to the whale. It had been a twelve-client week, so I was in a good mood. A great deal of the flesh was gone. I smelled more salt than decomp. Funny little white critters, crablike, skittered around in the belly of the carcass, busy at their task. What was the whale to them but a structure to scavenge, a lucky windfall—hey, over here! Look at this! Or whatever crablike critters said to one another, whatever their business was. In my scarf and hat and mask, I bent over to look at the ocean through the exposed ribs of the whale, like looking through a tall fence. A clump of dark-green tubes of seaweed lay at my feet. Gulls rested on the surface of the water, watching me examine the dregs of their buffet. During the storms of the winter, the beach, already narrow, had eroded significantly. The water covered the whale's head, uncovered it, covered it again. The long, angled bones of the whale's head, the hinge of the jaw, lay half-revealed, half-submerged in wet sand. Some bones had been knocked loose, scattered on the sand; the emerging skeleton had gaps. I had no idea what went where, but I set the heavy, loose bones inside the arch of ribs.

Exposed, the length of the animal was sublime. From head to tail it was three times the length of my car, at least. The vertebrae were thick, curvy squares, each one the size of a hatbox. In some way, the skeleton looked bigger than the living animal had, majestic in its openness to sky and air. I thought of Wallace Stevens's jar on a hill in Tennessee, a college favorite of mine. Like that jar, the skeleton of the whale seemed to organize everything around it in relation to itself. It comforted me that the animal had this life after its earthly life had ended, this power.

The case was still unresolved. I enjoyed the possibility that by the time the case was over, the whale would have long since been taken back by the sea, bones scattered for miles over the ocean floor. I wanted it to drag on and on, so that neither side would win, so that the ocean would win. That would be justice. In the *Chesham News*, an article had said that the whale had scars from past fishing-line entanglements, like most whales. Those must have been the scratches I had seen on the whale's side that night we got it out to sea. Those scars were gone now. In the article, there was a picture of Annie sitting at a desk, which seemed like an awkward place for her to be. I wondered who else besides me knew about the smiling octopus on her back. "These things happen," said Annie. "There's so much about these animals and their world we don't know."

However, Annie continued, things like this were happening more often and in places where they hadn't happened before. She went on to talk about how Cetacean Hall could do so much to educate the public, especially children, about the incredible beings with whom we share our precious and unique planet. She talked about the importance of donations. I hoped that some of the money I had given to the marine-mammal global organization had made its way to the NAOI. I imagined her surprise and pleasure when the unexpected bounty turned up, from an anonymous benefactor.

LATER, AFTER THE worst had happened, Sylvia wanted to hear about the good part of my life with Alan—the years before it all went bad. She was the one who found me. Well—I had found out where she was, for Lydia, but then Sylvia reached back through the airwaves for me. Our first conversation, on the phone, went like this:

"Suzanne? This is Sylvia. I'm sorry we never met."

"Yes, me too. Hello, Sylvia."

"I don't understand."

"I don't understand, either."

"But you were with him, all those years. What happened?"

"I don't know. I hadn't spoken to him in quite a while."

Pause.

I wanted her to hang up, disappear. I wasn't in the mood for this. But then she changed tacks.

"I want to know about the good part," she said.

"The good part?"

"With you. And your son. All that time. You owe me that much, at least."

"The good part."

"Yes."

By then, it was almost hard to remember about that. "It was a good life," I began, but then I stopped. "Listen. Okay. I'll talk to you about those years you missed. Fair enough. But you need to talk to me, too. I don't know you."

Pause again.

Finally, "Yeah, sure. I'm an open book."

"All right. Well. We met through friends, at college. When we first got married, we lived in a little apartment and we had our son, and then Alan became successful.

We moved up, you know—we needed more room for our family."

"You never asked him where I was." It wasn't a question. Sylvia's voice was sweet and clear. She had a landline; I always pictured her sitting in an armchair next to a fireplace, although that didn't really make sense. She was in southern Virginia by then for one thing, but for another, she definitely isn't an armchair-by-the-fireplace sort of person.

"He didn't talk about you," I said.

Pause. Then, "I don't understand that."

"He kept a lot of things to himself. He compartmentalized. And, I don't know, he worked a lot, and he kept getting more responsibility, taking care of bigger accounts for more important people and organizations." That sounded vague, even to my ears. I tried again. "It was just the three of us, and we would have liked to have another kid, but it didn't happen. But with only one, one nice thing was that we could go places and Noah was a really good little traveler."

"Where did you go?" asked Sylvia, and there was palpable curiosity in her voice. "I'm a traveler, too."

"Oh, gosh—so many places over the years. Europe, of course, many times. But also Africa, that was amazing, and Vietnam one year, Bali, Mexico. Iceland. A lot of the people we knew had summer places, right? On the Vineyard or whatever. We were different. Not so stuffy. More international. And we thought it was good for Noah to be exposed to all these other places, other kinds of food. So, for me, life was busy with the house and Noah's school, all that, but then I also did a lot of the trip planning, because Alan worked so much." Phone calls in hotel lobbies, in restaurants, in airports; that husband and wife in Zurich we always had to have dinner with on our way between northern and southern Europe. They were impeccably solicitous, and thoroughly opaque. We never went to their home.

I didn't know how to explain to Sylvia that it felt like we were famous people, the three of us and our luggage in the car on the way to Logan so many times, Noah reading a comic book, Alan on the phone, me checking the itinerary I'd created for us, which had always entailed a lot of research and many phone calls and emails. We were the family that came and went to cool places, and saw more things than I had ever dreamed of in my cheap Catholic schoolgirl uniform. Noah might have been bad at reading, but he liked to go on trips. We loved being able to give that to him, those experiences. It was so important for his development.

And then the arrival back home, weeks later, the key in the lock, and our high-ceilinged rooms, hushed and clean. Opening the curtains and the shutters on every floor. Sitting, jet-lagged, in the garden with a cup of coffee on the first morning home, noticing the good work the gardeners had done while we were away. Our gardeners were superb; artists, really. It was heartbreaking when we had to let them go, after. We all cried. I hate to think what might have become of that garden. The housekeeper had always stocked the fridge with fresh groceries, the bread that Alan liked, the cream-top milk. Once, we landed just three hours before the first day of school. Noah was eleven, and we let him have coffee with his breakfast in the bowl from the South of France I dug out of my suitcase. I have a picture of him, smiling in his coffee mustache, Alan on the phone in the background, waving, early-morning light drenching the kitchen, my suitcase open on the floor.

The three of us—we were like our own private club. People think that having money means you get to have lots of people serving you day and night, but for me, for us, it meant that you didn't have to be around lots of other random people all the time getting in your way, blocking your view. It could just be us, our little light-footed family, where we wanted to be, when we wanted to be there. Off the beaten track. Sometimes, Alan told me stories about the ridiculous things his rich clients got up to, all the ostentatious crap they piled on their houses and their bodies, and we laughed. We weren't like that. We were never like that.

I tried to tell Sylvia some of this, and then about Noah's reading issues, but before too long I could tell I'd lost her. "Sylvia? You there?"

"You were his wife," she said. "How did you not ask about me?"

I was glad we couldn't see each other. "You had been gone from his life for so long. It didn't seem like you were coming back into his life anytime soon."

"I was always planning to come back. Always."

"Okay, but, Sylvia—"

"But what?"

"Nothing. Nothing." I told her about the garden.

After that first call, every now and then we Skyped—Alan's birthday, maybe—but she liked telephones much better. Holding my phone to my ear, sitting in a chair myself, I told her about the various turquoise rooms of our life, hoping she wouldn't ask me again what she really wanted to know. And I found that I was curious about her. I wished I had known her, back then. I would have understood more, earlier, about what Alan came from. Then maybe I wouldn't have been so surprised.

But I'm getting ahead of myself. I think about that first conversation with her a lot, the way she asked for the story of the good part. I understand now how she felt. The good part can get so overshadowed by the other parts, and those parts can make it all seem so inevitable, even though it wasn't. People make choices. Still, I probably just should have stopped there, describing Iceland to her.

NOT LONG AFTER Alan and Lydia got back to Boston, Lydia was fairly sure she was pregnant, but she waited a few weeks even to buy the kit in the drugstore for fear that she'd jinx it by testing too soon. She didn't want to make an oracle cranky, even if the oracle was a dubious-looking plastic stick in a cardboard box. She didn't tell Alan, either, for fear of the same jinxing, the people dancing at the wedding just before they all get struck by lightning, drinking champagne on the deck of the *Titanic*, that kind of thing. She felt the glow, though, and the queasiness, and a weird sense that time was slowing down, stretching out, and other people really talked a lot. She wished they would shut up so she could nap. Her fingertips often felt quite warm, and she thought with considerable pleasure about the fact that the baby wouldn't inherit her bad hand, the bad side of her face, but emerge whole and unmarked. If it was a girl, her name would be Ava; if it was a boy, Daniel. Every time she peed, she felt a little burble of joy, because soon she'd be peeing to win, as it were.

On a Monday afternoon she finally bought the kit and hid it in her underwear drawer. On Wednesday morning, she peed on the stick. She was pregnant. She felt that she'd gotten away with something, that they'd gotten away with something, she didn't even want to tell a soul until the baby was born, pretty much. She ran into the kitchen, where Alan was making toast in his underwear, brandishing the stick.

"What?" he said. "What?" He grabbed the stick, studied it, smiling with delight, and then he kissed it. He pulled her into his arms and held her so tightly she nearly lost breath. "You are the best. You are a wonder. Tell that God of yours thank you."

LYDIA DID FEEL like a wonder, like a superhero. She tied and untied all the little knots at Hill, Hill and Adams, her belly moving her inch by inch away from her desk. Her feet were bigger, her breasts were bigger, her hair was thicker, her fingers were swollen. Peeing became fairly autoerotic, which was a plus, because she peed constantly, pushing away from the increasingly small-looking desk and padding down the carpeted corridors to the women's room and back. Every pregnant woman becomes an expert in bathroom location.

She had become a bit of a celebrity around the office. It was as if her pregnancy was the resolution to the story her face told that they had been waiting for, the happy ending in which they were all involved. The lawyers offered cushions, crackers, advice, offers to leave work early. She didn't leave work early. In fact, she worked better than she ever had, furiously even, building high, strong walls of finished tasks and precompleted documents so that when the baby came, he or she (but Lydia was sure it was a she) would have Lydia's full attention.

There was one lawyer, though, an older guy, comb-over, who ate peanuts in his office all day, who had a different attitude. Jeff. As Lydia was coming back from the bathroom one day, Jeff called out from his office to her. Lydia paused in his doorway.

"Come in, sit down," he said, jumping up to usher her in. He closed the office door behind her.

Lydia sat. "Everything okay?" She tried to remember if she had anything overdue to him, but she was way ahead on everything. She put her hands on her taut belly.

"Peanut?"

"No, thanks."

"Water?"

"I'm okay."

He moved a few empty shells around his desk. His office
was linty, which was strange, because the cleaners came in
every night. It was as if he brought the lint in with him, as if
he exuded lint from his dull pores. "Lydia, I just wanted to,
well, I don't want to intrude." He smiled beneath his comb-
over. "But. Your husband. You are aware—"

"Of course. Thank you, Jeff. I know about all of that.
And, honestly, what's a justice system for if it doesn't matter
that people did their time?"

"Good point. But, Lydia. We've been working together
all these years. Let me put my cards on the table here."

"All right." Did she have to pee again already?

"My sister was one of your husband's clients. She had a
small business, these special candles she made, and she was
really doing quite well. She's the artistic one in our family."
He smiled his linty smile. "Anyway, the thing is, it turned
out that what she gave him—it never went into any sort of
legitimate fund or investment instrument. It just went into
this sort of soup pot of money that he was ladling out until
he got caught." He moved a few more peanut shells around;
they made a skritching sound. "And that's a, that's a crime
of a certain *quality*, do you see what I mean? That kind of
person—" He shook his head. "My sister will eventually be
all right. She's very clever. But, Lydia, I can see that you're
very involved here, and—maybe I should have said something sooner."

"I know him."

"I know you think that." His gaze was surprisingly sharp. He billed quite a few hours for the firm.

Lydia shook her head. "I know him. I'm really sorry about your sister, and about what happened—all of it. I am. He is, too. But people get caught up in things."

"They do, indeed," said Jeff. Then he fell silent over his field of peanut shells, which exasperated Lydia. Like she didn't know what he was thinking. People thought that her face must mean that she was either an idiot or a savant, and she was neither. She was a normal, intelligent human being, no more, no less. "Has he," said Jeff, "asked you to sign anything?"

Lydia stood up. "Thank you for your concern, but you're really barking up the wrong tree. It's nothing at all like what you think." She nodded politely and walked out.

Back at her desk, she wasn't sorry. She felt bigger and stronger, and her own hands on her belly felt bigger and stronger as well, like gorilla hands. No one would ever do to their baby the things that had been done to Lydia. She understood so much more than she ever had before about life and death and teeth and blood and bone. She understood about coming from earth and returning to earth. What Jeff obviously didn't get was that she loved Alan deeply, but when she woke up next to him in the morning, their child ripening between them, she hardly felt as if she even needed to talk to him. The thing was done, and would be, forever, whether they were in the same room, the same country, or even on the same planet. She wondered if her baby would see the first colonies on Mars, the drowning of cities, airplanes without pilots. Probably so. Lydia's strong gorilla hands would make sure her baby was ready for all of it. She would build her baby a spaceship if her baby needed one, or an ark, or a bunker.

UP IN PROVIDENCE, Babette the nice, laid-back manager was replaced by Stewart the thin-lipped corporate clown. "That guy," Sylvia told me later. "I walked into his office one day, you know what he was doing? Sitting in there with butterfly clips all up and down his arms. Get your jollies however, but Jesus Christ. And I was the problem?"

Maybe it was the absurdity of those butterfly clips, or of Walmart in general, or just feeling her age, but Sylvia suddenly felt that it was time to gather her flock. It had been so long, and it was never right, what happened with Alan, and she could stand there in that drafty doorway until she dropped dead in it, or she could bring the different parts, the lost parts, of herself together. However the realization occurred, she walked out of Stewart's office that day formulating a plan. It was time for a reunion. Past time. She called her son Andy that night.

IT WASN'T UNTIL Lydia was four months along that she realized that Alan had a secret. He and Noah had meetings with people, meetings that involved driving places and getting back late. When Lydia asked what they were doing, Alan said, "I'll tell you, but not yet. There's a lot involved."

Sometimes his phone rang in the evening, and Alan would step out into the hallway, speaking in a low voice. Lydia pointedly didn't listen, didn't try to overhear. Caprice, over lunch in her scrubs—she was a dental hygienist—said, "What the fuck?" But Lydia said, "He'll tell me when he's ready. Do you want to feel the baby kick?"

Also, Lydia didn't entirely care. She was happy. She luxuriated in her happiness; she wallowed in it; she felt like she could have walked down the street naked, clothed in nothing more than her happiness. All she wanted to do was eat and have sex, pretty much. She, Alan, and the baby were making a single chord of life, a deep, low organ chord. She was a church, tall and strong and full of them all. So when Alan came back some nights with new energy and dirt on his shoes, when he talked to whoever and whoever in a low voice in the hallway, when he texted Noah late at night: she could wait for the explanation. It was good to see him happy, too—lighter, easier within himself. Caprice said, "*Ly*dia," but Lydia was rolling in her happiness.

As it turned out, Caprice was wrong. Lydia and Alan went to dinner at Mark's one evening, and there was Noah, beaming, with blueprints. Noah's face seemed to have sharpened, but that wasn't it, Lydia realized. It was as if his being had sharpened. He wasn't shifting from foot to foot; he exuded energy and purpose. The men sat her in a chair with a pillow on it, and Noah unrolled the blueprints before her on the dining room table. Six houses were drawn on the blueprints, with a compass down at the bottom right edge of the paper and, at the top edge, beyond the houses, lines of waves and, in capital letters, CAPE COD BAY. On the left side of the paper it said THE HARBORAGE.

"This is happening," said Noah.

"What is happening?" asked Lydia. "Are we going to live here?" How would she get to work from the Cape every day?

Alan, a hand on her shoulder, said, "No, this is a development project. We're going to build this."

"It's my development," said Noah. "I'm the director."

"In name," said Alan. "He's the front man." He unrolled another blueprint on top of the first. This one was of a single house, with arrows and numbers and little aerial drawings of toilets and tubs and the diagonal lines of doors swung open. "We're going for a New England look, traditional, but opened up. This is the living/dining room, and then the kitchen in the back—there's a second stairway here. Every house will have a view of the Bay."

"Wow," said Lydia. "It's big."

"Not for the Cape," said Alan.

Mark said, "We got approved for the construction loans this week. We didn't want to tell you until it was all squared away."

"We can break ground *next week*," said Noah. "You can come. Come on, let's open the champagne."

"None for me," said Lydia. The house would be very pretty, she could see that, but it stung, just a little, that Alan hadn't shared the plans with her until now. The baby moved, as if trying to press an ear to Lydia's walls to overhear the conversation. She rested her hands on her stomach.

Alan, leaning over the blueprint, said, "What do you think?"

"How does this kind of thing work?" asked Lydia.

"It's simple," said Alan. "The construction loan pays for building the model house, basically, then we sell units based on that, and once we've sold three of these babies we pay the loan back, and we're in the black."

"Like a mortgage?" said Lydia.

"Not exactly," said Mark, easing down into another chair at the table. Noah went into the kitchen, came back with a bottle of Veuve Clicquot. Mark continued, "With a mortgage you're on the hook for thirty years. Construction loans are a few years."

By the time the baby was walking and talking then. Lydia said, "We're going to need a bigger place, too. I mean, not out there—"

"Already done," said Alan, putting a set of keys down on the table. "We're moving to Medford."

Noah popped the cork. "Surprise!"

"Oh, my," said Lydia.

Noah poured champagne into glasses for the men, opened a bottle of sparkling cider for Lydia and handed a glass of it to her with an attempt at a little flourish. "May the Force be with us," said Noah, holding up his glass to toast. Did he still believe that? But he looked as if the Force was with him, actually.

"My kid," said Alan.

They all toasted and Lydia sipped her cider. This was a new world, for sure. The buoyant energy of the three men was infectious, uplifting. They enthusiastically pointed out features to her on the blueprints and watched her face for her approval. It was easy to give it to them, like handing out candy to trick-or-treaters, but a part of her, a quiet part, was already in another room with the baby. Medford. She'd have to look up the school situation in Medford, later.

Mark served dinner, and they toasted again. The baby flipped inside her, a duckling, a second heart. The illumination of the secret that had been visible in Alan for the last few weeks kindled to a hot glow now, and he laughed and drank and teased and ate steak, leaning back in his chair, more handsome than Lydia had ever seen him. "Let's go dancing," he whispered in her ear.

She pointed to her stomach. "With this?"

He caressed her belly. "*Particularly* with this. The baby needs it."

"The baby needs to sleep," said Lydia.

"Nope," said Alan soft and low in her ear. "Trust me on this one."

Noah, flushed, said, "What are you guys talking about?"

"Your father is being crazy. He wants to go dancing," said Lydia.

"Abracadabra," said Noah. He tapped on his phone in two swift moves and the apartment filled with a slow, smooth song. Alan stood up and held out a hand to her.

Lydia, with a bit of a heave to stand up, took it. He put his hand in the small of her back and moved with her out of the dining room, into the living room, gliding them both around furniture, down the little hallway and back again, and all the while he was saying things to her that only she could hear about how beautiful she would always be, and how astonishing their baby would be, and how houses didn't matter, big plans didn't matter, not really, the only thing was the three of them and the future and couldn't she feel it? The way they were at this minute. Everything was going to be all right now, he said, and she could feel the relief in him, some obstacle gone, one bad story ended. He held her bulk effort-lessly, like a man balancing the world on a finger. It was wonderful. Baseballs, worlds, women heavy with worries: all so light in his hands.

ON THE DAY they moved out of the studio, Lydia took one last look around at the squares and rectangles of unfaded paint where pictures had hung, at the messy nail holes, at the stained wall behind the compact stove, and saw that this had been a chrysalis for the creation of her family. The stain on the wall behind the stove was faintly heart-shaped. Lydia took a picture of it with her phone. Noah had signed the lease for them on the Medford place: a three-bedroom apartment with a foyer, a fireplace, and big windows that looked out on a leafy street. It was the biggest place Lydia had ever lived, and such an easy train ride to Boston that they wouldn't even need a car.

The baby was a girl, born in December. They named her Ava. They baptized her in a local Methodist church, then, at Lydia's insistence, in an Episcopal one that had beautiful stained-glass windows. They took a picture of Ava when she was tiny, fast asleep on an orange triangular throw pillow, like a fairy child found on a pumpkin. They took many pictures of her. Her favorite thing was to bounce back and forth; they took videos of that. Alan actually got paunchy; Lydia was soft all over; Ava's rhythms and needs organized their days and seemed to change time itself. There was both more of it, and never enough. Lydia loved the way Alan looked carrying Ava in the chest harness, Ava facing front in her little hat, waving her arms, Alan the proud new father with graying hair bearing new life forward. He liked to get all suited up with the baby and take her downstairs with him to get the mail. Ava never tired of the tiny outing, and if Lydia said, "I'll go," Alan always said, "No, it's our thing," and buckled Ava in with increasing expertise.

When Lydia was explaining this part, she said, "Do you see what I mean? Do you see?"

But I already did. I knew what this part was like. Alan's joy in babies was so pure, so natural, that all that work of child-rearing seemed, not easy, but entirely good. With him, being a family felt like being a lantern carried through the dark of the world. Not like being *in* the lantern. Being the lantern itself. Incandescent.

● ● ●

OK, I KNEW family life wasn't like that, not even ours, but still. I warmed myself by that semi-illusory light—the way Alan saw it. One of the worst things about going to see my mother, as I do every few months, even though she'll forget almost immediately that I've been there, is the repetition. It seems so minor, considering, but it depresses me unreasonably. I tell her some innocuous story of something I passed on the road—a flock of geese in flight, say, heading south or north—and she'll smile. Five minutes later, she'll ask, "How was the drive up?" And then I'll have to tell the innocuous story again, as if the previous five minutes never happened. Time evaporates behind us almost immediately. I've never told my mother what happened with Alan and how it all went down, because I would just have to repeat it to her over and over. I'd have to hear myself saying it endlessly. I'd have to explain about currencies and exchange rates, and she wouldn't understand any of it even before she forgot that I said it. In her mind, none of this has ever happened; it's a parallel universe of only the good parts. I admit that sometimes I like being in that universe, that lantern, with her. For a few hours every few months, I can almost believe that none of the bad parts ever happened.

NOAH LIKED AVA well enough; they let him hold her, showing him how to support her head. He didn't exactly feel related to her, even though he was. The weight of her in his arms was pleasant, like holding a purring cat.

It turned out that Noah loved work, which was a side of

him that had never blossomed with me. During that winter, Noah never stopped working, it seemed to him. He didn't *want* to stop working, which was weird. He'd never been like that before. He stayed on with Mark, living on his tuition refund and shadowing Mark and Alan in everything they did with the development. He set his alarm. He drank black coffee. He made lists and calculations. He took it seriously that the business was in his name, even though the two older men emphasized to him that this was a technicality, nothing more. It wasn't a technicality to Noah. He felt so right, as if, without his knowing it, he'd been preparing his whole life to do this, to go into business with his father. All those grueling hours spent on his reading, his time organization, blah blah: what a waste of everyone's time and money.

It was obvious to Noah: all those years, we'd been (I'd been, I supposed) prodding and testing him on the *wrong things*. He read blueprints and spreadsheets and invoices just fine, better, even, than Mark, who was a worrier, which could be a drag. He never picked up when I called. *Not yet* was his thought, apparently. Noah had the idea that when it was all done and sold and profitable, he'd allow a brief dinner with his mother/me. (Thanks!) He'd pick up the check. Not only were they going to get their old life back, they were going to get more, better, bigger. In his opinion, the government had made an example of his father, they had taken too much, it wasn't fair. For the first time in his life, Noah had a cause he believed in, and he hurled himself into it with all the energy that had never found a cause before.

When, later, Noah finally did tell me all this, he still knew every detail of the two jobs they gave him: driver when they all went out to the work site, and keeping tabs on the construction manager, Gordy, and how the money was being spent. Noah had a clipboard, the car keys, and wore a pair of heavy work boots adequate to all weather and terrain. He got to know the names of the guys at the site and used them as much as he could. "Mi amigo, Victor," he'd say, "how's it going?" and Victor would give him the status of various aspects, all of which were tough going. The ground, the weather, a particularly stubborn tree with crazy roots: Noah wrote it all down in meticulous detail. He met regularly with Gordy—in person, if they were at the site that day, or on the phone, if they weren't—to go over that day's doings and costs. Gordy, an extremely orderly man, neat as an envelope with a bill inside, answered each question with a forbearing expression in as few words as possible. Noah wasn't intimidated. He caught things, too, mostly small things, but every bit counted, plus there was the pleasure of sticking it to Gordy.

Alan and Mark took Noah's accounting seriously, and as the months went on, they even gave him some of the vendors to manage. "Watch out for these guys," advised Mark. "Trolls, every last fucking one." He meant *trolls* in the old way, Noah understood.

"Some of them even look like trolls," said Alan. "Seriously."

"What about Gordy?"

"Biggest troll going," said Alan.

"That's why we hired him," said Mark.

They gave Noah the concrete and roofing accounts, and he actually read up about concrete, roofing, and accounting, underlining and highlighting. It was the happiest time in my son's life. The blow that severed us from our old world liberated him. And maybe it's true that he was made more for blueprints and work sites than reading lists; maybe, for all his naivete and awkwardness, he liked being the muscle for Alan and Mark's operation. Finally, he had an assignment he liked: being his father's lieutenant. Maybe he always had been.

The very best part for Noah was being with Alan in Mark's car, especially on those days when Mark had to stay in town so it was just the two of them on the drive to and from the site. Noah always drove so his father was free to wrangle trolls; every time his father trounced a troll, they high-fived. Sometimes Lydia called with a baby bulletin, but mostly it was a troll-shoot all the way out, interspersed with pessimistic observations about the state of the world, which had too many trolls to count. It was a troll apocalypse out there. When Alan asked him about the most recent expenditures and overages, Noah had them all right off the top of his head, tight and clean.

"Jesus, Noah," said Alan on one of these drives, "I wish I'd had you working for me when all that shit went down."

"Forget that, Dad," said Noah. "It's over."

"Yeah, right," said Alan, but with that distracted look he got, like a man seeing a ghost.

"Dad, come on," said Noah. "Maybe you should write a book. Tell people how it really was."

"People don't want to know how it really was. They don't understand money. They don't understand financial instruments. They don't even understand *compound interest*, for Christ's sake. And, believe me, I'm way too small a fish for anyone to care. I'm a soccer dad now."

Noah, eyes on the road, laughed. As if.

When they got out to the site, they walked around with Gordy in the mud and dust, taking turns asking the sharp questions that kept Gordy annoyed and working as hard as he should.

"All right," said Gordy.

"I see," said Gordy.

"We could do that," said Gordy.

When Gordy's back was turned, Alan gave Noah a nudge in the ribs and a thumbs-up. Troll-training. Keep 'em hopping.

By the time winter set in, the house had a foundation and the beginning of a first floor. Winter would slow the pace to a crawl, but they had a good start. On a drive back when night had already fallen, Noah said, "Dad, what are you going to do with the money?"

"What are you going to do?"

"I asked you first."

"The money," his father said, as if the fact that they were doing this for profit had just occurred to him. He drummed his fingers on the dashboard. "The money. I don't know. Buy a horse."

"Buy a *horse*?"

"Yeah," said Alan, with that distracted look. "I've always wanted a horse."

Noah laughed, neighed. "Well, I'm going to get a car. It moves a little faster than a horse."

Alan nodded. "Good man. What kind of car?"

They considered various possibilities of wheels all the way back to Boston.

THAT WINTER, I was doing well, holding my own with my two shifts at Waves and my clients. The money in the strong-box went *shushshushshush*. I had been a poll watcher in the local elections that fall. Julie was my friend. I'd joined a book club; we were reading a book, a true story about a woman being held captive in a cave in Appalachia for five years. Her suffering was amazing. I wished I could talk about mine, but I didn't. It would require too much explaining. I thought that, in the summer, I'd go for a training at NAOI. I had held the whale to me alone for a long time, but I thought I might be ready to join up with the people fighting for the oceans and the life there generally. No one would ever know that I, the anonymous benefactor, had helped support our work.

I was walking down the street with Julie toward the other bakery and coffee place, Misty's, which wasn't nearly as good as Delilah's, but would have to do. Delilah closed for most of the winter in Chesham when she went to stay with her sister in Arizona. Everyone remarked on her midwinter tan when she came back and said they were jealous, though it didn't seem that they were, really. She wasn't popular.

Julie and I were talking about how to weather-strip the drafty shotgun shack. Julie was explaining the weather-stripping options, particularly the eco-friendly ones, with her usual thoroughness. She was up to bamboo when I saw, coming toward us, my former suburban neighbors, Matt and Rose. Both short, curly-haired, verbose doctors. Round and ruddy in their winter coats, they looked like watercolors from a children's book.

Matt and Rose were walking happily along the sidewalk, peering in windows, holding hands. Their winter coats were the expensive, black long ones, and Rose had draped a black scarf gracefully and cleverly around her head. Round-faced and makeup-free as she was, she looked like a Vermeer painting. A winter Vermeer. It would be obvious to anyone that they didn't live in Chesham. No one here wore their scarves like that. Nearly all the women wore makeup in every weather. It was too late to cross the street so I arranged my face in a conciliatory expression. What were they doing here? Although that was the kind of thing they did, in their generally jolly way, just driving off on a cold day to the Cape to look at not much of anything. They liked to drive places, eating snacks and listening to NPR.

As they came abreast of us, I looked down and away. "It's because of the sealant," said Julie.

"Suzanne?" said Rose. Everyone stopped. Julie cocked her head.

"Yup," I said.

"You fucking bitch," said Matt.

"Hey! Whoa!" said Julie.

Matt and Rose stood there together on the sidewalk, glaring at me like Tweedledee and Tweedledum on a very bad day. "What do you have to say for yourself?" said Rose, her words making clouds in the cold. "What do you have to say?"

"I didn't know," I said. "I wasn't aware—"

"You didn't *know*? Who are you kidding? It built your *house*," said Matt, leaning toward my face as if I couldn't hear him. "You slept on it, you ate it, you drank it, you fed your kid with it."

"Do you know what happened to us?" said Rose. "Do you want to hear the number?"

"Who are these people?" said Julie. "Who are you?"

"Ask her," said Rose, crossing her arms over her long, black coat. She flicked a glance at me. "You look like shit."

"You got paid," I said. "You're *doctors*. It wasn't like—"

"You have no idea what it was like," shot back Rose. "What it's still like. And you know what else? You're worse. He was bad, but you. You're worse. You should have gone to prison, too, you parasite, you shitty collaborator. Like butter wouldn't melt in your mouth."

"I'm not like that. You don't understand." Even to myself, my voice sounded limp and defeated.

"What's going on here?" asked Julie. "Suzanne?"

All I could manage was to shake my head, staring at the ground. I was like a rabbit in the presence of hungry foxes, flattening myself and going still.

"Do you know who she is?" Matt asked Julie. He had hardly any lips, that Matt. Never had.

Julie frowned. "She's my friend Suzanne Flaherty, that's who. Who are you?"

"*That* is *not* her *name*," said Rose.

"Yes, it is," I said. "It's the name I was born with. It's my name."

"You disgust me," said Rose. She and Matt pushed past me, marching away down the street.

"It's my name," I repeated to their backs. "It's my name." I began to cry.

Julie hugged me. "What the hell? Suzanne, what the hell?"

At Misty's, over coffee and sugar-coated pastries under fluorescent lights, I told Julie that my ex-husband had been a kind of whiz with currencies and exchange rates, but then he also made some bad business deals for people.

"Did you know?" asked Julie.

"Not really, I was so busy—"

"Doing what?" asked Julie, carefully not looking at me, pulling a bit off her pastry.

"Taking care of my mother," I said. "She has dementia."

"Oh, God," said Julie. "That's the worst. Where is she?"

"In a home now. You know, finally."

"I hear you," said Julie. "And those people are doctors?"

"Specialists."

Julie snorted. "Entitled much?" But then she said, "What kid?"

I couldn't deny him, even though he was still denying me. "Right," I said. "I have a son in college. It's . . . he's been distant recently. Since it all happened. Growing pains."

"Oh, Suzanne," said Julie. "A single mom putting a kid through college and with a demented parent?" She reached over for my hand. "I thought I was the biggest caretaker going. You've got me beat."

"What can I say?" I said. "Catholic-school girl all the way."

We ate our pastries and drank our bad coffee, and as darkness was falling I made my way back home, relieved that by now Matt and Rose would be long gone, eating their snacks and telling each other how horrible I was while getting all the answers right on that NPR quiz show they loved. I shut the door of the drafty shed behind me, feeling that I'd dodged a bullet, or maybe just been grazed by one.

But then my phone rang. It was my landlady, Annette. "Honey," she rasped out. "You and I, we need to talk."

"Okay."

Did she know who I was? I got dizzy. I put my head between my knees and took long breaths.

"Fuck," said Annette. "My sister's calling. I'll call you back."

I turned my phone off and locked the flimsy front door. Why couldn't everyone just leave me alone? Who was I hurting?

LYDIA'S CUBICLE WALLS grew crowded with pictures of Ava laughing in a striped sun hat, Alan's face alight from the glow of birthday candles, Caprice holding one of Lydia's heart photos (a heart made of soap bubbles in a tub) in front of her own heart, Noah asleep with Ava asleep on his chest on the sofa. When she sat in her cubicle, she felt surrounded by love. She was so grateful, every day, that it almost hurt. Sonny Swan had been right: everything was love, at the end of the day, or the lack of it. People died every day for lack of what she, Alan, Ava, and Noah had in such abundance. Ava's first word, in fact, was "more" and they laughed and gave her more peas and carrots. Alan had started running again, and now he was biking, too. He tightened back up, more than tightened back up. He became incredibly fit, for a man his age. Lydia felt that she finally understood what *enough* could really mean, and how much *enough* actually was. A lot. Everything. Winter slowly gave way to a messy, icy spring.

Because so much was now so clear to Lydia, when Alan confided that problems were coming up out at the site, absurd delays and construction problems, sections not built to spec, and bad weather and double-dealing creeps, she was able to remain serene. She had a job, after all, and their overhead was low, and their bouncing daughter was astonished by everything in the world. She kissed his furrowed brow. She told him not to worry. On another day, when Alan left the room to tuck Ava in, she quietly asked Noah if it was as bad as Alan had made out, and Noah nodded, squinted. Over time, Lydia had come to see that Noah had good sense about the way things worked.

Noah said, "I think it will be all right. I'm working out some deals with the vendors. We're behind, but we can do it." It was the deadline on the loans, he said. That was the problem. And Mark had gotten a little—Noah made a seesawing motion with his hand. The guy was no spring chicken. He missed things, and then they had to waste time cleaning up after him. Noah was clearly getting tired of Mark.

Lydia nodded. "We've got to band together to support each other. Your father thinks it's all on him."

"Right," said Noah. "Totally."

Lydia could hear the murmur of Alan reading Ava her favorite story, the one about the goose. She smiled, content. "Keep me posted," she said.

"Totally," said Noah.

YOU'D THINK, WITH the birth of Ava, that Alan might have thought about Sylvia. Maybe he did. I don't know. But Sylvia was certainly thinking about Alan a lot around then. She liked to knit in the evenings after her shift. She would open the window next to her elbow of a dining area, light up a joint, think about things for a while, then put whatever was left of the joint into the cobalt-blue ceramic dish Jay had made for her before he had his fall and his daughter took him away. Then she would set to work. Sometimes she didn't turn the lights on as the evening darkened, enjoying the feeling of the thread in her fingers, proud of the dexterity she still had.

It was time. She knew that it was time. It was time to tell Andy. It was time to find Alan. It was time for the three of them to be a family. She was going to knit two bedspreads, one for each of her sons, as Christmas presents. Sylvia was a fan of Christmas, which you might not expect from someone who's been a bit of a free spirit, but it might be the most truly renegade thing about her: she liked Christmas, and Christmas carols, and decorating Christmas trees, completely unironically. This coming Christmas, somehow, the reunion would happen. She would explain it all to Andy, how it all happened, and she would try again with Alan. This time, she would succeed. That spring, she smoked her evening joint, knitted, and was surprised how happy she was to have a plan.

IT TURNED OUT that Annette was concerned, apparently. Concerned about what? Well, she was concerned about my visitors. My visitors? People (what people?) had noticed (why had anyone noticed me? what had they noticed?) that I had these *visitors* at odd hours—short-term visitors. Annette coughed. I laughed, relieved. I said she couldn't be serious, it was just bodywork. What work? said Annette. *Body*work— massage therapy. There was a silence.

"Honey, listen to me," said Annette. "I know how it can get. I really do. And if you say you're giving these massages or whatever, then I'm sure that's true. But I have a reputation here, too, this is my property. So I need you to be more discreet."

"Annette, you're not understanding this practice."

"Daytime only. Nine to five. Like at an office."

"But bodywork doesn't work like that."

"I don't see why not," said Annette, and hung up.

THAT SPRING, WE had a major thunderstorm that was hard, dense, and loud, like it had a point to prove. It tore down store signs and pulled up trees, sunk a boat that wasn't firmly docked. Hail battered the clerestory window as I worked. Julie, there for her regular appointment, said, "Hope we don't lose power. Good thing you have all these candles." We lost power a few hours later and I opened the front door to get the last of the daylight. I sat in a chair in the doorway, silver light and downed branches in the street before me, a dimness behind me. The breeze was damp and almost cold. A siren was sounding somewhere. It was hushed the way it is after a storm, as if the world is taking a breath after shouting for hours. Two little girls went by on their bicycles, both drenched and barefoot, impervious to the chill, and singing some pop song I didn't know. They swooped along the empty street, their bare toes on the pedals, wet hair flowing down their backs. To them, I was just some lady sitting in a doorway, a blurry grown-up in a sweatshirt.

Although I didn't know it then, out at the site that same storm threw a tree down onto the house and flooded the new basement. Gordy, in a slicker, yelled into the phone, but the tree crew would get there when they got there, there were public roads to be cleared, higher priorities. Two walls were splintered and flattened, turned into nothing but a busted box for the tumbled tree. And more rain predicted for the next day.

I WORKED ON the bodies of the people of Chesham, but they worked on me at the same time, like water falling day by day. They built up my muscles. They put a crick in my back. They kept my fingernails short and they filled me out—hips, breasts, thighs. I could have tried to lose the extra, but I decided to keep it, so I would look more like them. Like someone they could trust, a local small-business person. The next time Matt and Rose, or anyone else from the old life, saw me on the street, they'd likely look right past me—a townie. I let my hair grow and I wore it in braids sometimes. I let the gray grow in, too. I switched to the local drugstore shampoo.

Summer came. I wore jeans and T-shirts most of the time, like everyone else; a windbreaker in the evenings. I could keep the windows open all day and night, which made the ceiling feel less low. The air blowing through smelled fresh and felt vast. Because it was summer, I didn't have to pay for the electric heat. I made sure to remark on that to people as I bought groceries or a new pair of sneakers. I did my best to keep banker's hours, but the days were long, and the town had its share of seasonal tourists. I had to save up for the inevitable winter dip.

The fight over the whale dragged on, but with less heat. Now nature was giving us sharks coming in unprecedentedly close to shore to get the gray seals, whose colonies were growing with strange speed; there had been a human death and many seals lost as well. Everyone monitored local shark activity on an app, as if the sharks were going to break into houses or vandalize cars.

I continued to go out to see the carcass. That spring's fierce storm had accelerated the removal of the remaining flesh from the bones. Bits of flesh still hung from them, draped like gruesome curtains in many parts, but most of the tailbone was clear. I touched it, and was surprised to discover the oil there. It was dark, sticky, the consistency somewhere between olive oil and honey, and it smelled both musky and, underneath, repellent, like something nasty rotting in a wet basement. That stink seemed capable of yet defending the whale, driving away predators long after the flesh was gone. How did the whalers of previous centuries stand it? Or did they just not notice after a while, surrounded as they were every day by animal death, boiling down vats of blubber? The exposed bones were darker and sticky as well where the oil was seeping. I looked up *whale oil* when I got back home. Whale bones seep oil—the first fuel oil, before petroleum was discovered—from deep within the marrow, for decades. At museums that display whale skeletons, tubing runs from the bones to glass flasks, collecting the dark oil that the whale continues to exude.

SYLVIA, SITTING IN the windowless break room at Walmart, wondered why she of all people had stayed in such a shitty place for so long. But it was all right now. It was going to be all right. She jotted down what she'd say to Andy, when she explained. She wasn't sure how to find Alan, but maybe Andy could help her.

IT WASN'T A good summer for any of us, except maybe Noah, who was stronger and more confident and out at the site every day. The site wasn't more than an hour from Chesham. He must have passed the exit to my town every day.

Back in Medford, the old itch pulled at Lydia all summer, very nearly pulled her in. It might have, too, if not for Ava in the morning, Ava at night, Ava astonished by a bug, Ava on her lap, Ava pulling at the buttons on her blouse, Ava with a fever, Ava maybe with a fever, Ava freaking out with joy when she saw other babies, trying to grab their hands from her stroller. Lydia just—and it made her a little angry— couldn't slip. Not anymore. Not even a bit of a bruising misadventure, and then the recommitment, the penitence, the self-aware laugh at meetings, the applause. Maybe if Ava had been older, but not now, not with Alan worried about his project and on the phone with Noah or out at the site constantly. She didn't understand exactly what was happening with Mark, the stories were unconvincing, but the bottom line was that he was around less. On her knees while Ava napped, she asked what she needed to do, and the answer was so loud and immediate it was almost comical.

So off she went, back to the folding chair, back to the coffee, back to the rooms, as they said, back to the rooms. She knew she could call Naomi, but she didn't. The room in Medford was a Unitarian church where all the pews had been taken out of the sanctuary. The folding chairs were padded; the coffee was organic and fair-trade. A dance company rehearsed there during the week. Lydia thought, *Better problems, better problems, better problems. Look where you are.* She'd been in far worse rooms, with people in far worse shape, when she was in far worse shape. She still had all her days, all her years. She wouldn't have to give back her ten-year chip. She touched it, as if to reassure herself that it was still there, beneath her shirt.

Lydia began her first share, "The problem is me. I mean, I really, really want to say that my husband is driving me crazy, my kid is driving me crazy, I'm worried about a lot of things, but one finger out, three fingers back, right? Life on life's terms. I'm the one standing in my kitchen wanting to hit the gin bottle, I'm the one going in the CVS and cruising the cough syrup aisle, I'm the one wondering what happened to the rest of the pain meds from my husband's root canal last winter. This disease." Lydia shook her head. "Jesus Christ. This disease. Anyway, a day at a time I haven't done any of that. But I am—it's hard right now. I need you people. I'm really grateful you're here. I would do a ninety in ninety—all right, I should, I know—but my baby isn't even a year yet." Lydia choked up. "Anyway. Anyway. I got here."

"Keep coming back," said the fireman, and the nurse, and the kindergarten teacher.

"Keep coming back," said the rabbi.

"Keep coming back," said the woman who said she was an artist. Lydia thought that maybe she could show that woman some of her photographs sometime. They could have coffee.

Lydia kept coming back. Tuesday night at seven, at First Unitarian. Open meeting.

WHAT I MEAN here is: we were all trying. We were all doing our best. But then official letters come in the mail, old habits sing their siren song, people in small towns smell the stranger on you no matter what you do or how much you help them—it's like nothing ever really leaves this world, it's just written where it doesn't usually show, sinking in until it seems like it was there from the beginning. I've seen it in clients many times: the scar from a father's belt buckle, the pinky that will always be crooked from a car door, the raised white marks of old burns, the permanent stoop in the shoulders. Do you know why Julie's feet were like that? Years and years of waitressing. She didn't go to library school until she was thirty-five, because it took her that long to save the money for the tuition. She changed her life, but her feet couldn't change back.

What I mean is, even with all the work I did and my gray-streaked braids, the cops showed up. Two of them, a man and a woman, knocking on my front door. I was eating a lemon popsicle when I opened the door, trying not to let it melt down my arm.

"Hello," I said in a friendly way, thinking they were selling raffle tickets or something.

"Suzanne Flaherty?"

"Yes."

"May we come in, please?"

I sucked at the popsicle. "Sure."

They were both young and square, flushed from the heat. They looked uncomfortable, but also dogged. The woman said, "We've had some complaints. You give massages?" I didn't like the way she said the word.

"Bodywork," I said, the way Eagle always did. That's what he called it. He was a *bodywork practitioner.* "I do bodywork."

The cops looked at each other.

"Ma'am, can we see your license, please?"

I took them into the room with the clerestory window, where the linens were neatly folded at the end of the table, the sun streaming into the room. It couldn't have looked more innocuous. I pointed to my framed certificate. I was getting balletic with the dwindling remains of the popsicle, lapping at the sweetness.

The man got up close to the certificate, read it, then took a picture of it with his phone. "Ma'am," he said, "this isn't real."

"Of course it's *real*, I did that course—"

The woman shook her head. "You know what we mean. This is some crappy online thing. A real license requires three hundred hours of training, or more. It looks like you had six. Can we see proof of your liability insurance?"

I put the popsicle stick down. "I help people," I said. "On a sliding scale."

Now the man shook his head. The woman glanced at him, shifted her weight, glanced at me, nearly fifty with my round hips and my knee-length shorts and lemon popsicle juice on my arm. All of her calculations and assumptions passed over her face. Finally she said, "Listen, in the state of Massachusetts, this is a misdemeanor. You want to help people, that's great. My brother-in-law is a physical therapist, he gets people walking again. But you need a real license, ma'am. You need to put that time in."

"And money," I said.

The woman looked at me with a bit less kindness. "Well, that is the law. We can't have people just running around calling themselves whatever. It's not safe."

"We could hit you with a five-thousand-dollar fine," said the man. "That's money, too."

"Oh, Christ," I said. "I can't."

"Should have thought of that," said the man. "Can I have a glass of water?"

I brought it to him, then said, "Okay. Okay. What do I do?"

"Stop," said the woman. "Stop today. Don't make us come back here."

"We'll get the health department out here," said the man, refreshed, handing me the empty glass. "They'll fine you, too. Every which way."

"Just stop," said the woman to me. "Get licensed. Then you can help people all you want."

"All right," I said. "Thank you." I showed them to the door.

Fucking Annette, I thought, dropping onto the couch. She just couldn't forgive me for . . . what? For the secret she was sure was there. For the difference I couldn't hide, no matter how wide my hips got. The other girls always know who you really are, even if you wear the nightgowns and the oversized men's shirts and buy drugs you don't want. They know, and, eventually, they get you for trying to trick them.

Ha ha, Suzanne Flaherty, you fake, said the secondhand couch that sagged. Loser, said the popcorn ceiling. The linoleum corner that always curled up smirked at me like that cop had. You're nothing, with nothing to offer, nothing to say. But the thing was, I *did* have something to offer at last, I *did* have something to say. It wasn't fair. Why should I have to stop and go back at exactly the moment when I was doing so well, and on my own terms? When I was with Alan, I never had to wait my turn, take a number, waste my time, settle. And, okay, I hadn't earned all of that. But I had earned this. Maybe Annette was jealous of something in me, some capability that she couldn't even name. Why couldn't she just leave it alone?

I would get the license, I decided, when I had time. Which wasn't right at the moment.

FALL CAME. THE storm wreckage at the site had been cleared away and not only had they rebuilt, they'd advanced. Noah, Alan, and Gordy were all relieved, which was part of the reason that Noah didn't tell anyone about the piece of mail he opened by accident. Sort of by accident. By this time, Noah had come to think of himself as responsible for the team, so he felt that anything that looked official was his business. He thought maybe they had a violation—Gordy's fault, undoubtedly—or something. And then he couldn't put it back in the pile, because he'd ripped the envelope, but it was clear that this was just the latest of a series and there would be more to come. The government didn't appear to be kidding. This is how Noah learned the word *restitution*. It was a Monday night. Mark and Alan were at a Red Sox game. Noah put the envelope in his pocket, went back to Mark's, took Mark's car keys, got the car, and started driving.

Noah didn't know what he would do when he got out there or even why he was going. He was terrified. This was how it had all been before, how suddenly everything disappeared, but this time it would be even worse. He had the ragged idea that he could burn the new house down for the insurance, but how much insurance did they even have? He couldn't remember. Driving, he fumbled for his phone, thumbing around to try to find the email from the insurance

lady, but he couldn't find it and he had the presence of mind
not to crash the car. The road narrowed, the towns grew
smaller. The scent of salt came into the air.

What was I doing that night? If it was a Monday night,
I was working at Waves. I had a lot on my mind that fall.

It seems to me now that the change in Noah must have
started here, that this is when he became the man he is now.
It's simple, isn't it? Alan got Noah's hopes up, and then he
took all those hopes away. What did he think would happen?

When Noah got to the site, he parked the car in the rut-
ted dirt. By then, some of the exterior walls had gone up
again along with a rough first floor. Plastic covered a few
openings for windows and what would one day be a front
door. The strange thing was that there were some lights on
inside and at first glance, to Noah, it was kind of homey, the
lighted house, part of a house, glowing in the darkness. He
put his head on the steering wheel, breathing hard, as if he'd
run all the way out to the site. *What the fuck*, he thought.
What the fuck what the fuck. What were they going to do?

He got out of the car and walked toward the house. He
heard voices. The ground was uneven, sandy. Salty air encircled him; the wind touched his cheeks, his hands, the tips of
his ears. He could smell the dope as he got closer; it smelled
good to him, like a bit of relief. He knew he had to kick out
whoever was in there, but just for a second the light and the
dope smell and the cold, wet night itself felt reassuringly
ordinary. Keg parties in fields. The sagging front porch of a
grad-student group house, back in Kansas. Pushing the thick

plastic aside, he climbed in through a window opening on the ground floor because that would be more surprising to the intruders. It was dim inside; two canister flashlights sat on end, directing light up toward the beams. Four teenage faces—two boys, two girls—turned to him, like faces at a campfire. It was parking-garage cold, but out of the wind.

"Hello," said Noah.

"Hello," said a boy leaning against a wooden pillar. "Can we help you?" The pillar boy was lean and canny-faced, in Docksiders. Another boy, larger with heavy-lidded eyes, lounged in an open window space on the other side of the room, leaning against the gathered plastic, smoking a joint. The scent was sweet. Melodic, folky music was playing on a little cylindrical speaker. The two girls, both slender as saplings, were sitting opposite one another blowing smoke rings, popping their jaws. They looked at him, smoke dissipating into the darkness around them. One was blond with a straight, thin nose; the other burgundy-haired, with streaks of blue in it. The smoke-ring girls were so pretty, like a pair of herons. The burgundy-haired one wore a black choker around her neck. Her eyeliner swooped almost to her temple.

"This is my house," said Noah. "My father is building this house—I'm building this house with my father."

"Oh, shit," said the blond girl. She stood up. "Okay, we're going." The girls turned off the music, started gathering up the cylindrical speaker, half of a six-pack of beer, and a pie in a pie tin.

"It's all right," said Noah. "Can I have some of that?" He gestured toward the joint in the larger boy's hand.

The larger boy left his window perch and brought the joint to him with a bow. "It's your house, dude."

Taking the joint, Noah glanced up at the beams, around at the few walls and window portals. "What do you think?" he said.

"Oh, it's great," said the burgundy-haired girl. Her friends nodded agreement. "Really cool space."

"Would you like some pie?" asked the blond friend. "She made it."

"No, thanks. But I would take a beer." Inhaling deeply, he handed the joint to the pillar boy.

That boy grabbed a beer from the girls, popped the top, and handed it to Noah. "Here you go, sir," he said. Sir? How old did they think he was? Or was the guy fucking with him?

"Thanks. Cheers." Noah sipped warm foam. The teenagers watched him, no one saying anything. "You kids from around here?"

The pillar boy exchanged a glance with the larger boy. "Pretty much. We're like cousins." He indicated the other boy. "He lives here. My family's visiting."

The larger boy said proudly, "He's from Boston."

The blond girl said, "We go to the same high school. Us three." She pointed to herself, the other girl, and the larger boy. "He's some foreigner," she said flirtatiously, nodding toward the pillar boy. "We don't even know if we like him yet."

Noah nodded. "Cool." He didn't know what else to say. He didn't really, he found, want to kick them out. It was a relief to party with people; how long since he had done that? Maybe he would just get wasted. Maybe he could get laid.

The lean and canny pillar boy said politely, "Would you like to sit down?"

Noah nodded, and sat down on an overturned bucket. The girls put the speakers and the pie back down. The teenagers resprawled on the plywood floor, looking as if they were settling in for story time.

The larger boy, big sneakers reddish from the dirt outside, said, "So, like, what are you doing here? It's kind of late." Flat on his back on the floor, he pulled another joint from his pocket, lit up.

"I needed to get my head clear," said Noah.

"I hear that," said the boy, offering the joint to Noah.

Noah puffed. He passed the joint to the pillar boy. He took a long swallow of the beer. It tasted yellow. God, he was tired. "You guys come out here a lot?"

"Never," said the girl with burgundy hair, brushing her bangs out of her eyes. "Sometimes. Once before."

"No, it's good," said Noah, as the joint came around again. "Houses need people in them. You're breaking it in. By breaking in." He smiled at his own pun.

The teenagers laughed. "Oh, yeah?" said the larger boy.

"Well, I'd like to have a house like this one day," said the burgundy-haired one.

"We're going to build more of them," said Noah.

"No shit," said the pillar boy, not looking as if he believed Noah at all.

The burgundy-haired girl looked around, clearly impressed. The blond one looked at her nails. "I might go home soon," she said.

But she didn't. No one moved much. The larger boy started the music again, then returned to the floor. The music was sad and spare. The joint came around a few more times. The burgundy-haired one began to sway lightly around the unfinished room. She looked as if she was dancing as much to the night itself as to the music. Her skin was incredibly pale, like she stayed inside a lot, making up songs in her room. Noah had always liked girls like that. There had been one like that at college, they had been having a little thing, before he left. What would she be now? A junior? Did she have a major? What did it matter? He was never going back there. The burgundy-haired one danced toward him, tapped him on the head like *duckduckgoose*, then danced away again. Noah took a deep drag on the joint, eyeing her.

"I think it's time for you to go," said the pillar boy.

"Excuse me?" said Noah.

"Go on," said the pillar boy. "We don't want to play with you anymore." He said it in a whiny child's voice.

The larger boy laughed and the blond girl laughed, too. The burgundy-haired girl was swaying alone at the open night end of the house.

"No, you get out of my fucking house," said Noah. "You're trespassing."

The pillar boy opened a beer and poured it on the floor. "Shut the fuck up, dickwad. Call your *crew*."

Noah stubbed out the joint in the pie. He stood up. "I said get out of here. This is my house."

"Prove it," said the larger boy with the reddish sneakers, at which point Noah picked up one of the canister flashlights and smashed the larger boy in the face with it, at which point the pillar boy and the larger boy, bloody-faced, beat and beat and beat Noah down to the dusty plywood floor. He lay on his back, gasping, the larger boy's foot on his chest, the weight driving him through the floor, his fingers scrabbling on the boards.

The pillar boy said, "You fucking psycho."

A female voice—the blond girl? where was the burgundy-haired one?—said, "Let's get out of here." Someone put some material on him, it felt like a sweatshirt, and then a piece of plastic over it. Noah told himself it was the girl with burgundy hair. The plastic smelled like old dirt and cement. His eyes were already swelling shut as he heard the muffled thumps of steps in the soft-packed dirt outside. Then it was dark and quiet everywhere except for the sound of the wind, rattling and rattling at the plastic in the windows, at the plastic draped over him.

Early the next morning, Noah felt a hand on the horrible, endless pain-field of his face and heard Gordy say, "Oh my God." Air slowly, jerkily whistled through him.

"Don't move," said Gordy, as if he could.

Not long after, people put him on a stretcher, metal doors

closed, and Gordy was there next to him, calling everyone. He smelled like soap.

Teeth.

Ribs.

Busted nose.

Every body tells a story.

No one called me.

No one called me.

No one called me.

What's the legal term for that?

AFTER THEY RELEASED Noah from the hospital, he convalesced at Alan and Lydia's in the spare room. He doesn't know what he was thinking. He was on a lot of painkillers. He had to eat soft food only, like Ava. He watched movies on his computer. He doesn't know what he was thinking, stop asking. When everyone asked him what happened that night, he said there were punks in the house, he'd just gone out there on a whim, and there was a stupid fight. The pie with the stubbed-out joint, the bloody pink sweatshirt not his size were proof enough. He didn't really remember what the punks looked like, it didn't matter. He told me the whole story only after years had gone by; it was part of his list of resentments. Sometimes Alan and Lydia and Ava, too, came in to keep him company while he ate his dinner of mashed potatoes and soup. Did his father know that Noah knew? If he did, he didn't show it. Maybe, Noah thought, his father had figured out what to do. Then they took his dirty

plates away, held Ava up to give him a tender—careful!—
goodnight kiss, he took a pill, and went to sleep.

On the day that he could finally have an actual sandwich,
and he was so hungry, he found his father sitting in the living room, his glasses on, reading through a sheaf of papers.
Lydia was at work. The woman who helped out with Ava
had taken her to the park. Noah said, "Dad."

His father looked up.

"Dad. So. The thing. The government thing."

His father blinked.

"The big thing."

His father nodded. "Right." He didn't ask how Noah
knew. He didn't flinch. That was one of Alan's best moves,
to behave as if you and he were both already in a conversation, a reasonable conversation about things you both knew
and for which you were both responsible and should probably find some sort of solution.

"Well. It's really—it's bad, right? I mean, we don't have
it."

"We don't have it yet," said Alan.

"But," said Noah. "Um."

Alan said, "Come sit down. Look." On the back of one
of the papers he wrote some numbers about the Harborage
and profit and comparables and then he subtracted, he even
extra subtracted for worst-case scenarios like tornadoes that
would never happen, and then there it was, a really fine, even
a bit of a proud number, a rooster on a sunny morning kind
of number. "Okay?" said Alan. "How was the sandwich?"

"Fantastic," said Noah, still looking at the rooster number, crowing. "Are you sure?"

"I'm sure," said Alan. "Keep getting better, we need you back on the job. Gordy's totally out of control."

"Trolls!" said Noah.

Alan was running a lot. He said he was training for a triathlon. He did squats and stretches in the living room after his increasingly long runs; he swam at the local Y; he rode his bicycle along the Mystic River; he joined a training group. Once Noah's injuries were down to yellow bruises, he took long walks with his dad from time to time. He says they talked, but about what, he's never said. If I had been there, if anyone had been there, they would have seen a father and son walking together, talking—an unremarkable sight.

THAT FALL, SYLVIA was on the train heading south, at last. As the train passed through Boston, she looked out the window, thinking, *Which street are you on? Honey, I'm coming. You have a half brother. You'll like him, even though he's a cop. I know. It's weird.*

Take a moment to look at Sylvia on the train. She is seventy-one, she has fine blue-green eyes, and she is doing a sudoku. There's something about Sylvia, and it isn't just her light sandalwood scent or the shaggy tousle of her white hair—there's something about her that makes you want to get close to her; there's a little cloud of energy around her, a focusing energy. Sylvia gathers intensity around her. She might be eating a green apple, and when you see Sylvia eating a green apple—or an orange, or a pear—it suddenly occurs to you how wonderful that apple is, how green, how round, how fresh its scent. It's amazing, isn't it?, how the earth produces something as glorious as a green apple—or an orange, or a pear—and that you can just eat it on an ordinary train on an ordinary day, heading south. She's also good at sudoku, she's making quick circles and she's smiling as she's making them. Now and then she glances out the window, taking in the rusted Northeastern landscape with her fine eyes. When Sylvia is looking at that landscape, it looks more resonant to you, too. You notice the colors, the shapes. It's because of the intensity of her gaze and the intelligence in it. That's Sylvia. That's part of Sylvia. There are other parts.

She tucks her feet, in their little brown suede boots, up on the empty seat next to her. She takes a bite of apple.

At Roanoke, Andy picked her up in the patrol car. Sylvia wanted to ride in the back, but Andy said, "Stop, Ma. I could get in trouble." Andy bent at the knees to put her suitcase in the trunk. Sylvia tried not to sigh audibly; he did everything as carefully as a first-grade teacher. Sylvia found it depressing. She got in the front seat, though, the way he wanted. He buckled his seat belt, turned the key in the ignition, and put both hands on the steering wheel. He smiled at her. "You're getting a police escort home, Ma. Like the president."

As they drove, Andy waved at passing townspeople, who smiled and waved back. How was this one my son? thought Sylvia, not for the first time. But he was handsome, and he was a good man, and she was glad to have him in her life.

Sylvia was still surprised that Andy had picked Virginia. They'd never lived there. The South was like another country to her, a backward one. She wondered if it was okay for Andy here, but he didn't like to talk about personal stuff with her, or anyone, as far as she knew. He had always been like that—in motion, building things, taking things apart, rescuing stray dogs, but not talking about any of it. She'd come home and there would just be a new mutt in the living room, staring at her, maybe peeing. That was Andy. Once upon a time, the two of them had been a team—he was great at packing even as a kid, it got so he could pack up his room in under an hour—but he didn't like to talk about that, either.

With both hands on the wheel, he drove them very safely to his house. He parked, got Sylvia's suitcase out of the trunk. His house was two levels: an entry floor and, above it, all the rest, with big leather-covered furniture, and a television set the size of a yacht. Another thing Andy never talked about: his love life. Sylvia said, "Wow, honey, what a place," as she looked for signs that any other human being, boy or girl or anybody, ever got past the living room. But not even traces of a mutt to keep him company. The floors were bare wood, waxed to a shine.

"Thanks," he said. "I like it." He wheeled her suitcase to the guest room. Sylvia slipped off her shoes. From the living room window, she could see his patrol car parked neatly in its space, as if it was arresting the house. Or maybe it was guarding the house. Every night that car would be parked right there, letting the eyes in the dark know that a cop lived there. A cop and his mother. What could anyone say about that? She was so tired of people saying things. All her life, people had been saying things. People had said things at Walmart, too, some of them right to her face. Her eyes were grainy from the train air. Her mouth felt dry.

Andy came back out and stood by the immaculate kitchen island like a real estate agent showing her the property. "Ma, are you hungry? Do you want a nap? Make yourself at home. I have to go back to work."

"I'm all right," she said.

"The lights are on a timer. They come on automatically at seven. If you don't want that, there's a switch thing under the sofa. Just turn them off."

Sylva nodded. "10-4."

"Peace out," said Andy, holding up his first two fingers in a V. "I won't be back until after midnight." He kissed her on the cheek and left. She liked hearing the sound of his big feet on the stairs, like old times. Click of the door.

She heard the patrol car pull away. She opened the refrigerator. There, in an oval glass dish covered in plastic wrap, was a roasted turkey breast with a Post-it note on it that said MA THIS IS FOR YOU. Next to the glass dish was a plastic container marked VEGETABLES and another marked POTATOES. It was like Thanksgiving. She took them all out and put them, one by one, into the sparkling microwave. She watched them go around, molecules popping. So fast. She never did like it that much at Walmart. It was like everything she did, and how fast she wasn't, was causing a stoop in everyone else's walk. They wanted a microwave world, with microwave employees that could heat up and check out a customer in thirty seconds. Sylvia preferred to get to know people.

She ate her entire microwave Thanksgiving, all of it molten at the center and cool at the edges, standing up at the kitchen island. She thought it was good for her ankles to stand and then move around. She lifted one foot and twirled it, then the other, as she ate. She could hear birds chirp outside. The lights in the living room came on, ta-da.

She opened the dishwasher, which had one white cup in it, and put in her dishes. She sat down on the big leather sofa and tried to turn on the yacht television, but she kept ending up at a vast blue screen with options that all dead-ended at another blue screen. Then she couldn't figure out how to turn it off. The yacht was lost at sea. After a while, she gave up and lay down on the sofa, moving toward the back of it so she wouldn't roll off the slick leather. She woke up to Andy in his uniform touching her shoulder, all the lights still on, saying, "Ma, it's late. It's time for bed." She never thought she'd be glad to see a cop looming over her, but she was. He held her by the elbow as she walked toward her room. He didn't have to do that, but it felt comforting, anyway. The shiny floors felt cool and smooth on her bare feet. Tomorrow, she would tell Andy. She knew just what she would say.

• • •

SOME THINGS ARE just wrong. Some acts have consequences that compound. They rot, and they stink, and they leak everywhere for years and years. They weigh so much that not even great teams of people and machines can carry them away. If he had called me before, I could have told him that. But he didn't, and, once again, I didn't know.

ON A COOL, bronzed day in early November, Alan crossed the half-marathon finish line at the back of the second third of the pack, making very good time for his age group. Lydia, Ava, and Noah waited for him in the crowd, carrying water, oranges, a sweatshirt. Alan came out of the finish-line tent draped in a silver Mylar cape. The silver rippled behind and around him as he came toward them, smiling. Noah clapped hard, holding Ava, who clapped as well. Lydia held out her arms to him. He paused a few feet away, a silver column, making a frame with his fingers.

"Click," he said.

Two nights later, he slit his wrists in the park not far from their house. He was dressed in his running clothes, having told Lydia he was going out for a run as she turned in for bed. She found the documents the following day: laid out on top of his desk were the life insurance policy and a stack of letters from the government, demanding in increasingly dire phrases what he owed in restitution. Lydia knew what restitution was. The number was very big. She had thought they had both paid up with all they had lost, the fires they had been through, the hell in their eyes, but it seemed she had been wrong. Also clear were the insurance company's terms regarding suicide: they would pay if the death occurred two years or more after the policy was taken out. It had been two years and three months.

Lydia carefully folded up all the papers and put them back in their respective envelopes, just as she would at work. She organized them by postmark date. She felt calm, although she knew that she wouldn't feel like that anymore very soon. It was funny, in a way: the man had been so smart financially, everyone said so, but in the end the math he did was very, very simple. A child could have done it. After the restitution was paid, there would be a small amount left over for her and Ava, enough for a little nest egg, but not the kind of money that would make anyone suspicious. The business was all in Noah's name. She would have to ask Noah about what that meant.

Three months. What made Lydia feel ill, what began to sweep over her calm and drown it, was knowing that he must have hoped against hope during those three months. She counted back. He had taken out the policy when she told him she was pregnant with Ava. He had spent the last two years and three months hoping he wouldn't have to do it, hoping he could stay, trying to get ahead of the fire that was still advancing. He must have been running day and night for his life, orphaned emotionally once again, filled with shame, a mortally wounded lion. That night at the lecture, she had thought they were both enthralled by stories about love and transformation, but now she wondered if Alan had been looking at Sonny Swan's scars and noting the length of the cuts. Even worse was the feeling that somewhere within her, she had suspected that this could happen all along. She, too, had hoped against hope, ever since they met. Ever since she was born, maybe. Slowly, she tilted out of the chair and lay down on the carpet, her forehead to her knees. The tears, she knew, were only the beginning of it.

PART THREE

The Whale's Bones

Sylvia will tell you that a lot of casinos are run by Indians—excuse her, Native Americans. The poker sites are run by the Mob—it doesn't matter which Mob, it's someone's Mob. The horses are owned by billionaires who made their money on child labor, or worse. Elections get won by whichever candidate has the most money. Everyone's got a team, a leg up. Total randomness, total fairness, is a fantasy. Never happens. Sylvia says she's just one lady scrapping out there on a tilted board, balancing on the tilt with her swollen ankles and her crinkly lungs. She ran away from home when she was sixteen and it was the sixties and she did all the things runaways do. At nineteen, she met Alan's father at a blackjack table. He was an older man named Gary with a lot of cash who was perpetually amused by how crooked the world was and how bad at hiding it. He was, he said, a food importer. She thought her ass had landed in imported butter, and he married her and at twenty she gave him Alan. But then something went wrong, Gary had all these suspicions, and he threw her out. Right out, on a Wednesday. Why did he throw her out? Sylvia will say, He was nuts. His whole family was nuts. Crazy jealous people. You won't get any farther than that. But then Sylvia will lean forward, and she will put her hand on her heart, and she will say, "I always planned to go back for him. Always. Gary knew things about me. He made me sign over custody. But I figured once Alan was of age, you know, we could reunite." You will, in that moment, believe her. You will believe that she believes this, absolutely. And why not? What mother wouldn't hold out the hope not only that she could find her son again, but also that there is no way the universe *wouldn't* allow them to find each other? A while after Gary, she met a better man, a kinder man, with whom she had another son, Andy. She and Andy's father stayed together for a good long time until he got very tight with Christ. That was a bit of a dealbreaker, and her life took some turns, and she got delayed. It never seemed like quite the right time to tell Andy, who took the divorce hard. But she was determined, she had always been determined, to set it all right. It was only fair, to everyone.

When you hear all this, you will forget what Sylvia just said, which is that fairness is a fantasy. The universe isn't fair. Never was. But when you're with Sylvia, both these contradictory ideas can seem entirely possible: that the universe is never fair, and that it had to play fair with her and Alan—the road-weary young mother with the blue-green eyes and the baby. You will wish that they could find each other again, that time might be reversed.

ON HER FIRST morning in Roanoke, Sylvia said to Andy, "I need yarn." She wanted to tell him, but it seemed to her that she needed more yarn, to have a good start on the second bedspread.

"What?"

"For my knitting. I'm making a bedspread. There are these special green diamonds—it's too hard to explain to a nonknitter. Isn't there a craft store in this town?"

Andy's eyes were deep brown behind his glasses, with the long eyelashes that always made Sylvia worry about him, if he was getting picked on. Maybe he did get picked on, and that's why he became a cop. He wouldn't have told her. "You knit?" he asked, furrowing his brow.

"Honey, I told you that. Ever since I quit smoking."

"How long has it been since we've visited?"

"Well." She thought back. "You came to Providence for Christmas three years ago. We went out to the place with the biscuits. With Jay."

"Right. Jay. You still see him?"

"Not so much. He had a fall. He went to live with his daughter in Delaware."

"I'm sorry," said Andy. "Wow."

"'Wow' is right. That daughter is a Nazi. She's probably pillowed him by now."

"Ma," said Andy, but he was smiling. "Jesus." He took out his phone and poked around on it. "Okay, there is a place. Kiki's Krafts, with two Ks. I'll take you." He closed the binder. He took off his glasses, and put them into a case, which he snapped shut. "On to Miss Kiki's," he said. "When in doubt, ka-nit."

Sometimes Sylvia wondered what Andy meant by things, but she didn't ask. She did think that if he knew how hard it was to do stranded colorwork and steeking, he might not be so snotty.

WHO WOULD HAVE imagined that Roanoke would have a place like Kiki's Krafts? You went down a few steps to the door. It took Sylvia a minute, holding on to the handrail. The front of the store was all sorts of glitter and glue and little straw baskets, all that shit that breaks in five minutes, but at the back was an entire room, floor to ceiling, of every color of yarn in the world, skeins and skeins divided by color, each color in its own cubby. The dark colors started at the bottom and then the colors lightened as the cubbies went up, like a sunrise. A woman sat knitting at a little table, very cozy. Andy said, "Whoa. That is one hell of a lot of yarn. I'm going to get a coffee."

Placed in front of the shelves and shelves of yarn were three high wooden stools so that a yarn lover, a group of yarn lovers even, could sit down and have time to contemplate it all. Which Sylvia did. The diamond pattern called for a shade of green named "emerald," but at Kiki's there were fifteen shades of emerald, easy. One you might call bluish emerald, another jungle emerald, another cool emerald, an emerald with sparkles woven in, an emerald with tiny gold threads, an emerald that was almost aqua. There were so many shades of emerald, so many shades of everything, every single one elegantly wound and in its own little cubby. It was like a museum of yarn, like every possibility of yarn was there, in Roanoke. Of all places.

A half-smiling woman of about Sylvia's age, but with no makeup, a head of curly salt-and-pepper hair cut close, and glasses on a braid of red silk around her neck, came into the room in black slippers with big black bows on them. This was Kiki's Krafts, and Sylvia thought she must be Kiki; she looked like a tall sheep. Her ankles were perfect. She said, "Can I help you find anything?" .

"Are you Kiki?"

She inclined her head, like a sheep queen on a balcony. "I am."

"Where did you get all this?"

She smiled fully, looking around at the shelves with satisfaction. "Everywhere. The internet really helps. Do you knit?"

"Yes. I'm doing this one." Sylvia showed her the pattern.

"Wow. That's complicated. What's your usual yarn?"

"Brick. Smith's, three-gauge."

"Oh, okay. Well. Are you local?"

"I'm visiting my son for a while. He's a cop here."

"Right. So, what's our color story here?"

Sylvia wasn't sure how to answer that.

Kiki put on her glasses. "Well, given what you've been working with, I might go—" She reached up and pulled down an emerald like the spot on a butterfly wing. "Here, feel it."

Sylvia ran two fingers over the skein. "God Almighty."

Kiki laughed. "I know. They know what they're doing in Delft."

Sylvia laughed, too, as if she'd spent summers in Delft, and said, "Yeah!"

"Is it for your son?" asked Kiki, tucking the emerald butterfly skein back into its spot. Sylvia hated to see it go.

"I have two sons," Sylvia said. "I'm making one for each of them," she said. "For Christmas." She was practicing saying it out loud: "I have two sons." Kiki the sheep queen was the first person she'd said that to in a long time. She looked like someone who'd been places, maybe that was why. Sylvia had been places, too, though probably not as far as Kiki. A lot of places.

"You must come here before you start the second. I have a red you're going to love that plays really well with the emerald."

"Which one?" Sylvia pointed. "That one?"

Kiki shook her head, took her glasses off. "Not telling. You'll have to come back. What's your name?"

"Sylvia. I'm Sylvia."

"Welcome, Sylvia," said Kiki. She shook Sylvia's hand. Hers was cool and strong, maybe the way hands were made in Delft.

Sylvia bought the butterfly-wing-spot emerald. In the evening, she sat knitting on the slick leather sofa, listening for the sound of Andy's patrol car pulling in for the night, as Roanoke birds chirped outside. She'd brought a stub of joint to Roanoke, but she refrained, since Andy probably wouldn't like that, being a cop. Plus the smell. The click of the needles and the chirp of the birds made a song. She made up little words to it as she moved swiftly down the emerald rows. When Andy got home that night, she meant to have the conversation, but he looked so tired. He was very concerned about budget cuts and something about an after-school neighborhood program. Maybe Saturday.

IT ISN'T HARD to see the Alan in Sylvia. The innate grace; the way with numbers; that intensifying gaze from his beauty to what suddenly feels like the abundance of yours; that lightning energy at the core that sometimes flashes smarts and sometimes sex and sometimes secrets, rooms with closed doors. The difference is that, with Sylvia, the other rooms in her seem like places she passed through and then forgot about on her way somewhere else, somewhere sunnier. Alan never forgot a room or what was in it or what it was all worth, down to the penny. Andy is only the sweetness in Sylvia, none of the gambler or the wanderer. Different fathers: sure. Different eras: sure. But a knife can be used to cut flowers or cut flesh and all three of them, mother and sons, have that gleam. Had.

ON HER FOURTH morning in Roanoke, sometime around the bronzed day, Sylvia asked Andy where the gambling was. He was reading something in a binder, wearing glasses, which made him look more like his father than he probably realized. He was thicker, too, around the middle, just a little. How strange was that? How could her child, her sweet little boy with the mutts, be forty, with a thick middle?

"Ma," he said.

"Legal gambling."

"Ma." He looked at her through his glasses. "There's one bingo parlor. That's it."

"I like bingo."

"Like the way you like poker? Like the way you like twenty-one?"

"That was different. And Roanoke, Andy, is not Laughlin." He tapped his pen on the binder. "Why are you here?"

"Because you're here. I'm visiting you."

"And . . ." He looked like such a cop. It made her tired.

"Come on, honey, let's just have our visit. We don't see each other enough." She thought about how she'd planned to start: I have something I need to share with you, something I've been meaning to tell you for a long time.

"Yeah, okay." He closed the binder, left the room, and came back with a thin computer. He pulled out a chair for her at the dining room table. "C'mere, I want to show you something. Prepare to be amazed." She sat down, and he sat down in the chair next to her. His chairs were big, like the couch, with chrome on the sides.

"Look at this," he said. "You won't believe it."

On the screen was a chart. At the far left were the names Maria Djacjalewicz and Stephan Djacjalewicz and the words *LABORERS, m 1562, Chrudim.* Next to them were five little rectangles with the names Maria, Stephan, Johannes, Gretchen, and, again, Maria. The first baby Maria, along with Stephan and Gretchen, had brief dates: *1563–1564, 1565–1567, 1569 (3 mos).* The second baby Maria went up to 1651. Sturdy lady. Johannes only made it to 1607. Maria the mother, to 1608. Did the second baby Maria miss them all? What did she do all those years? No other lines descended from her.

"What is Chrudim?" Sylvia asked. She didn't even know how to say it. And what did it have to do with her, anyway? Stephan and Maria in Chrudim, hundreds of years ago.

"It's a town. It was in a place called Bohemia, but now that's part of the Czech Republic." He pointed along the rows, rolling the image along so she could see how the chart flowed through many names, all strangers to her, until it came to her name and Andy's father's name with one line toothpicking Andy's name and the date *1978–* followed by a blank space.

"Where did you get all this?"

"Dad gave me the names of his greats, and then, see, someone else was working on this, too, from another part of the family somewhere, could be anywhere in the world. They filled in all this stuff." He rolled the image down, pointed. "Minsk. Russia. Isn't that incredible?" He nudged her. "This must be why I like winter so much." He smiled, moving the cursor around the boxes, showing her all the different names with all their *z*'s and *j*'s and *w*'s, all the marriages and children, centuries of them, and every last one of them, Sylvia noted, dead. "You know what I wonder?"

She folded her hands in her lap. "What?" He was so into this. She could say, *About that line from my name and your father's* . . . She could say that.

"I think some of these people must have been Jews," continued Andy. "On Dad's side. He didn't know, and his parents were so—well, you know how they were. And we can't ask them now. But these names—" He moved the cursor in a circle around one patch. "I looked them up. They're Jewish names. And here—" He moved the cursor again. "See? He went to America, right around the time of some really bad pogroms in that area. I've been reading about it. Changed his name to Simonson." He tapped the screen. "He's the hinge, this guy. He's where it all changed."

"Your father and I never talked about religion."

Andy said, "So, Ma, I need names from your side—your mother's maiden name, her mother." He looked bright and happy. "Grandpa Frank's part is coming along okay, I'm up to the Sicily greats. But I need Grandma Zelda's info. So we can fill it in." He moved the cursor again and some empty boxes, like empty coffins, popped up on the white field. The little arrow hovered there, waiting. Jump in. It spooked her. It felt like bad luck. But she should tell him. She took a deep breath. She really should.

"I don't know," Sylvia finally said.

"You don't know your mother's maiden name?"

"Honey, I just don't know—why do you want to do all this?"

He looked as hurt as he had looked when she'd asked him why he'd brought home the one-eyed cat that was clearly dying. "Because it's who we are. Their blood runs in our veins. We're part of a history. I want to know what comes to me from your side." His brow wrinkled. "Don't you?"

"History isn't really my bag." What she wanted to say was: No, I don't. Not at all. Believe me, neither do you. She had never wanted to know much about where anyone came from, even way back. Sylvia just thought of herself as a fifties–sixties person, like the two decades were her parents. Better that than Zelda and Frank, frightened of everything and stingier than dirt. Powdered milk. Balls of saved string. Books of green stamps. Rochester winters, worse, even, than Boston winters. And that ugly suspicion in both of them that you were probably up to something dirty until finally you were. Who cared what made their scratched-up linoleum insides? She got out of there and kept going. But she knew she couldn't say that to Andy, who believed in history and the law and the bright futures of skeletally thin one-eyed cats. If she started the whole Alan conversation now, it would lead very quickly to how she ended up with

Gary in the first place, and she had hoped to swoop around that part. The genealogy chart was so clinical. It fixed people forever, stuck on their little lines like butterflies on pins. They needed a different setting for what she'd come all this way to say, and to do.

"Grundheisen," she said. She owed him that much. She coughed. She tapped her chest. It felt crinkly all the time these days.

"A German!" Andy began typing away. "Jesus, maybe they were all Jews. Wouldn't that be incredible?"

"They were Protestants, through and through."

"Might have converted. A lot of people did." He was hot on the trail now, already at an image of old birth records in tiny, fancy, illegible cursive.

"Sure," she said. "Stranger things have happened." She stood up. "I'm going to go lie down a bit." She'd ask again about the bingo hall tomorrow.

"Could it have been Grundhoven?" He was peering at the screen.

"Grundheisen."

MARK BROUGHT ME the news in person. I agreed to meet him on a bench in the small, picturesque graveyard of a church in town, which was apt, as it turned out. I didn't know that, though; I just thought it would be more discreet in this big-eared town, because whatever he wanted to tell me had to be serious for him to come all the way back out to Chesham. I certainly didn't want him in my house. I was sitting on that stone bench when he pulled up and got out of his car. He walked toward me, waving, but for a moment I hardly recognized him. He was markedly thinner. His jowls were more pronounced, his eyes seemed to be more deep-set, his earlobes were longer, and his gaze was more intent. He seemed to have aged, to have jumped forward a decade, or backward a century or two. He looked like some ancient Eastern European version of himself, someone way back who lived badly through long winters.

I stood up. When he reached me, we sat down, he took my hand, and he told me. There would be a funeral, he said, and he told me where it was. We sat shoulder to shoulder on the bench. He kept looking at me as if he had asked me a question and was waiting for the answer. But I was the one with the questions.

"Why did he do it?" I said. I couldn't understand it, although, in another way, from some other part of my brain, I could. Something had been chasing him all those years; I had done my best to help him. The news made me feel sick, though, hunted by the past. Would it never end?

Mark told me about the development and clocks ticking on construction loans and finishing loans and vendors with bills, and if it had all gone right, the restitution would have been paid, the loans and the vendors would have been paid, and everyone would have been in the clear. But they didn't finish even the model house in time, there was insane weather and bad turns of fate and thieves everywhere, and it must have been—Mark winced, as if he still couldn't quite stand it—that in the end Alan saw only one way out. The guy, said Mark, was the captain going down with the ship, the soldier throwing his body on the grenade to save the platoon. As he explained all this, he was looking at me with that same expectant expression.

"It's terrible," I said. "I'm, well, I'm shocked—I'm shocked that he didn't think he could find another way. I mean, Alan, right? Our Alan?" I tried to squeeze Mark's hand, but he drew it away.

"What other way, Suzanne? What other fucking way?" Now he looked angry. Why was he angry?

"I don't know. You two were the money people. With Alan, there was always another way." I wondered if Mark was all right. Had he had a heart attack or something, to be so thin? His breath didn't smell very good. Maybe he was ill.

"No, Suzanne. Don't you get it? What you did? I told you. I explained it to you when I was here before. You ruined him. More than him. More than him, Suzanne. Noah—"

"Noah? Noah's a child."

"No. No," said Mark. "He's the director of the project." Mark shook his head. "It's not that far from here. I don't know what will happen to it, the bank will foreclose, I guess. I gave Alan money," Mark said, very low. "And the kicker is—wait for it—he fired me."

"What?"

"Oh, yeah." Mark laughed. "Six months ago. Said it was time for a fresh start. I think he knew it was all going to shit. But he said he wanted to run things with just Noah. Not me."

"But everything you're telling me, I mean, yes, it's horrible, but I didn't do any of that. It wasn't my development. I didn't put Noah in that position, or you. I've got nothing out here except what I earn—I gave it all away, all those ill-gotten gains. You know that. There are bigger things going on in the world." I was beginning to get angry myself. No one had been planning to cut me in on the profits of their scheme, so how was I to blame when it went south? Underneath my anger, I also felt as if I were being chased; beneath that was something dark, moving slowly. It was looking at me.

"That money wasn't yours to give away, Suzanne. It was already owed. Your whatever-the-hell gesture, whoever it is you're pretending to be—it cost a lot of people." Mark's breath was truly bad. The smell of it frightened me. I wondered if he had gotten a bit demented, like my mother. How old was he, exactly?

"But how could I have known that?" Why were we even talking about money at such a terrible time?

"How could you not? Who do you think you are?"

"I'm different now."

"What, you live in some little shit town and you don't dye your hair? That's different? We all lived off the fat of the land for a long time, Suzanne. You, too. And one day the bill came due. You just didn't want to pay it. What's so different about that? You stole money that wasn't yours and used it to buy yourself a ticket to the moral fucking high ground. That money could have saved a lot of people a lot of pain. And you call us crooks." He laughed. Then, "Are we sitting in a graveyard?" He laughed again. "The poor bastard," he said. "What the fuck was the point?"

THAT AFTERNOON, I went down to where the whale lay, pausing on the dune. Nearly all the flesh was gone, and with it, the smell. I almost missed it. I walked down to the whale, unmasked. I took off a glove to put my hand on the curve of a rib and my hand came away oily, probably smelling of it. The bones were so real in a way that the things Mark had told me didn't feel real, entirely. I thought I should have brought Mark down here to show him the whale. If he saw how magnificent and vast it was, if I explained to him about the larger picture—but that could never happen, of course.

If I had stayed. If I had stayed. That was what Mark meant: that I should have stayed. Would Alan be alive then, would all of those things Mark told me about not have happened? Would I have been there, the faithful wife waiting at the gate, when Alan was released? Would the debt have been paid? Would I have driven him home to whatever apartment we had to live in? Would we have loved each other through to the end, two old criminals giving out Halloween candy to the few trick-or-treating children in the building?

Why did that scenario seem so impossible to me? A closed door I would never open as long as I lived.

The dark thing gazed at me, unblinking. I wiped my oily hand on the sand. If, if, if. If I had known more about currencies and exchange rates. If wishes were horses, then beggars would ride, as my mother used to say, before her brain melted.

An older African American man with two little pointy-nosed dogs came walking down the beach. He veered up the sand toward the whale, keeping the little dogs, sniffing wildly, on tight leads. White flecked his hair. He had an earring in one ear. He nodded as he got close.

"Hey," he said.

"Hey," I said. I tried not to look as possessive of the carcass as I felt.

He eyed the whale. "Wow." The little pointy-nosed dogs whined and pulled. He grimaced. "Guess that's the head there."

"Yeah."

"It's kind of like a shipwreck, isn't it?"

"But no treasure," I said. I didn't say what I knew: the wreck *was* the treasure.

"Will you hold these guys a minute?" He handed me the dogs' leashes, then moved away a few steps and took out his phone to get a picture. "Look at that," he said, showing me. He'd gotten the whole shape of the whale resting on the sand, with the blurry little nose of one of the dogs, lunging, jutting into the frame. Without the stink or the feel of the oil, the whale seemed an ancient, peaceful structure, abandoned and decaying on the beach, the violence of its death centuries old rather than a few years.

I handed the dogs' leashes back to him. "Would you put it in a museum or just cut it up and haul it away?"

"Me?" He scratched his jaw. "Neither. I'd leave it here. This is the place it picked."

"That's what I think, too," I said.

"They won't do that?"

"No," I said. "It's one or the other."

"People," he said. "They just don't see."

The man and his two little dogs walked away down the beach. I lingered by the carcass, not wanting to leave it, as if it could give me the answers I sought.

What is restitution?

What is restitution?

What is restitution?

Money drowned in water.

THE HARBORAGE WAS just two towns away, on a piece of land not far from the water. On a Saturday morning a few days before the funeral, I pulled up and parked in the roughed-up dirt near the only house that yet made up the Harborage, a half-finished structure wrapped in blue Tyvek. This was the show house, the dream into which buyers were supposed to insert themselves, their lives, their holidays, their views of the ocean over morning coffee. This was the house that the storm had brought down, which shouldn't have been a surprise. It had flooded more than once in the storms along here. The land was too low. I wondered how Alan and Noah had gotten permission to build at all, then I didn't wonder, because it was the kind of shady thing Ted, he of the springy amnesiac muscles, arranged all the time, with pride. Probably, Alan had found a Ted.

I made my way over the ridges and valleys of dirt to the house, which was more or less an outline of a house: beams, rafters, subfloors, a staircase, a deck off the back, work-lights strung throughout. I pushed aside the heavy plastic hanging over where the front door would be—would never be, now—and went in. I half-expected someone to stop me, some man in boots and a hardhat to stomp over and throw me off the property, but no one was here. No one at all. When the plastic fell back down behind me, it was quiet the way the inside of a tent is quiet. The light inside was dim, grayish. The place smelled of raw wood, dirt, cement, and something chemical.

I was standing in what would be the foyer. I walked around the ground floor. On the right of the foyer, a space that would probably be a living room, and beyond that, a big kitchen; behind the kitchen, the deck. There was a brownish-reddish stain on the living room floor. I didn't know about what had happened to Noah yet. I thought one of the workmen must have had an accident. On the left of the foyer, another area, cozier, and beyond that, contiguous to the kitchen on its left side, a high-ceilinged room: the dining room. I looked up at the second floor, but I already knew how the rooms would be arranged there, and the way that the steep little back staircase in the kitchen would sidle up behind the second floor, appearing just to the right of Noah's bathroom.

I knew it, because this house was laid out exactly like our old house, the one that was taken away by the government, even down to that awkward second staircase. A hundred years ago, that would have been a servants' staircase. Now, it was in just the right place for teenagers in socks, carrying their shoes, to slip down and out the back door without waking their parents at the other end of the house. He had put it here, they had put it here, as if another teenager was about to slip down those stairs—and with that teenager, another life, another chance at a different history.

I walked through my old walls, through my kitchen island, up the stairs through the ceiling to the second floor, where I passed from room to room, unseen, unheard. They would have painted the walls that luminous, liminal white/yellow/pink I had chosen. They would have hung the big mirror here, the framed pressed flowers there, the tiles in the bathroom would have been the ones from Portugal. The basket of rolled towels would have gone there. The master bedroom would have had north-facing light coming through the shades instead of east light, but otherwise the ample bed with the grand carved headboard reaching halfway up to the ceiling—to us, it had always been sort of ironic, self-mocking even, but out here no one would have seen it that way—would have gone along that wall, to get the view. Before we looked into trees; here we—they—would have looked at water.

Standing on plywood, I looked through the sawed-open window space at the water.

Every choice Alan and Noah made—and they would have made them all, I knew they would have—would have been a choice I had already made, choices that had been lost when it was all lost. It was our life the two of them had been rebuilding, minus me. This was the future the two of them had been making, the dream they were going to sell to strangers: the past we thought we were living in.

I ran downstairs, pushed through the thick sheet of dirty plastic, breathed in great gulps of air. If I had known. Alan insisted on that awful night that I knew it all, but I've explained about that. What do I know about the intricacies of how money works? My job had been just this house and planning our trips. I took a certain grim satisfaction in the fact that they couldn't, in the end, create the house without me. Not the first time, and not the second time, either.

IN HIS COFFIN, Alan looked like the show-house version of himself. Lydia wanted an open casket at the funeral, so there he was, in a good suit, with a rubbery face. The suit was too big for him, though, because he was so taut and thin. All that running. His quick fingers were still and folded on his chest. His eyebrows looked tinted. Dead, he looked cheaply made. The coffin was thin, too; the black paint was chipping away on one corner, revealing plywood underneath. His slight smile was fixed. His cuffs, bright white, covered his wrists, of course, but everyone in the room had to know what was under there. He gave off no scent, except a slight artificial-floral perfume that must have been added by the undertaker. I couldn't cry, but I couldn't walk away, either. Idly, I counted the white flowers in a vase nearby. An even number, so that was good. I kept looking at his rubbery face, its lines, its shrewdness visible without the padding of fat and motion, as if he might finally sit up and explain it all to me. What happened. Why. What it meant. Who we really were to each other.

This perfumed Alan with the tinted eyebrows and the immaculate cuffs didn't answer, though, just continued to smile fakely with closed eyes. Looking at him, I realized that I had changed in the aftermath of the revelation of his crimes. I knew the whale, but this man, the man with whom I had once shared my life: I barely knew him at all. I had no idea why he did all those things he did.

ON HER SIXTH morning in Roanoke, Sylvia asked again about the bingo hall, and Andy said, "Sure, why not?" He seemed more relaxed about her general motives now, clearly pleased to come home and find his old mom knitting on the sofa every night the way old moms are supposed to do. She had knitted herself a day pass, apparently. The next day he came home for lunch, then dropped her off on his way back to work. As she got out of the car, he said, "I'll be back at four." Then he winked. "Go easy on them, Ma. It's a small town, and I live here."

She laughed and shut the patrol car door.

Her fingertips tingled as she pushed open the heavy door of Roanoke Bingo Play. She stopped at the bouncer and shook his big hand. "I'm Sylvia," she said.

"Hello, Sylvia. Please step through the metal detector."

She glided through. A thinner guy checked her bag. She bought five cards that looked pretty good to her and settled into an open seat at a table. She spread out the cards on the table and studied them—the patterns weren't bad, not spectacular, but entirely possible. She wouldn't buy more, or any extras, yet. She scanned the room, did a rough count in her mind. Not too many people. Good. This was a weekday afternoon; she'd have to come back at different times of the day and evening, if she could get Andy to take her, to check out the crowd and the cards. She also needed to get the feel of this place and how the numbers moved there.

Bingo wasn't Sylvia's first choice; blackjack was her game. Marlboro Light 100s were her smokes. But bingo would have to do in Roanoke. Bingo parlors have all the charm of warehouses: big rooms, lots of tables, that bingo hall hush as everyone concentrates, in the old days a haze of cigarette smoke. At night in some of them, drinks on the tables. The faces intent as birdwatchers, but unfriendly birdwatchers, maybe more like they're waiting to shoot the birds. Roanoke Bingo Play was the same, plus the smell of sweet pretzels from a concession in the back. Worse chairs than the place in Providence. Fatter people than the ones in Jersey. No Indians—sorry, Native Americans—running things. Florida had been so good to her, once upon a time. At the front, the bingo caller was a guy who looked like a farmer on his day off. He sat in a folding chair turning the handle on the rotating drum of balls, calling out numbers loudly, but like it was the bad news he'd always been expecting. Sylvia began putting markers down.

You'd think—I certainly did—that it's entirely chance in bingo, but that's not necessarily true. The difference in bingo is the way the numbers tend to fall in different halls, and whether they're being generated by a computer or old-school, with some old guy in a bow tie or a gal in a little dress, or in this case a farmer pulling the balls from a big rotating drum. It's supposed to be that all the little balls are equal, but they aren't, because of wear and tear or who knows what spin the puller might be putting on the ball. You had to get a feel for that; you had to get to know a place.

And there's another factor, too. There's the stuff someone like Sylvia can silently count and calculate, like the number of people and cards in play, the kinds of numbers on her cards, and so on, but then there's the part that's like geography, or plate tectonics: numbers do run in patterns, the way rivers flow, no matter what they say about randomness. There's a tilt to them, and once you catch on to it, you can lean in its direction. Sylvia can't explain it better than that. I've asked. She just has some kind of internal divining rod for the tilt. She always has to be patient; she never catches on to it right away. But before too long she usually knows, the way people who fish—not the amateurs, the real ones—have a feeling about rivers. She didn't know yet what kind of river Roanoke Bingo Play would be for her, so she watched her few starter cards and listened for the numbers, watching the room, waiting to feel its tilt.

At the next table, a man in a straw hat, a geezer with sexy turtle eyes behind his glasses (she'd always been a sucker for that), caught her eye. She tossed him a small smile. He was wearing a vest hung with a rabbit's foot, some kind of big cross thing with flared arms, a plastic rose, a little plastic pig on a string, other trinkets: he was one of those lucky charms people. Everyone had their own bag, okay, but nothing about this was luck. It might feel like luck, but actually it was patterns and getting your markers down fast. Sylvia had always had quick hands and a knack for patterns.

And so the question arises: why wasn't Sylvia rich? She had a gift, obviously. A mathematician in the rough, always happy to pull up a chair as the cards are being shuffled, as the wheel is going around. When she put the bingo markers down at Roanoke Bingo Play, she smiled and hummed. She didn't look hungry or avid; she looked content, at home. Sometimes, when she plays this game or that, she takes her shoes off under the table and puts her bare feet on the floor. She leans back in her chair, humming, barefoot, deftly reorganizing her cards.

Sylvia wasn't rich, because she thought of herself as a sunflower, following the sun from Rochester to her life; also, she got bored easily. You might think that everyone who's good at gambling is a gambling addict, but that's not true, if Sylvia is an example of anything larger (which is doubtful). Sylvia was good at gambling because she was good at gambling, and she treated her gift as a trust fund. When she needed money, she could pick up a game wherever and walk out with lined pockets, toward the sun. Sometimes she got a job, for a while. Mostly, Sylvia liked to go. Mostly, Sylvia went. She worked as a dealer for about six months once, but it made her too sad, all the drunk people losing every night, telling themselves they were having a great time. She was glad to get out of that town. Sylvia can buy a bus ticket like nobody's business. Escape artists, both Alan and Sylvia. Gamblers. She didn't raise him, but it was still in him. Did he know? Did they talk about her after Gary kicked her out? What did they say? He almost never mentioned her. Not to me, anyway. The longer he's been gone, the more I see how much I didn't know about him, or about anything, really.

THAT NIGHT AT dinner, Andy said, "How was it? Did you win?"

"Not yet," Sylvia said. "What is this in the salad?"

"A cornichon."

"It tastes like a pickle."

"It is a pickle. You doing okay? Not bored?"

"No, honey. It's a nice town." Andy of the cornichons. No wonder he was single.

He gave her a sharp look. "You want to go back."

"It's just bingo."

"Mmmm," he said, as if it was up to him.

"Is there a bus?"

"I'll drive you."

• • •

SYLVIA, OF COURSE, wasn't invited to the funeral. No one besides me knew about her, and I hadn't thought about her for a long time. I am collaging the three of us together here, cutting up time this way and that, trying to understand. In reality, Sylvia moved bingo markers around and worked on her presents for the Christmas reunion, not knowing yet that her older son, her firstborn, was already dead. The three of us didn't grieve together, nor in the same way. I'm not even sure we grieved the same man. If I could do it all over again, though, Sylvia would never have found out what happened to Alan, because, like my mother, why did she need to know that? In her mind, he could have had the life she'd imagined for him. If I could do it all over, this moment when Sylvia has all her cards spread out in front of her would be the only glimpse of Sylvia, and she would stay suspended there, like a constellation. But she, too, exists in ordinary time.

ON THE DAY of the funeral, I turned away from the casket. In the front pew was a willowy woman—Lydia—with a little girl—Ava—standing up and leaning hard against her mother's leg. Next to Lydia was a tall woman in a long, black sleeveless dress, with tattooed arms. Lydia and the little girl seemed so terribly young, both of them. And the damage to Lydia's face. What had done that? The two of them looked like refugees who had just arrived at some port of entry and were waiting to be processed. I walked up and introduced myself.

"How are you holding up?" I asked.

"I'm fine," said Lydia.

"Hello," said Ava.

"Where's Noah?" I said.

"On his way, I'm sure," said Lydia with an expression that clearly said, *Please go away.*

"Is he all right?"

"No."

I stood there awkwardly, waiting for her to say something else, but she busied herself fixing the barrette that was sliding out of Ava's hair. I retreated to a pew toward the back. The church—it was Episcopal—had elaborate stained-glass windows. I leafed through a hymnal that seemed to have songs for every occasion, keeping an eye out for Noah at the church door. A corner of my eye, really, because I didn't want to see any of the friends from the old days. I needn't have worried. There weren't many people, and those who were there were strangers to me. One man wore a yarmulke. There was a burly man with a crewcut, and a woman wearing a ceramic frog pin on her flowing blouse. As they came in, they went straight to Lydia and Ava, with hugs and pats. They sat in the pew behind Lydia, talking to one another. It was like being at a wedding with no one on the groom's side, except me.

Where was Noah? The service started, an old priest in a beret said something or other, and then it was over. We all stood up to move to the reception in a room off of the sanctuary. It was then that I saw that Noah was there, he must have come in late and been sitting behind me, with Mark, who gave a guarded little wave.

"Noah!" I said, and he looked at me without speaking. He opened his mouth. He closed it again. I thought he looked pale. I headed toward him, but he ducked his head, down and away. I kept going into the reception, thinking I would find him there.

At the reception, Lydia and Ava were sitting in chairs, receiving condolences. The tall woman with the tattoos was standing near them like a guardian. The room was small enough that it looked full, but it hardly looked like that mattered to Lydia, whose face was closed up tight with grief, her feet flat on the floor in front of her, one hand on Ava's head. I hesitated in the doorway, feeling like an intruder; I would have left then, except for Noah. I went over to the long table in the back and put a few cookies on a plate, waiting for my moment.

The old priest in the beret was circulating around the room, taking people's hands in both of his, his expression alert and sympathetic. He looked like an elderly beatnik. Had Alan known this priest? I couldn't understand why we were in a church at all, since I'd never known Alan to go to any place of worship. What did Episcopalians believe? For a moment I felt as if I'd entered some parallel universe where a parallel Alan had made different, parallel choices and become a churchgoing family man. But this wasn't for Alan, of course. This was clearly all for Lydia, and right then I hated her, just a little. It was, after all, for love of her and the child that he had done this, made this horrible sacrifice. It was with her that his despair had been so overwhelming that he would give her himself, utterly broken and naked in death. He'd never done that with me.

The beatnik priest got to me, unfortunately, and I reluctantly put the plate down so he could hold my hand in both of his. "I'm so sorry for your loss," he said. He smelled like licorice. "What is your name?"

"Suzanne. I'm the ex-wife."

"Ah. Okay. So then young Noah—"

"Is my son."

"Ah," said the priest again, as if now he understood something that had confused him. "I see the resemblance."

"Do you?"

"Yes." The priest regarded me carefully. He was smart, this old priest. It made me uncomfortable, and I wondered how much he knew. "The shape of the eyes."

"He won't talk to me," I said, and suddenly I felt myself tear up.

"He blames you?"

"It's not my fault. I wasn't even there. He hasn't wanted to talk to me for so long."

"Really," said the priest. "And if you had been there?"

Oh, fuck *off*, I thought. This wasn't the confessional booth. "Look, it wouldn't have mattered—it was about the money, that the money was gone."

The old priest furrowed his brow. "Where did it go?"

I caught myself. Was there a statute of limitations on this sort of thing? I pulled my hand from his grasp. "I'm sorry. Never mind." The room was so small. The only place to go was another corner just a few feet away. "Is there a ladies' room?"

The priest pointed. When I got to the ladies' room I sat down on the tiled floor for a few minutes, my hands at my temples. *What now what now what now?* I wished that I believed in priests, in or out of berets. I made myself stand up, splash water on my face, and go back, because I didn't want Noah to slip out and away from me again. Blessedly, the priest was gone when I got back to the small room and the few mourners were even fewer. The burly man with the crewcut was talking earnestly to Lydia, who was nodding. Noah was standing at the long table, his back to me. I wanted to lean in and hug him. But instead I stood a few inches away on the brown carpet, waiting for him to turn around, willing him to turn around.

Finally, he did. He was clean-cut. He was taller, heavier, and he held his funeral-clean hands as if they were peculiar constructions he'd been given to hold by someone else. His nose—what had happened to his nose? Had he been fighting? He was, indeed, pale, as I'd noticed before, and his eyes were narrowed. In that millisecond when I saw him anew, I saw the bitterness and disappointment in him. It is so much a part of him now that I don't notice it anymore. But that day I did, and I thought I could pluck it out.

"Noah, please," I said.

He tilted forward ever so slightly. "You've been calling."

"Noah, we need to talk."

"Nah."

"Noah. I'm your mother. For God's sake."

"You left us," he said. "You didn't help. And I'm on the hook for all of it. I have to file for *bankruptcy*."

"That was your father—" I began, but stopped, because as the syllables left my mouth, what remained of the light in Noah's eyes went out. I saw it happen. When things fall apart, you see how they're made, and in that moment I knew, too late, that Noah's secret, irrational hope that his mother still believed in his father deep in her heart was the last thing he had left to lose. And then it was gone.

"I'll call you," he said, and loped out of the room. I didn't go after him. I didn't know what to do. I thought that with Alan gone, and with time, Noah might come back to me at last, of his own accord. At least we'd have each other.

The room was nearly empty now; no one had stayed long. I still hadn't offered my proper condolences to Lydia and Ava.

I crossed to where they were sitting, the tall woman in the long black dress still standing by them, watching over them. "Listen, I know this is awkward," I said. "I'm sorry."

"You don't have to do this," said Lydia. Ava began hopping up and down.

The tall woman leaned down. "Ava, do you need a potty break?" The little girl nodded.

"Thanks, Caprice," said Lydia as Caprice slowly led the child away.

I sat down next to Lydia. I wanted her to understand me. "It's just—we both married him. We both had children with him. I'm a mother, just like you. What he did—it was heartless."

"No," said Lydia fiercely. "You're wrong. He had a big heart. A huge heart. We were happy."

I flinched.

"We were," Lydia insisted. "He was at a different place in his life. He changed. That can happen, you know."

I said, "My dear, I didn't mean to insult you."

"Don't fucking call me 'my dear.'"

I held up a hand, palm out. "Sorry. Sorry. If there's something I can do to help. Were you able to track down his mother? Even with everything, I think she'd want to know." So, you see, I was thinking about Sylvia there. I remembered her.

"What are you talking about? All of his family have been dead for years. Could you excuse me—"

"No, Lydia, that's not true. Is that what he told you? His father and stepmother, yes—a long time ago. But as far as he knew, his birth mother was still alive. I think she was cocktailing or something somewhere. She got in touch with him when Alan and I were first married. He was excited, but it was awful—it turned out she just wanted money."

"Did he give it to her?"

"God no. He cursed her out. But he was crushed."

I needed Lydia to understand something. I needed her to listen. I said, "I could try to find her name—it had changed, maybe she'd gotten married again, I can't remember. I think she wrote him a letter. You probably have all his papers."

Lydia sat up straight, feet parallel, planted firmly on the floor. "I don't want to know her name. I don't give a shit. He didn't leave any papers." Caprice and Ava were slowly making their way back. Lydia held out her arms. Ava smiled, quickening her pace.

"Lydia," I said, "she deserves to know."

Lydia leaned forward as Ava accelerated toward her, arms outstretched. "I don't even know her name," said Lydia.

"I'll find her," I said. "Please."

Lydia shrugged, but I could tell she was softening.

And so I found her. It was like the whale, in a way. I could help.

AFTER THE FUNERAL, Lydia went home and slept dreamlessly for two days. Every once in a while she surfaced, heard the small domestic sounds, the voices of Ava and Caprice, ate some of whatever Caprice had left by the bed, and fell back asleep.

On the third day, she woke up, knowing what needed to happen next. Any lawyer at Hill, Hill, and Adams could do it. She could do it herself, really. But she needed their names, their stationery, a licensed signature, which was annoying. She wouldn't ask linty Jeff, that was for sure. On the fourth day, I called her with the information she needed right when she had finally admitted that she did, in fact, need it. Kismet.

• • •

MEANWHILE, SYLVIA WAS moving bingo markers and knitting and resolving to have her Talk with Andy, which she planned to do when she handed him his finished bedspread and showed him the other one. But before she could do that, she got an email with a phone number. This Lydia person who said she was Alan's second wife. His post-prison wife. Sylvia called her on a break between bingo games. But what Lydia said: it couldn't be. None of it. Sylvia's mind felt like aluminum foil crumpled in a ball. We have to meet, Lydia said. I have a child. Sylvia said she was sorry, but she just wasn't interested in the child, not yet, not now. She was still trying to understand what had happened to her child. Lydia said that it wasn't about the child, and for a moment Sylvia thought she meant Alan and she was angry. Because it was only about Alan. Lydia asked again if they could please meet, but it wasn't really a question. She needed to explain in person.

Sylvia leaned against the wall at the back of the bingo parlor. Her legs were shaking. Her lungs crinkled hard and she tapped and tapped at her chest like the way you used to tap those little buttons on landline phones to get a dial tone.

The geezer with the turtle eyes and the lucky charms pinned all over his vest came up to her and said, "Ma'am, do you need a glass of water? Do you need a chair?"

Sylvia shook her head. He brought them, anyway. She sat down hard in the chair. She drank the water. "It's my son," she said. "There's been an accident. We've been estranged."

"How long since you've seen him?" asked the geezer, crouching in front of her.

"A long time."

Sylvia tried to catch her breath. She felt so old. Why would a rich man like Alan do such a thing? He had made mistakes, okay, but that was behind him. What could have happened? She had held him in reserve in the back of her mind for so many years, a kind of last, sunny island where they would be reunited and she would live out her days, with both of her strong sons. Sylvia leaned her head against the wall of the bingo parlor. The smell of the sweet concession pretzels was stronger back there.

"Chicken legs." Pause. "Eleven," said the bingo caller. "Two little ducks." Pause. "Twenty-two."

Sylvia tapped and tapped her chest, trying to understand.

SYLVIA HAD SEEN Alan once when he was grown. He'd found her. She was living in Los Angeles then, her favorite place of all time, making good money. Andy was at the police academy in Virginia, working hard and doing well. It seemed like the tough times were over. Sylvia worked for a man named Kevin who often needed things delivered from one part of the city to another, or sometimes from the city to the Valley, now and again outside LA, never more than a day's drive. She was always home by dinner. The things to be delivered were always boxed up or wrapped up in some way, completely wrapped up, and she never looked. She let Kevin put them in the trunk and never so much as lifted a corner of the paper or shook a box. Once you look, they'd know you looked. They'd see it in your eyes. And you wouldn't be able to forget what you saw, either. At the other end of the trip, all she did was open the trunk for whoever was waiting. She tried not to look at them, either.

Sylvia didn't need drama in her life. She just wanted some peace and quiet. Really, her whole life she'd just been looking for peace and quiet and warmth, trying to keep two steps ahead of the darkness that lurked in so many places, in so many people. That light out there. She couldn't get enough. Above all things, she didn't want to screw up that gig. It was the late nineties, and she was still using an answering machine. She got a message from Alan on it that said, "If this is you, and I hope it is, I'll be in Los Angeles on business next week and I would like to see you. Please leave a message for me." He gave her the name and number of a hotel. She played that message over more than once, listening to his adult voice, which was new to her.

It was like time collapsed. It was as if the baby she had been forced to abandon was leaving a message on her answering machine. She felt so strange during that whole week before she got to see him again, like her hands were the wrong size or her eyes were too small, or too big, and sometimes she couldn't breathe right. Driving, doing her deliveries, she forgot where she was going more than once and stared out the windshield, blinking in the light.

At last the day came. She did her hair, she did her nails, she took the car to the car wash as if he was going to see it, as if they were going to drive somewhere together, go on the road together this time. She cleaned her little apartment, even the bitsy balcony that overlooked the highway. You would think she was bringing a baby home instead of going to see her own son, a grown man, who had words. She didn't know why she was doing what she was doing, but Jesus Christ Himself couldn't have stopped her. She was an animal, digging, nesting.

He had said to come at four. She got to the big hotel at five to four, she gave her car to the valet, and she walked through the glass doors at four on the button. She proceeded to the front desk. The man at the desk eyeballed her, and picked up the phone. He continued to eyeball her, listening.

"No answer, ma'am."

"I'll wait," she said, and sat down in a zebra-striped chair. She crossed her legs at the ankles and sat up straight, the way her mother always had. It was the one thing Zelda taught her that was worth anything. She was prepared to wait a century in exactly that position, but a few minutes later, the glass doors opened.

In he came, her son, her son!, her Alan, so gorgeous and strong, walking out of all that light. She practically had to shield her eyes. She couldn't even stand up right away, he hit her heart that hard. He walked toward her with his arms out, big smile, hair hanging over one eye, that curl near the hairline, like Gary. But like Gary strained through a golden sieve. A Gary that never was. He was wearing an open-necked shirt and a light suit jacket, no tie. The beauty in him: it was everywhere, it flooded the lobby.

She stood up slowly. She felt like she might pee right on

the thick black rug, like one of Andy's mutts. She laughed, which was weird. He laughed, too. "Where have you been all my life?" he said, hugging her. She couldn't move her arms to hug him back, and then she could. His cheek was incredibly smooth, not a trace of stubble, as if it was still a baby's cheek. She held him tight.

"Let's go upstairs where we can talk," he said, putting his arm around her. "I want to know everything."

She walked with him like that, in his embrace. He held her with such confidence. It was like the entire hotel, or all of Los Angeles, was his and Sylvia was his honored guest. She was so relieved that he wasn't furious with her. She had already made up her mind not to tell him everything like he said he wanted, but she could explain some of it, finally. He needed to know her side of the story, his true life story.

His room was deluxe. Sofas and chairs. A bar on the side, thick glasses on the bar. A winter coat, from back East, tossed over the arm of a sofa.

"Warmer here, I bet," Sylvia said, making stupid conversation just inside the door. She couldn't seem to get any farther into the room. She was having a hard time looking at Alan and she couldn't look at him enough.

"Sure is," he said. "Do you want a drink?"

She shook her head.

"I need one," he said, walking over to the bar. "This is quite a day." He pulled a few little bottles out of the half-fridge, clinking them together in one hand. He shot her a smile. It was his baby-smile, exactly. She managed to sit down in a chair. She watched him, astonished. It was like finding the actual treasure from a dream you had once where you'd found treasure.

"You're so beautiful," he said, not at all shyly, as if it was just a fact.

"I don't know," Sylvia said, although when he said it, she felt that way, so beautiful. Like it might be her name: Sobeautiful. Princess Sobeautiful of the West. "Tell me everything about you. Please."

He poured them both drinks and he told her that he had a wife and a son named Noah and a brokerage business and his business was booming. He had a big house and a big office and every day he was busy, incredibly busy, with many people who relied on him. He probably didn't sleep enough. He smiled, he sipped. But that's life on the planet, he said. Right?

Of course, that was true, as far as it went. Back in Massachusetts, I was, what? Choosing curtains. Working with Noah on his reading. Alan was on a business trip to Los Angeles. He said his mother had found him, so he had agreed to see her. As if she were the one seeking—and, of course, she had been hoping to see him for years, but she hadn't sought him out.

In Los Angeles, Sylvia nodded. Gathering her courage, she asked about Gary.

"Oh," said Alan. "Oh." He shook his head. "He's dead," he said shortly. "They're both dead now. Him and Marjorie both." Marjorie was the wife after Sylvia, it turned out; it pained her to think that she had been Alan's mother all those years, but Alan was staring into his drink, not looking very sentimental as he explained.

"When?"

"Years ago."

"Jesus," Sylvia said, pulling a sad face, but inside she was relieved, because she thought that at last it was over. No one could get between her and Alan now. She wanted to meet his wife, his kid, walk in the garden at his big house.

"I have to show you something," he said, coming over with his drink to kneel next to her chair. He set his glass on the carpet and took an envelope out of his jacket pocket. He took a photo out of the envelope. It was creased through the middle, as if it had been folded, but someone—him?—had laminated it, crease and all.

"That's the day we brought you home," Sylvia said. "Your father bought me that dress just for that day." In the photo, she was stepping out of the car holding out the baby, all wrapped up, as if she was serving him on a tray. She looked about twelve years old, smiling with her brand-new baby in her brand-new dress and heels. All the hippie in her was gone by then; she looked like she was auditioning for Miss America. False eyelashes, even. After having a baby! It was such a different time.

"Dad doesn't know I have this," said Alan.

"I won't tell," said Sylvia, and they both laughed. Then she began to cry. "Oh, honey," she said. "Oh, honey. I'm so sorry. I'm so sorry."

He scooted around to the front of the chair, held her legs, and looked up into her face. "Don't cry," he said. "Hey. Hey." His hands on her legs were a man's hands, but his upturned face was like a child's. Sylvia tried to stop crying, but she couldn't, still holding that picture. She had the funny thought that she was glad it was laminated, so she couldn't get it soggy.

And then Alan put his face in her lap, turning his cheek against her skirt. Sylvia, his mother, smoothed his hair, traced the line of his ear. "No, no," she said. "No, no. It was all a long time ago." From outside the window, the sound of cars passing.

They sat like that too long. But, like with the wrapped packages she never unwrapped, she didn't want to say anything. She didn't want to peel back the paper by saying anything. How could she explain that moment? He was her son, her long-lost son, and he was also a stranger to her. She didn't want to let him go, and he didn't seem to want to let her go, either. She leaned down and lay her cheek on his back, smelling his sweat, feeling the muscles along his spine on the side of her face. Her arms lay along his arms. She was still crying, dampening his suit jacket. They were all folded up like that, him inside the curve of her, and there was such a feeling between them, like a hot needle sewing them together. Her heart was beating very fast. He tightened his grip on her legs.

A ripple of sunlight on the wall.

Sylvia could have stayed like that, and he wasn't letting go, but she knew it wasn't right. With a great effort, she sat up. "Maybe I'll take that drink," she said. She had to explain; it was what she had come here to do.

WHEN ALAN GOT back, he told me that it had all been a crashing letdown, that Sylvia was a shady older woman who just wanted some money because she had continued to fuck up her life. Let's not forget that he was a liar. I accepted it, telling Alan that the plum curtains would be better, and what Noah's math tutor had said. I was in the thick of our life then, and frankly, I didn't care. I didn't think I had anything in common with people like Sylvia. But then, so long after, I finally met her and we had so much to say to each other.

HE STOOD UP, nodding, pushing back the wayward curl. She could still feel the place on her legs where he had gripped. The back of his suit jacket was wet. His face had gone still.

He made her a vodka and cranberry juice, mixing it with his finger. She near-gulped it, for courage. "Listen," she said, "listen." And she tried to explain it all, who she was back then, how impossible it got to be in that house with Gary, his suspicious nature and the weird rules he started to make, how he threw her right out on a Wednesday and then all the years since then, how she'd always thought she'd be back. Every place she went, somehow she thought she was lighting out to get her kid back. She had been saying all this in her head to Alan ever since she was thrown out of her own home, but now, in the moment, she kept feeling like she was leaving out the most important part, except she couldn't remember what that part was. He sat across the room on the sofa, his head in his hand, sipping his drink in the other. He never looked up. She wasn't sure if he was listening.

She stopped talking after a while. She studied the place where his hair swirled on the top of his head. She realized that one day it would be gray there, and nearly began crying all over again. She wanted to see that, the gray swirl on his head.

He looked out the window at smoggy LA for a few minutes. Then he set his empty glass on the carpet. "I still don't understand."

"What?"

"Well. How you could have done it. Left me there. Who leaves their own kid?"

"I told you. He threw me out, right out on a Wednesday because he was crazy jealous of I don't even know what. If I had fought him for custody, I would have lost. He had lawyers on lawyers. He—he wasn't always a nice guy. "

"So you ran away again." He said it so softly. "You had another child, that you kept."

"I'm so happy to see you. I mean, I've wanted to find you all my life—"

He looked up, and his face was different now. Flat, somehow. Like his father's on a bad day. "You didn't look. Did you?"

She didn't know what to say. It seemed like anything she said, he could just say, *That's a lie*, and in way he would be right. "I always wanted to see you again," she said. "I always thought I would, and, look, here we are." She tried to smile.

"Right. Wow. Right." He laughed to himself. "Right." He shook his head as if there was water in his ear.

"Alan. I know I didn't explain it the right way, there's more—"

"I bet," he said, and laughed that grim laugh again. "And the bottom line is that you didn't give a fuck. Did not. Give. A fuck. For years. If I hadn't found you and called, I never would have heard from you. You just wanted to be free of me. You started over."

"That's not true," she said. "Listen to me." She explained about Andy, how it all went down, how hard a struggle it had been to get that kid raised, the shifts she worked and the shit she took. Now Andy was at the police academy, he was happy there, and she could tell just from looking at Alan that his life was great, that he'd had the best of everything, anyone could see that, look at him, so successful and everything, the house, the business—she stopped. His expression was worse than ever.

"Are you fucking kidding me?" he said. "Is that what you think, that you left me in the lap of luxury? Don't you know?"

"Know what?"

"He lost it. All of it. Whatever he was doing, one day, poof. Gone. We had to move *overnight*. Literally overnight to a shithole apartment in a shithole town. Marjorie just about lost it, she took it out on me, most of the time. Our old house

burned down two weeks later. I think he did it himself, for
the insurance. All my stuff I couldn't carry, it just burned."
Alan rubbed his head. "That's what you left me with. You
did that. I can't believe you didn't even fucking know."

"Honey," she pleaded, "how would I have known? Who
would have told me? They took you from me forever when
you were just a baby. After that, they didn't even know
where I was."

"Convenient."

"No. It was hell. Look at me. Can't you see it?"

But he wasn't looking at her. He was crossing the room
to his coat. He took out a checkbook and began writing a
check.

"What are you doing?"

He tore off the check and held it up in the air like a man
at an auction holding up a number. "This check is a contract.
It means you stay away from me forever. Take it. I mean it,
Sylvia. Take the fucking check." He pushed it toward her.

She took it from him, to get it out of her face. "You're
the one who called me," she said, crumpling the check in
her hand. "I didn't come here for your money. I don't want
your money."

"This was a mistake," he said. "I don't know what I was
thinking."

He threw the old photograph on the ground. "Fuck!"
he yelled, rubbing his eyes hard, and then, much quieter,
"Fuck." He wasn't looking at her anymore. It was as if she
wasn't there to him.

She didn't dare cross the room to hug him goodbye, for the second time in her life. It was like an invisible bodyguard had her by the shoulders and was escorting her from the room. She was dismissed. She couldn't understand it. She felt like she could barely walk.

"What did your father say about me?" she said when she'd made it to the door, but he didn't answer. He just kept staring out the window.

She did cash that check, though. She uncrumpled it and used the money to buy a new car with a bigger trunk. She had some fun in those years, she won't lie. But after that day, nothing felt the same and she missed him twice as much as she had before. She's never understood it. It's funny—she went there feeling like she needed to explain to him, but she left wanting him to explain to her. Even so, she wrote him a letter explaining it all again, trying to get him to understand, but he never wrote her back. She sent it to his office, she found the address in the phone book, but who knows? Maybe she had the wrong address. Maybe he never opened it.

Ever since that day, she told me, her voice breaking, she'd wanted to finish the conversation with him, to go through it again and get it right this time, to give the money back, with interest. She'd imagined him so many times, with his lovely wife and son in his spectacular house, sitting in his big garden, thinking the worst of her. And now he was gone, because he was stubborn in his misconceptions just like his father, he was bullheaded under all that smoothness. It could have been different, if only he had listened. Why didn't he listen? It broke Sylvia's heart that the only conversation she was ever going to have now was with a woman she'd never met before, and in fact, she hadn't gotten to meet anyone from Alan's life. She'd never been to that big house. She'd never sat in the garden. None of it ever happened and now it never would.

This is the way damage moves, the way it seeps and wanders. How much of the damage began with Gary? From any perspective, he didn't seem so great. A real genealogy chart would trace damage back and back, map the radiating lines. It would look like a kaleidoscope.

IN ROANOKE ON the day Sylvia spoke to Lydia, after she left the bingo parlor and got into the patrol car, she didn't say anything to Andy right away. She was afraid, honestly, that he'd turn on her the way his brother had all those years ago. She couldn't bear to lose them both. It felt unreal, and she wondered if this was one of those scams they pull on older people. She had heard they were getting more elaborate. The woman on the phone, this Lydia, knew things about Alan, but with the internet now, you could pretty much know everything about someone. Except, if it was true, why had he done such a destructive thing to himself? Leaving his own child—and the grown one, to boot. Wasn't that why he was so mad at her on that terrible day in Los Angeles?

Andy, both hands on the wheel, said, "How much did you take them for today, Ma?"

She shook her head. "The house usually wins. You know that."

LATER THAT NIGHT, when she finally did tell Andy, his jaw set. She tried to explain about what her own plan had been, how great it was going to have been, this wasn't how she'd wanted him to find out, but now, now—and could it be some kind of scam? She hoped against hope that it was a scam. They could still have their Christmas. He nodded slowly, then said, "Well, there's one way to find out." He opened his computer. It took maybe ten minutes. Maybe nine. He must have used some cop sites. He said, "It's true. Everything that woman said is true, but what we don't know is if she is who she says she is. She'll need to bring a government-issued photo ID." He closed the computer.

"You think I should meet her?"

His gaze was hard, even with those long lashes. "You have to meet her. We have to meet her. If she even shows."

"Honey, I'm sorry," said Sylvia.

He turned away and began loading the dishwasher. "We'll talk about it some other time, Ma. Go to bed."

Sylvia lay on the bed in all her clothes, for a long time. Should she have told Andy about his half brother before this? She had known what would happen. He would have found Alan before sundown, and she wasn't sure she wanted those two times in her life to connect. Also, she wasn't sure Andy could handle knowing that his mother had left another child in her wake. He was so tender-hearted, with his peeing mutts. If loving a child's innocence is a sin, then, okay, she was a sinner. She had thought that now was the time, finally, but fate got there first. The house does win most of the time, even when it's Sylvia at the table.

A WEEK AFTER Alan's funeral, Noah came to see me at last. When he walked through the door of my house, he said, "What the hell is this place? This is where you live?"

He didn't seem to see the tall vase with the fresh lilies, the expensive cheeses on the little coffee table, the clean windows. I had nailed down the curling corner of the linoleum, even. "It is," I said. "I'm so glad you're here." He let me hug him for a few seconds.

Then he sat down, sliced himself a thick wedge of cheese, and ate it, glaring at me. I sat down opposite him. I had so much I wanted to say, but I had resolved to let him begin.

But he wasn't saying anything, just continuing to eat cheese as if that was the reason for his visit. His eyelids were swollen. He moved slowly, toward the little coffee table and back again, eating. Finally, I said, "Honey, I know this has all been terrible. I know."

He just looked at me, chewing monotonously.

"We can get you back to college. We'll find a way."

"Back to *college*? Are you kidding me? What are we going to be after all this? Regular? Come on."

I had no answer for that.

"Right," he said.

Behind me was the room with the clerestory window and everything that had happened there. I wouldn't tell him about that now. He had Alan's jawline, my eyes, and an inner weight that was his own; he'd always had that.

"Noah," I said, "what are you going to do now? What do you want to do?"

"I don't want to do anything," he said. "I'm done." He was large on the sagging sofa, large in the drafty room. His expression was impassive.

IN ROANOKE, IN the two weeks that Sylvia and Andy had before meeting up with Lydia, Sylvia was determined to finish both bedspreads. They ate Thanksgiving in a local restaurant, not talking much. There was so much to say, but Sylvia didn't know where to start and Andy didn't seem to want to talk at all. Nearly every day, she brought her knitting things into the Roanoke Bingo Play, set up her cards, and knit as she played. It was sort of like patting your head and rubbing your belly at the same time—once she got the rhythm going, she was good for hours. The numbers ran one way down the emerald and rose-colored rows, a different way across the dull white cards. Clicks and clicks, taps and taps. She planned to give it to Lydia, a gift from the past to the present, a place to start. It was very important to her to get it finished; it seemed to her that something would be set right once it passed from her hands to Lydia's, something would be completed.

THE THREE OF us never agreed on how much magic he really had. If we had ever been in the same room all together even once, we would have talked about it, I'm sure. I wanted that to happen in the time when I was talking to both of them but they weren't talking to each other. I thought they could, eventually. I thought I could bring us together. He passed, after all, from Sylvia to me to Lydia; each of us held him, touched him, loved him, believed in him and what he could do. So was he that handsome, that smooth, that smart? Was he a genius, a psychopath, a hypnotist? Was he such a fantastic con artist? Sylvia said he was a golden child. Lydia said he was a good man who had accounted for his mistakes. I said, He had a . . . quality. Right, he shone, said Sylvia. An old soul, said Lydia. No, I would say. That's not it. Then what? I didn't know. I only knew that we were all just ordinary now and the one thing we would never say to one another is that we hated our ordinariness and always would. Alan gave us his scent of the extraordinary, of possibilities for lives we had never thought we would have. In that time when the three of us almost met all together, we sniffed for it on one another even as the scent grew fainter. But why did he want so badly to make those lives happen for us, ordinary and dented as we were? And then why did he do what he did? I understand the amount. I understand the logic of the money. But there's something else that's left over. Something I can't figure out. The thread winds and winds, and the row is never finished.

• • •

ON ONE OF the days before Sylvia met up with Lydia, she
noticed that the geezer with the sexy turtle eyes was watching her from the next table. Why did he go to Roanoke
Bingo Play at all? If you're lonely, there are better places than
a bingo parlor to go. No one even talks at bingo parlors.
Abandoning his sad heap of losing cards going every which-
way, he walked over and sat down next to her. It looked like
he had added a new good-luck charm to his vest: a pair of
dice appliqué. She could have told him those weren't going
to help.

"I'm Pete, by the way," he said.

"Sylvia."

"How do you keep track of all those cards?"

"Practice."

"You win?"

"I've had my good days."

"Huh. Do you want some help?"

"This isn't a team sport, Pete."

"Okay. But you only have two hands. I could move some
markers for you. You keep all your winnings."

Sylvia looked at turtle-eyed, charm-bedecked Pete.
"Sure."

He took off his hat and set it on the table, flexed his fingers, and smiled. "Away we go."

Sylvia didn't mind, and after a while she could see that
Pete didn't seem to be a man who required a lot of conversation. If talk were rain, he was like a cactus. Which was
good, because she didn't seem to have many words right

then, just sounds and little hand movements, and numbers making their patterns in her head, pretty as waterfalls.

She won that day, won again. Fifty dollars, seventy-three dollars. Pete put his hat on, leaned back in his chair.

"Guess you're my good-luck charm," Sylvia said.

He tipped his hat. "Ma'am."

Sylvia gathered up her knitting, collected her winnings, and when Andy pulled up in his patrol car outside, she gave him fifty bucks.

"Oh, my," he said.

"It's all legal. Listen, this Lydia person. What do you think she wants?"

Andy stopped to let an old lady on a walker cross against the light. He leaned out of the window and called out, "You be careful now, Theresa. Mind the traffic signals." She waved, rocking along on her four metal legs. As they started to move again, he said, "Could be for the kid, reconnecting with her grandmother."

"Why didn't she do that, why didn't they do that before—"

"Before Alan passed?"

"Well." Sylvia didn't want to say it, but they both knew. Anyone could see why.

Andy removed one hand from its three o'clock position on the steering wheel to squeeze her hand. "Look, he was obviously troubled, to have done what he did. You don't know what happened to him in life, and from what you've said, his choices—he didn't make good choices."

"He was rich."

"Ma. Rich like a thief is rich."

"You don't understand the world."

Andy laughed, gesturing around at the interior of the patrol car. "Yeah, I do. Believe me, I do."

Sylvia didn't say anything, because she didn't want to upset him. He was a good kid. He didn't have the same special temperament as her and his half brother, and that was just the truth of it.

When they got home, they both left their shoes at the front door, the way Andy liked. Not a spot anywhere in that apartment. Her son Andy, keeping the world clean and safe, one square foot at a time. After dinner, he sat at his computer, working on his chart of the dead, straightening out their lines and dates, like a man sweeping tombstones.

FOR DAYS AND days after that, with silent Pete at her side moving markers like it was his job, Sylvia kept winning. In one week, she won almost two hundred dollars. She had the thought that it was Alan, waving to her from the other side, saying he was sorry, he was so very sorry, he was terribly sorry, he understood now the mistake he had made, the chance he had missed. Or maybe he was showing her patterns for some other reason, like on a Ouija board. Maybe the numbers were supposed to be spelling something out, a message from him to her. She couldn't read it, though. She collected her winnings at the end of each day, stacking the bills on top of the dresser in her room. The emerald rows grew, too, as easily as the cash. It all gave her a feeling of hope, although she couldn't have said what exactly she was hoping for, since it was all over now.

One day, in the quiet of the bingo hall, Pete said to her, "You're good at this."

"That's true."

"Do you have a system or something?" He moved a few markers. He was getting better at keeping track.

"More like a vibing sort of thing."

"Huh," said Pete, studying her face as if he could maybe see through it to how her brain worked, get some lessons.

"The thing about me," said Sylvia, casting off the end of a row, "is I'm not really a money person. I'm more like a life person. Also," she said, starting a new row, "if you win in one place too long, they start to get suspicious. I can't tell you how many times I've been hauled into some shithole manager's office to admit I'm cheating."

"And you aren't?" Pete looked as if he might like her either way, and that told her something about Pete.

"No. But I guess I have a natural advantage. I don't think that counts as cheating. You missed the seven there."

Pete moved the marker. "You're a complicated lady."

"Not really," Sylvia said.

TED WAS THE one who told me about it. He was putting on his shoes in the living room, the indentation from the face cradle still visible on his forehead, his cheeks gently flushed. Was it the massage or the nap he inevitably took on the table?

He looked so young and sweet, like he'd just trotted off a college rugby field on an autumn day. Noah would never be that kid now. I poured Ted a glass of water and he drank it all down, then stood up with a little hop. He handed me two twenties and a ten, which I put in my pocket.

"It's going to be a good week," he said.

"Oh?"

"Yup. The county won. They're going to cut up that fucking mess out there."

"Oh. When?"

"By the end of the week. Not a moment too soon. I've got a client wants to look at that stretch. If I could tell you the brand, you wouldn't believe it." He was beaming. "Thanks, Suze. See you next time."

"See you next time," I said, showing him the three steps to the door. He bounded down the steps and into his car, which played rap music, loud, as soon as he turned it on. Phone at his ear, he peeled away from the curb.

A few minutes later, a car pulled up and two people from the health department arrived at my door. Why did they all operate in pairs? They shut me down and charged me all these ridiculous fines. For helping people! Hope you're happy now, Annette, I thought.

SYLVIA AGREED TO meet Lydia in Philadelphia. She couldn't bear to go to Boston. She'd never wanted to go back to that town; in her mind, it was always the ass-end of winter there. Rochester-esque. On the train going north, Andy and Sylvia didn't talk much. He read a mystery with a picture of shattered glass on the cover. She looked through a magazine about movie stars, but she didn't know who most of them were. They all looked like high school students to her, in their T-shirts and flip-flops, and she didn't care, really, who was breaking up with whom, although she used to follow that stuff, she used to be a big movie fan. How many of those movie stars, though, were on a train with one son, a cop, while going to see the widow of another long-lost son, a major crook who'd killed himself? Someone should make a movie about her life. Plus all the other stuff, and Kevin, those years. Los Angeles light, wrapped packages in the trunk. Out the window, little towns went by. Smaller than Roanoke, even. She wondered how many of them had bingo halls or maybe blackjack tables.

They got off the train in Philadelphia and made their way to the restaurant Lydia had picked out. Andy carried the bag Sylvia had brought. It wasn't all that heavy, but she found she didn't mind the gesture. She was more nervous than she'd thought she would be, as if Alan himself were going to be there, as if she were going to get another chance. It was a little bit comical, too, big, tall Andy carrying the bag that said Kiki's Krafts, with its picture of a cat holding knitting needles in its paws, particularly since Andy's expression was dead serious. You'd think he was on his way to some sort of craft arrest. Or kraft arrest.

"She said she'll be wearing a green hat," he said.

"I know, honey. I remember."

"This is weird," he said, glancing around the street with all the people going here and there, so ordinary, an ordinary day for most of them.

"It is. But she knew my son, your half brother, and I have two grandchildren. You're their uncle."

"Right," said Andy, nodding. "Okay, then."

They arrived at the restaurant, and already, through the front window, she could see a woman at a table, wearing a green baseball cap. Blond, head bent. Sylvia squared her shoulders.

"Let's go," she said, opening the restaurant door.

Lydia looked up as they approached and Sylvia's first, terrible, disloyal thought was that Alan had done that to her face, that he had his father's temper in him. "Oh," she said before she could stop herself.

"It's okay," said Lydia. "A fire, long time ago." She reached out with her five-fingered hand to grip first Sylvia's, then Andy's. When she smiled, she was pretty, even with the scars. She was lanky and she didn't look rich. She gestured for them all to sit down. Sylvia tried not to stare at her other, messed-up hand and the side of her face. The poor thing, scarred like that. And now this. Andy had already sat down and was holding the menu upright in both hands, like a shield. Lydia was looking back and forth from Sylvia to Andy, and Sylvia wondered what she saw.

They ordered things Sylvia doubted any of them wanted and then Lydia said, "You must have questions."

"You, too, right?"

Lydia blushed, ducked her head again. She teared up. "Sorry. Yes. I—I'm still, I don't know what. And it's all . . . it's not what you might have seen in the paper, before. That's not the man I knew. And when I found out you were still alive—"

"Why wouldn't I be alive?" Sylvia said.

Lydia glanced away. Andy, next to Sylvia, shifted his weight in his seat. "Oh, just—Alan never said much about his family. I didn't know a lot about you. I think he would have, you know, eventually."

"Uh-huh," Sylvia said. Andy put his hand on hers. "How did you find me?"

"Suzanne—Alan's ex-wife? his first wife? She tracked you down."

"I didn't realize I was missing," said Sylvia.

Sylvia wondered—was he still alive when she was passing through Boston, or was he already gone, or was he walking around thinking about death? Could she have stopped him if she had gotten off the train in Boston that day and found him? What if she had refused to leave the hotel room in Los Angeles that day, insisted he sit down and listen? Or if she had gone back the very first time, drawn a line in the sand with Gary?

"But I want to tell you something," said Lydia, "something important. To everyone else, I know he was a criminal—"

"A felon," offered Andy. Sylvia sighed in his direction. No wonder other kids hadn't liked him. Maybe the mutts were his only friends. "I'm sorry to ask this, Miss," continued

Andy, "but could we see a government-issued photo ID before we go any further?"

Lydia looked surprised, but she got out a driver's license and handed it to Andy, who scrutinized it, then her, handed the license back, and nodded. She was allowed to drive on.

"I don't care about the crime part," Sylvia said. "Why did he do . . . what he did? Do you know?"

"He did it for me and Ava, our kid. Your grandchild. I think he must have thought it was the only way out. I'm not saying it was right, I'm not saying he didn't cause a lot of pain, but he was trying to fix things and you should know that."

"What things were those?" asked Andy in the careful cop voice that made Sylvia nervous. She didn't want him to scare Lydia off.

Lydia explained about the restitution. At first Sylvia wasn't sure she believed Lydia, because she'd never heard of that, since when was there payback in this world? Since when did anyone put back what they took? But Andy, nodding, obviously had heard of it. "Fuck," he said, which was odd, because he rarely swore. "Oh, Jesus."

Lydia was crying, both hands, like a broken gate, held up to her face, her lunch untouched. "He waited the right amount of time. They can't come after us. But Ava and I—we can't have anyone claiming things. Do you know what I mean?"

"Shame on you, lady," said Andy.

"What?" Sylvia said. Andy was shaking his head.

"Listen to me," said Lydia to Andy, as fiercely as if they'd known each other for years, "we don't have *anything*, all right? Anything beyond the basics. I have to protect my kid." She put an envelope on the table. "It's a simple thing."

"What do you mean, you don't have anything?" asked Sylvia, but neither Lydia nor Andy answered her.

"You got me and my mother up here for this?" said Andy. "Are you kidding me?"

"How else could I have done it?" asked Lydia. "Through the mail? Online? Over the phone? These aren't exactly normal circumstances."

Andy put the Kiki's Krafts bag on the table. "She knitted him an entire blanket. A Christmas present. We were all supposed to be together." He yanked out a few emerald and rose folds. "Look at this. This is who this woman is. Look at her, for Christ's sake. People have taken advantage of her all her life. She wouldn't hurt a fly."

"I'm not here to judge," said Lydia. "The blanket looks very pretty. I didn't ask for any of this. I don't want any of this. I didn't even know you existed until a few weeks ago. I want my husband back. I know now that there are things I will never understand about him, but this part—" she tapped the envelope. "This part I know about. I have to get this done, for me and Ava."

Andy spoke softly, but in sharp syllables. "Ma, she wants you to sign something that says you have no claim on whatever is left. Whatever he left."

"Which is hardly anything," said Lydia.

"I don't understand," said Sylvia. She tried to catch Lydia's eye, but Lydia had turned her face away. Sylvia could only see the unmarked side, some Before that Sylvia didn't know about. Or the After, for that matter. "Is that true? Is that what you want?"

"Yes."

"And that's all you want? You don't want to get to know each other?"

Lydia carefully refolded the quilt, smoothing it as she folded. A red diamond disappeared into a green one. She neatly tucked the bedspread back in the Kiki's Krafts bag. "First things first," she said. "I'm sorry, Sylvia."

Sylvia didn't think she should be saying her name, this Lydia. If someone doesn't want to know you, they shouldn't have your name in their mouth. The envelope lay on the table between them. A little water had gotten onto the corner and was soaking it, darkening it from beige to brown. This made the third time Sylvia was losing her son, and how could that be, when she had always loved him so much? How was that fair? What was *her* restitution? Some strangers somewhere were going to get checks from the government, signed by a machine, and that was what was left of her own son, made out of her very body. Sylvia would never even see his ashes. This Lydia said she'd already scattered them in some river in their town. And what had happened to all the money? Was Lydia lying?

"What happens if I don't sign it?" Sylvia asked Andy.

"Are you a lawyer?" Lydia asked him, looking worried.

"He's a cop," Sylvia said, and that hit home, she could tell. Because what Alan did—*that* was the scam here. His final, biggest scam. Sylvia knew it and Lydia knew it and suddenly Sylvia understood that that was why Lydia was there: to get Sylvia to help her cover it up, once and for all. Bury it.

Andy sighed. "I guess, technically, as next of kin, you could try to sue for something or other. Her house, I don't know."

"I don't own a house," said Lydia. "But my daughter is only three. I have to take care of us. Sylvia, you're a mother."

Sylvia saw then that she had the winning hand. Lydia clearly didn't know that Sylvia had signed away custody already, years ago, and that must have ended her official status as kin. Sylvia knew she could bluff and bargain with this woman, the last person to see her son alive. There was a granddaughter, a grandson—a grown man. People who had been in that garden. Sylvia could play for inclusion in their lives. Sylvia imagined Pete was next to her, hands poised over the markers. She saw the board, and everything that would follow, how she would be bargaining to be included in the circle of her own flesh and blood.

She opened the envelope, took out the pages. Some of them were marked with those little translucent flags that said SIGN HERE SIGN HERE SIGN HERE. Lydia handed Sylvia a pen. "I loved him," she said as Sylvia signed, signing away her child for the last time.

"So did I," Sylvia said. She pulled off each flag as she signed and stuck them on the table. What could she say?

Maybe it was her whole job just to deliver him into this world, and not look back. Close the empty trunk and go.

As she was signing, Lydia said, "Hey, one thing—what was it with that one tooth of his?"

"What?"

She tapped her bottom teeth. "The funny one, in front. What did that? Was it like a childhood thing?"

"I have no idea," Sylvia said. "He was perfect when I left." She handed Lydia back her pen. She left the little heap of plastic flags stuck on the table. Then she got up, picked up the bag from Kiki's Krafts, motioned to Andy, and they walked away.

The tears didn't come until the long train ride south. Andy sat next to Sylvia with the Kiki's Krafts bag on his lap, the emerald-and-red knitted bedspread neatly folded within it. He handed his mother tissues; they didn't talk much. Sylvia wept for so much that had been lost, and she cursed Gary again for his cruelty. But she knew that, in Lydia's place, she would have done the same thing to protect her child. Of that much, she was sure.

ANDY SHOWED SYLVIA on his chart where he added Alan to her name. He had to move the digital toothpick from where it was at the center under Sylvia's name over to one side, to make room for his half brother. He had to make room for Gary, too. Before, on that chart, that vast graveyard, Sylvia had been like a ballerina in a music box, balanced on one name; now, she was more like a table, with a child on each side of her. Andy, on the left, with one open side. Alan, on the right, closed, a date on each side of him. Husbands flanking her, too. The story on the chart looked so simple: a good-guy husband and a good-guy son on one side; a not-so-good-guy husband and a shady son who went to prison on the other side. Except the shady son who went to prison had such a light that shone out of him. Everyone who knew him saw it. From Alan's name, the descending lines of two children, a boy and a girl. Their names hung fresh and new on the page, open on one side to the future. For many years, Sylvia had thought she was a sunflower, turning and turning toward the sun, but she could see on Andy's dust-free, glowing screen that she was actually a stitch in a row, and the rows made patterns of their own. The origin of it all might have been in Chrudim, but she didn't know how to say the name of that town or even where it was.

The next day, she said to Andy, "I want to find that other one, that Suzanne. You have to help me."

The day after that, she called me.

HERE WAS MY mistake. I just shouldn't have said. At that time, the time just after Alan was gone, I wanted to talk to Lydia constantly, I wanted to talk to Sylvia constantly, and they wanted to talk to me just as much, even though they weren't talking to one another. We were all part of one another's stories and now we were putting the whole thing together, finally. We were all so hungry for details. All the pieces he'd compartmentalized. It went on for months, all the stories back and forth, although I was the only one of the three of us hearing them all. Lydia gave me that photo of the bread-bag heart. Sylvia sent me the bedspread she'd been knitting for Alan. I had just framed the two photos of whales breaching to send to them, so I was explaining what had happened and what it had meant to me, and then the part about the donation—I had gotten so close with each of them, and I thought they would understand. About the earth, and humanity, and the larger picture. About living an authentic life. And I didn't even know either of them when I gave the money away, or what was going on. This is what I'm saying: I didn't know. And I wasn't the one who took all that money from those people in the first place, people like Matt and Rose who were already, let's be honest, rich. They just wanted to be richer. They were greedy and they kidded themselves in their greed.

If I had known how the other two would react when I told them, how brief that time would be when I was talking to each of them, I would have never said. We were the ones who were left. A found family. The ones who knew his heart, each in our separate chamber of it, but, really, separated by so little. A thin, thin curtain of flesh and blood. Whenever I talked to each of them, it was almost like he was there, in the next room. Secretly, I thought it wouldn't be long before the three of us were actually in one room together, a turquoise room where we would all sit, and finally know the entire story, and see it whole. That could have happened.

But they didn't see it that way, neither of them. And so the opportunity for the three of us to be together and understand the whole story—that window, like the whale's window on the beach that night, was gone.

The things they said, the names they called me. So much for Sylvia's hippie ethics. Lydia had this whole line about making amends and paying your debts, but how were they my debts? She said, and here's where her earnestness tipped over into self-righteousness, "I'm sure you felt terrible about your complicity, but—"

I corrected her right away. "No. He made it sound different than it was. It isn't the way you think. I don't know anything about money."

There was a pause on the other end of the line.

"Okay, Suzanne," she said in that patronizing tone people get when they don't believe you. And then she nearly sued me. Sued me! For what? She only stopped when she realized I truly had nothing. It's like they think they were cheated out of something that I got, but I wasn't the one who cheated them. I had just wanted to help.

I kept trying to explain—on the phone, on email, by text; I said, I'll come to Medford, I'll come to Roanoke—but they both backed away from me as if I were some sort of monster. Lydia, face pinched and blurry on FaceTime, said, "Suzanne, I think I need to draw a boundary here. Please don't contact me again." Sylvia texted me: "you have broken my heart. i wish i'd never met you or that other one. wish my son hadn't, either."

I see Lydia's photograph of the heart-shaped plastic bread bag every morning as I eat my breakfast. I sleep under Sylvia's bedspread at night. If they ever changed their minds and came to visit, they would see their gifts here. I wonder how they would feel then about their judgments and assumptions. It seems to me that the two of them could also be called complicit, with each other. They've both agreed to the story that I messed up their lives, but that isn't true. I wasn't even there.

WHEN I WENT out to the whale the day after Ted told me the news, I was pleased to see that nearly all the architecture of the animal was visible. It didn't look like a cathedral, though, as I had expected. The ribs curved, the tailbone extended, the long bones of the head arrowed, all oil-streaked, sinking into the sand. More random bones were piled against one side. Someone else must have done that. A gull perched on a rib. Several ribs were spotted with bird shit. Bits of stick, dune grass, and seaweed lay within what had been the belly of the creature. What the skeleton looked like was a whale, but a whale pressed out of the landscape, like a bas-relief. It was still magnificent, but it was part of the land now, not the ocean. I lifted my face to the strong sun, smelled the salt in the umbering air, mixed with a faint whisper of rot. Winter would be coming soon, with those impossible heating bills. The clerestory room was empty, futon stripped of sheets. The walls were bare. I had my period, first one in a few months. The gaps would be getting even longer, of course, but today I enjoyed the blood, the bone, the heat, the ache, the smell. I am alive, I thought. I am alive. I am alive.

THREE DAYS AFTER Ted told me the news, the men with chainsaws arrived on the beach. It didn't take long.

I'VE WONDERED—IF EVERY body tells a story, what does mine tell? I am white, with my whiteness marked by little red dots here and there, particularly on my torso. They're called cherry angiomas and they're harmless, but a few more appear every year, dappling me. Stretch marks, like silver vines, run from my hips toward my belly button. My stomach is pouchy. My legs are thin, muscular, for no reason that I know of except that my mother's are the same. There are two little lines near my ears that I've decided, unprovably, are the traces of the anorexia bout when I was sad and thirteen. My shoulders are broad and my arms, as I've said, are freakishly strong. I made swim team in high school—just. I never won anything, but I loved that glide, that kick, the yielding silken envelope of the water. On my left calf is a burn mark from the time my older sister threw the hot curling iron at me because I wouldn't stop teasing her about the stoner boy she was curling her hair for. My feet went up a size when I was pregnant with Noah and they stayed that way. My toes and fingers are squarish, and on my right index finger a subtle but perceptible bump has started to grow; one day, my fingers, like my mother's, will bow at the top. My breasts were always smallish; they swelled with pregnancy, then shrunk again; now they are neat, with small nipples. My eyes, like my father's, are hazel, and they turn ever so slightly downward. On him, this looks shrewd. On me, it has a melancholy cast.

If I look at myself naked in a mirror, front and back, I see them: the German and Dutch farmers, the Scottish laborers. Sturdy feet, sturdy hands, broad shoulders, a strong back. Naked, I look like a woman who could pull a plow, or forge one. Unlike my ancestors, though, who were undoubtedly chipped and twisted by tools and accidents and weather and homesickness, my skin is smooth, my bones unbroken, my back straight. My teeth are straight, too, and white—braces, dentist, periodontist when I still lived in Boston. I wear contacts most days, glasses in the evening to rest my corneas. For a little while, a circlet of skin was lighter where I had removed my wedding band, but now my hands are all the same pinkish-white shade. My shoulders are freckled from the summer sun. Those freckles, I've noticed, take a long time to fade after summer is over. Every body tells a story, but not all the stories. This whole story—it doesn't show. No one can see it. I suppose that's why I've needed so badly to tell it. I've been working on it for a while, trying to explain. If I could, I would give this story to Lydia and Sylvia, but I know they wouldn't accept it. They wouldn't even look. What's the word for a gift that can never be given?

EPILOGUE

~~~~~~~~

Luna

Sylvia stayed in Roanoke, at least for the time being. She got a job at Kiki's Krafts, working behind the counter. Kiki is an okay boss, less persnickety than she looks, and Sylvia gets an employee discount on all that gorgeous yarn from Delft and many other places, too. Pete comes around to see her at Andy's, and that's good. Sylvia likes to walk by the river, it's maybe a little crowded on weekends, but the trail is easy and she likes the smell of the water and earth. People stand out in the water with their fishing rods, and she thinks they catch things, because often the lines go taut and the people struggle to keep a grip on the rods. If you stand and look, sometimes you can see surprisingly large shapes moving under the water, like maybe something big is going down the river on its way to the sea.

Sylvia never really wants the people to catch one of those big ones. She thinks it should stay free, and, often, it seems like it does, because the line suddenly goes slack and the people with the fishing rods shake their heads. If you keep looking, you might see a large tail-shape just under the skin of the water, gliding away.

BACK IN BOSTON, Lydia began the long process of getting her college degree, and then her law degree. Night school, loans, and, with a silent apology to Ava, just a little bit off of the insurance money. They moved to a smaller place on a ground floor, but still in Medford. Lydia was determined that no one would ever blow her house down again. She goes to the Unitarian church on Sunday mornings for services and on Tuesday nights for meetings. She stopped making heart photos. She says that she just doesn't have the time, and, anyway, she doesn't notice them the way she used to do. She has other things on her mind.

AVA IS A skater girl and a math girl and an earpod girl. She's very fond of purple. She doesn't remember much of her father: not his voice, not his face, not the things he said to her or the stories he read to her, not his funeral. She has a sense memory of being lifted up by him and flown through the apartment. She remembers that feeling of being aloft, moving effortlessly through the upper air.

• • •

I'M MAKING THIS all up—well, a lot of it. Noah keeps in touch with Lydia and Ava. I hope that's what happened to Sylvia, after she stopped speaking to me. I still have it in me to wish them well, even though they wouldn't return the favor.

WHEN ALL THAT was left in the sand were bone fragments, boot prints, spots of oil, strands of flesh, and a paper coffee cup, I got the fuck up and got the expensive, time-consuming license. I couldn't really make a go of it, though, especially since I needed to help Noah. The room with the clerestory window is Noah's room now, until he can go out on his own, although things are so pricey on the Cape. He got his real estate license. You might have seen his face in the ads in the *Chesham News*. After work at night, he seems to spend a lot of time on those websites where men share jokes and conspiracy theories and have all these special emblems and codes. He thinks the world has gone wrong in ways large and small. He never seems to get around to renewing his passport, although he loves to watch soccer. He is devoted to the memory of his father.

I got hired at Hyannis Spa and Wellness Center. The uniforms are pretty tasteful, sleek and black with a side-tie. I was able to quit Waves. At work, for the clients, I call myself Luna. That's what it says on my name tag, and there's even a little image of a half-moon there, too, because they take care with the details here. It makes things more personal, and our clients feel that. When I extend my hand to you,

you'll probably carefully note the name and say, "Hello, Luna." You'll be impressed by my grip. "Yes, hello," I'll say to you, also careful to use your name. You'll like me and my strong hands, already confident that I can take care of you. I'll smile at you, and show you into the darkened room.

ACKNOWLEDGMENTS

THIS BOOK WAS a long time in the making, and took me to many new places in all senses of that phrase. It benefited enormously from the myriad forms of love, support, patience, expertise, and input of the following: Mary Bly; the Brown Foundation Fellowship Program at the Dora Maar House; Maud Casey; Chris Castellani; Ava Chin; Bill Clegg; Alice Elliott Dark; Paul Doucette of the New Bedford Heritage Fishing Center; Allison DePerte, Kimberly Durham, and Rachel Bosworth of the Atlantic Marine Conservation Society; Fordham University; Sarah Gambito; Brunson Hoole; Linda Johannes; the New Bedford Whaling Museum; Cynthia O'Neal; Richard Palmer; Laura Pinsky; Janice Pinto; Kathy Pories; Elizabeth Povinelli; Chris Stamey; Suzanne Thurman of the Marine Education, Research, and Rehabilitation Institute; Meg Tilly; and Gary Weiner.

Daiken Nelson, beloved partner, went above and beyond more times than I can count. Endless gratitude.

The Complicities

An Interview with Stacey D'Erasmo
Questions for Discussion

OUR TENDENCY TO ELIDE THE TRUTH
An Interview with Stacey D'Erasmo

CATHERINE BARNETT: What is your informal working definition of *complicity*?

STACEY D'ERASMO: If you look *complicity* up in the dictionary, it means the state of colluding with a crime, and it comes from the Latin *complicare*, "pleated together." In the novel, I wanted to get at what happens when you're involved in something that you *know* is not right and yet you are, with full agency, going along with it. You may not be the primary actor, but you're *an* actor. You have agency and you're in some way betraying your own conscience.

CB: Apologies happen infrequently in your novel. Why are the characters so reluctant to apologize, and what would you say is the relationship between complicity and apology?

SD: It's the most basic thing: you can't really apologize unless you actually think you did something wrong. In order to apologize sincerely, you have to feel that you have something to apologize for. And that's what Suzanne doesn't want to deal with. My interest in questions of complicity has come from what I've seen, over and over, especially in the last decade: just stunning examples of horrendously bad behavior, pathologically bad behavior. Yet, in almost every case, everybody around them knew what was going on. I think the January 6 hearings should be called "Complicity: The After-Party." Show me any of those people who say "I'm sorry. I helped create this, I'm sorry." I want to see Ivanka Trump say to the man who was bashed with the fire extinguisher, "I'm sorry, this was in no small part my fault."

I'm also thinking of Weinstein, Epstein, Madoff— situations where literally battalions of people knew something wrong was taking place. What are the internal conflicts within them? What did they have to do to try to square themselves with themselves as they were hurtling along in these scenes? As a writer, these characters interest me.

CB: I admire the way your characters are flawed, which makes me want to see how they will—if they will—come straight, do the right thing. But I'm often unsure how to feel about them, especially Suzanne, who keeps denying her role in the crime at the center of the novel. Am I supposed to believe the denials, or take them with a grain of salt?

SD: Oh, with a big grain of salt. Suzanne doesn't want to know what she knows. In an odd sort of way, I have empathy for her in the torment of her denial. And there's a lot of denial going on. Past a certain income threshold, you have to know that you are getting over at the expense of others, right?

CB: Because she's our narrator, I feel like I have to like her.

SD: No, you don't. She's a soul in torment. I don't excuse her, but I feel for her. But this is to me the highest compliment: that you didn't know how to feel about these characters. Yes! I want it that way, and I want it that way because I truly and deeply believe that we are all very mixed creatures. So with Suzanne, whether or not I like her isn't exactly the point. I'm fascinated by her.

CB: Maybe part of your empathy is that you think she's trying to believe in her own innocence?

SD: You have to look at the difference between what she says and what she does. What she says is, "I didn't know." But what she does is leave her husband, go somewhere else, and then get involved in what we might call helping, healing others. She becomes a masseuse. She tries to help rescue a beached whale, whose presence in the novel is equal parts metaphor and narrative fact. Much of the book finds Suzanne paying homage to (or seeking redemption from) the whale, whose death and decomposition both torment and compel her. It's as if she is trying to make amends while not admitting what she has to make amends for. I didn't know until long after I'd finished the book that Ghislaine Maxwell set up a marine mammal charity; I have no idea why. I thought, well, that's perfect—she's not going to cop to what really happened with all those poor girls and women that she abused and exploited, but she's going to give money to the dolphins. That kind of split happens quite a lot. In the novel, Suzanne is saying, "I'm going to be this good citizen of the planet," while unable to admit to what happened in her past. She doesn't intend her way of telling to be a confession, but the reader begins to understand that in a backwards way it is a confession.

CB: I was thinking about the difference between conscious and unconscious complicities. What are some unconscious complicities that you see us participating in?

SD: One of the biggest ones in this country, which we all know about, is the phenomenal wealth gap that now exists. We've all seen the statistics that since the 1980s the wealth gap in this country has metastasized. Past a certain income threshold, you have to know that you are getting over at the expense of others, right? Systemic racism is obviously a huge area of complicity, a net in which we're all caught. I feel it's important to zero in on when you feel your hand's in it—right? That's hard to do. Those are places where we would rather have things be unconscious.

CB: Do you separate yourself from these kinds of actions, choices, truths?

SD: Absolutely not. How could I? What is difficult to come to terms with about power is that it is (as Foucault explained) diffuse, incredibly sticky, pervasive. It is neither easy nor simple to operate ethically within big systems of power, which is what we're all in. One of the reasons I'm not really interested, as an artist, in the Big Bad Wolf is that the Big Bad Wolf is not the power system; the Big Bad Wolf is, let's say, the worst *actor* in the power system. We like to make power individual. That way we can say, "Well, the Big Bad Wolf is bad, but the rest is good, so all we need to do is kill the wolf and then we'll all be good." But of course we know that's not true. In this sticky web that we're all in, behaving decently is no small task. No small task at all. It is not just one person; it is not just one institution, it is not just one night; it is a very, very deep system. It makes me think of *The Matrix*, as a pop culture example. Try getting out of the Matrix. What are you going to do?

I'm very fond of Ursula Le Guin's brilliant fable, "The Ones Who Walk Away from Omelas." Everything is lovely in Omelas, but this state of affairs depends upon one condition: there is a child in a basement, completely tormented, and as long as that child is tormented, everything in Omelas is great. Everyone in Omelas takes the bargain, but at the end of the story, some of the citizens walk away, out into the wild. You can see the metaphor. In the world as it is, it sure as hell is not just one child in the basement. And the thing about the story is, you know, where are they going to go?

CB: In the novel's opening paragraph, Suzanne says, "Besides, facts only take you so far. And even facts look different next to other facts." This vibrates with questions of "facts" and "truth" in our moment.

SD: She's self-justifying, right? What I would say in our actual moment is: how many more facts do we need? We have bales and bushels of facts. The oil companies knew about global warming in the 1950s. They had the facts. The facts are not the problem—it is the use and misuse and concealment of facts that is the issue, and again, going back to the idea of complicity, it's not just one person concealing those facts.

CB: What about approaching the issue of complicity from another angle—whistleblowing?

SD: Obviously this is a book of the not-whistleblowers! Recently I did an event with the journalist Eyal Press, who wrote *Dirty Work: Essential Jobs and the Hidden Toll of Inequality in America*, about who does America's dirty work in places like slaughterhouses, and *Beautiful Souls: The Courage and Conscience of Ordinary People in Extraordinary Times*, about people who essentially did the right thing under extraordinary pressure. He makes clear that being a whistleblower—even just not being complicit—is very, very hard and generally comes with a very high price. In the movies, the whistleblower is heroic and the judge at the end bangs their gavel and compensation is triumphantly awarded to victims. But in real life, whistleblowers suffer greatly. Financially, spiritually, emotionally. Being a whistleblower entails not just one heroic act going against the prevailing power systems; it is a choice that sends you down a much different path for years and years. You have to be prepared for significant loss. Press makes the point that part of that loss could be the loss of your community, which can be more heartbreaking than any sum of money you might ever lose.

For a very topical example, look at Liz Cheney. What I find incredibly moving about her is that she did something that almost no one does—which is that she changed her mind, she paid the price, and she took significant meaningful action. There is a kind of sinister beauty in both the sound and meaning of restitution, which is a legal term.

CB: Can you think of writers who are models for you in that way?

SD: I think of writers who had tremendous integrity, who didn't go along, who followed their own paths, despite the cost. Adrienne Rich, for example, who won the Yale Younger Poets Series while she was still in college and then hit all the conventional marks: the marriage, the children, the prizes. But then in the '60s and '70s she made choices, both personally and professionally, that weren't valorized: the increasingly "confessional" poetry, her lesbianism. She took a major hit, on all levels. Or Gwendolyn Brooks, who really broke her life in half in the 1960s. Her style went from being very accessible and much lauded—she won the Pulitzer in 1950, when she was 33—to being incredibly dense and often difficult, after she attended the Second Black Writers' Conference at Fisk in 1967. Both Rich and Brooks were very successful when they made choices that they knew would lessen their cultural power. How many people ever do that? It's so rare. I think that is very inspiring. And not easy, not easy at all.

CB: Throughout *The Complicities*, the characters—even when they've participated in, contributed to, and benefited from the inequities—keep trying to insist that things should be fair. What do you make of this contradiction?

SD: Sometimes I think the characters are right and sometimes I think the characters are wrong. Alan's mother, Sylvia, says, "Look, you know, everything's run by somebody's mob." And on some days, I would agree with her on that point. Alan's second wife, Lydia, says, "I thought we paid our debt," but she's overlooking the fact that if you don't pay the restitution, you haven't paid your debt. And it is actually true—what really breaks some white-collar criminals is not the jail time but the legal demand for restitution, which tends to be such a lot of money they often can't repay it all. So they've taken something they can't give back. This may be where some of my root empathy for the characters comes from. They have unleashed forces that are out of their control now.

CB: I love the lyric moments in the novel. In one of these moments, it's as if Suzanne is trying to comfort herself with what could almost sound like a lullaby, though the meaning of the words is definitely not soothing: What is restitution? What is restitution? What is restitution? Money drowned in water.

SD: Perhaps there is a kind of sinister beauty in both the sound and meaning of restitution, which is a legal term. People are told in courts to pay restitution all the time, and if you don't pay it, it quickly piles up, accruing interest. The ever-widening circles of damage done are really what can't be paid back; for instance, think of something like climate change. If every industry, every country, every airplane, every individual, did exactly what they need to do starting today, even if they go above and beyond the Paris Accords—the damage is still going to reverberate for centuries. The way that debt grows, like something organic, is part of what the characters in my novel are up against.

CB: The novel is divided into three main sections: "The Whale's Breath," "Whalefall," and "The Whale's Bones," each of which has a title calling our attention to the beached whale, a creature whose suffering and death compel Suzanne to take dramatic steps. When I imagine the whale's "enormous eye, so eerily human but so much bigger, enfolded in flesh . . . half-closed," I'm reminded of Rilke's poem "The Archaic Torso of Apollo," which ends with lines that could be spoken directly to Suzanne: "there is no place / that does not see you. You must change your life."

SD: When I began writing the novel, I had this very strong image of a woman in Suzanne's position—that kind of life, that kind of husband—being in the presence of a stranded whale. She watches it decompose. The whale is not just one thing. The way in which Suzanne has to keep showing up for the whale as it decomposes works in tension with everything she doesn't want to know; she's just going to go and watch this ever-expanding rot. She doesn't know why she's doing it; she's just doing it. There's something really human about that. I didn't know until I was deep into writing the book that whale bones seep oil for decades. Decades. The reverberations do not end.

CB: The most vivid part of the whale is that eye.

SD: Yeah, Suzanne longs for, and yet doesn't want, the whale to look back at her.

CB: Toward the end of the novel, Suzanne says, "We all kind of wanted to be special." What does it mean to you, to her, this "being special"?

SD: People will do a lot of cruddy things to themselves and others for a little bit of magic, and to feel special—and I include myself in that company. Greed is only one part of it, as is another wise unattainable beauty that people gravitate toward. It's crack. I'm sure that you and I have both been in rooms where X amazing and powerful cultural figure is behaving badly, maybe even *really* badly, and people are letting them get away with it. Do I, for example, believe that Susan Sontag was a beast? Yes. Yes! I believe she was ruinous to people. Was there a time in my life when as a figure she meant something important to me, providing an oxygen in scant supply elsewhere? Yes. Yes! And if when I was 25, I had been invited to a dinner party where she was chewing off the hand of the person next to her, would I have called her out? Probably not. And I want to emphasize that everything we're talking about, everything I was trying to write into in this book—I have these demons within myself. I am not excusing myself from these deeply human, deeply complex conditions. And if I can't reckon with that, in myself, what does it matter who I "cancel"? You can cancel until you're blue in the face, but our own profound and very complex yearnings cannot be canceled. This is where novels happen.

CATHERINE BARNETT is the author, most recently, of *Human Hours*, which won the 2018 Believer Book Award in Poetry. A Guggenheim fellow, she received a 2022 Arts and Letters Award in Literature. She lives and teaches in New York City, where she also works as an independent editor.

This interview first appeared online in *The Yale Review* on November 7, 2022.

QUESTIONS FOR DISCUSSION

1. What is the meaning of complicity to you?

2. Do you feel that any of the characters in the novel are complicit? If so, who? And in what way? Are some more complicit than others?

3. Why does the whale stranding have such a big impact on Suzanne?

4. What do you think of Suzanne's decision about the money? Would you do the same? Why or why not?

5. Why does D'Erasmo describe the death and decomposition of the whale in such detail?

6. The story of Suzanne and those around her is told through different POVs. Why do you think the book is narrated in such a complex way?

7. Why do you think D'Erasmo chose not to give Alan a voice? What do you think he would say if he were telling his side of the story?

8. What is the role of money in this novel? If it were a character, what sort of character would it be? How does class affect the people and events in the book?

9. What would be the most just outcomes for each of the characters in the novel? How often do we see just outcomes in situations like this, and why do you think that is?

10. Throughout the novel, the characters all find themselves in risky, compromised, or dubious circumstances. Why do you think they make the decisions that they do? What are the value systems of each character? How and why do these sometimes clash?

11. Suzanne, Lydia, and Sylvia are all mothers. How does motherhood influence their characters, their choices, and the trajectory of their lives in general? What are the differences among them, as mothers?

12. Of all the characters in the book, Noah has perhaps the most vulnerable and sincere relationship with Alan. What kind of father is Alan to Noah? How does the father-son dynamic affect what happens in the book? How is it different from the mother-son dynamic? Have you seen that difference in your own experience?

13. In *The Complicities*, the past just won't stay in the past. Why do you think the past has such a grip on these people? What makes it so sticky?

14. Which character do you find the most sympathetic? Why?

STACEY D'ERASMO is the author of four novels and one book of nonfiction. She has been the recipient of a Wallace Stegner Fellowship in fiction, a Guggenheim Fellowship in fiction, and a Duggins Outstanding Mid-Career Novelist Prize from Lambda Literary. Her essays, features, and reviews have appeared in the *New York Times Magazine*, the *New York Times Book Review*, the *New Yorker*, and *Bookforum*, among other publications. She is an associate professor of writing and publishing practices at Fordham University.